Reginald Hill is a native of Cumbria and a former resident of Yorkshire where his outstanding Dalziel and Pascoe crime novels are set. He says he always regarded himself as a writer of some sort, but until he wrote *A Clubbable Woman* (1970), which introduced Chief Superintendent Andy Dalziel and young DS Peter Pascoe, he had managed to avoid putting his theory to the test. Since then it has received ample confirmation. *An Advancement of Learning* (1971) introduced Sergeant Pascoe to Eleanor (Ellie) Soper, and Pascoe's subsequent police career and his private life have been unfolded with wit, drama, suspense and impeccable style in *Ruling Passion* (1973), now a major TV series, *An April Shroud* (1975), *A Pinch of Snuff* (1978), *A Killing Kindness* (1980), *Deadheads* (1983), *Exit Lines* (1984), *Child's Play* (1987), *Under World* (1988), *Bones and Silence* (1990), which won the CWA Gold Dagger Award, *One Small Step* (1990), *Recalled to Life* (1992), *Pictures of Perfection* (1994) and *The Wood Beyond* (1996).

REGINALD HILL

Ruling Passion

A Dalziel and Pascoe novel

HarperCollins*Publishers*

HarperCollins*Publishers*
77–85 Fulham Palace Road,
Hammersmith, London W6 8JB

This paperback TV tie-in edition 1997
1 3 5 7 9 8 6 4 2

Previously published by HarperCollins in 1993
and by Grafton in 1987
Reprinted six times

First published in Great Britain by
HarperCollins*Publishers* 1973

Copyright © Reginald Hill 1973

The Author asserts the moral right to
be identified as the author of this work

ISBN 0 00 649990 2

Set in Times

Printed and bound in Great Britain by
Caledonian International Book Manufacturing Ltd, Glasgow

For Pat again – with love and thanks

Search then the ruling passion: there, alone,
The wild are constant, and the cunning known;
The fool consistent, and the false sincere;
Priests, princes, women, no dissemblers here.
This clue once found unravels all the rest . . .

Alexander Pope

PART ONE

Chapter 1

Brookside Cottage,
Thornton Lacey.
September 4th.

Well hello, Peter Pascoe!

A voice from the grave! Or should I say the underworld? Out of which Ellie (who gave me the glad news of your existence when we met in town last month) hopes to lead you, for a while at least, back into the land of the living.

Ironic, thought Detective-Superintendent Backhouse, his gaze flicking momentarily to the pale-faced man who sat opposite him. He did not speak the thought aloud. He was a kind man, though he never shunned the cruelties of his job when they became essential.

He read on.

Doubtless she told you we've been doing up this rural slum to make it a fit place for pallid cits to recuperate in. Well, now it is complete and we'd love for you and Ellie to week-end with us in a fortnight (constabulary duty permitting, of course!). Timmy and Carlo are coming down from the Great Wen so there will be much nostalgia! Not quite as squalid as that other cottage in Eskdale (I hope) – but oddly enough life in Thornton Lacey is not without its correspondences!

'What's he mean by that?' asked Backhouse.

Pascoe stared at the sentence indicated by the superintendent's carefully manicured finger. It took him a second to bring the words into focus.

'When we were students,' he said, 'we spent a few weeks one summer in Eskdale. In Cumberland.'

'The same people?'

Pascoe nodded.

'Colin and Rose weren't married then.'

'What's this about correspondences?'

'I don't know. I don't remember much about it.'

Except one evening, the six of them, golden in the low-stooping sun, walking in companionable silence across a diagonally sloping field towards the distant village and its pub. The slope had separated their courses, pulling them apart so that they were strung out across the coarse, tussocky grass, only coming together again at the wooden gate in the lowest corner of the loose-stone wall.

Make it Friday evening if possible, but bright and early Saturday if not. Do not fail us in this our command or our wrath shall be terrible and you know just how terrible my wrath can be!

Seriously, it will delight me more than I can say if you come. It's not every day that we see Abelard reunited with Eloisa (and his vital equipment, I hope!)

Love from us both,

Colin (and Rose)

Backhouse finished the letter with a sigh, made a note on a slip of paper, clipped it to the single pale lemon sheet and put it into a bright green plastic folder.

'I'll hang on to this,' he said. 'If I may.'

Not that it had any value at the moment. Probably it never would. But he preferred to work that way. Meticulousness is the better part of serendipity.

'Would you like another cup of tea?' he asked.

The door opened before Pascoe could answer. An ancient constable creaked wearily in, holding some type-written sheets.

'Mr – that is, *Sergeant* – Pascoe's statement, sir.'

He laid the sheets carefully before Backhouse and retreated.

8

'Thank you, Crowther,' said Backhouse, turning the sheets round and pushing them towards Pascoe.

'Read it,' he said gently as Pascoe picked up a ball-point and made to sign at the bottom of the first sheet. 'Always read before you sign. Just as you always tell others to read before they sign, I hope.'

Without answering, Pascoe began to read.

Statement of Peter Ernest Pascoe made at Thornton Lacey police station, Oxfordshire, in the presence of Detective-Superintendent D. S. Backhouse.

On the morning of Saturday 18th September, I drove down from Yorkshire to Thornton Lacey. I was accompanied by a friend, Miss Eleanor Soper. Our purpose was to spend the week-end with some old friends, Colin and Rose Hopkins of Brookside Cottage, Thornton Lacey. Other guests were to include Mr Timothy Mansfield and Mr Charles Rushworth, also old friends, though I had not seen them nor the Hopkinses for more than five years. I do not know if anyone else had been invited.

It was our intention to arrive at nine-thirty but we made such good time that it became clear we were going to be there by nine . . .

It was a glorious morning after a night of torrential rain. A light mist lay like chiffon over the fields and woodlands, yielding easily to the gentle urgings of the rising sun. The roads were empty at first. Even the traditionally dawn-greeting farmhouses seemed still to sleep in the shining wet fields.

'I like it,' said Ellie, snuggling contentedly into the comfortably sagging passenger seat of the old Riley. 'There are some things it's worth being woken up for.'

Pascoe laughed.

'I know what you mean,' he said with hoarse passion.

'You're a sex maniac,' she answered.

'Not at all. I can wait till we reach a lay-by.'

Ellie closed her eyes with a smile. When she opened

them again it was an hour later and she was leaning heavily against her companion's shoulder.

'Sorry!' she said, sitting upright.

'So much for the attractions of the early morning! We're making very good time, by the way. You're sure they really want us for breakfast?'

'Certain. When I talked to Rose on the phone she was very angry we had to cry off arriving last evening and insisted on first thing today. Poor girl, she probably had a fatted calf roasting or something.'

'Yes. I'm sorry. It was a shame.'

Ellie put on her indignant look.

'Shame! That fat sadist Dalziel doesn't know the meaning of the word.'

'It wasn't his fault. It's this string of break-ins we've been brought in on. The phone rang just as I was leaving.'

'So you said,' grunted Ellie. 'Bloody queer time for a burglary. I bet Dalziel did it.'

'The break-in happened some time earlier in the week,' explained Pascoe patiently. 'It was only discovered yesterday when the people got back from holiday.'

'Serves them right for coming back early. They should have stayed away for the week-end. Then we could have enjoyed all ours too.'

'I hope we will,' said Pascoe, smiling fondly at her. 'It'll be good to see them all again.'

'Yes, I think it will be. Especially for you,' said Ellie thoughtfully. 'You've been cut off too long.'

'Perhaps so. I didn't do all the cutting, mind. Anyway, cutting's the wrong image. They were always there. Like securely invested capital! I've never doubted that one day I would see them all again.'

'It took an accident to bring me to light again,' admonished Ellie.

'There is a something power which shapes our ends,

10

rough-hew them how we may,' proclaimed Pascoe solemnly. 'Colin's not the only one who can quote.'

'Here's to it,' said Ellie, relaxing in the window-warmed light of the now completely triumphant sun.

We arrived at Thornton Lacey at eight-fifty. I noted the exact time as I looked at my watch to see how close to our forecast time of arrival we were. I suggested to Miss Soper that we should wait for half an hour before proceeding to Brookside Cottage, but after discussion we decided against this. Thus it must have been two or three minutes before nine o'clock when we reached the cottage. The curtains were all drawn and we received no reply to our knocks.

'We should have waited,' said Pascoe smugly.

'Nonsense. If they got so pie-eyed last night that they can't hear us knocking, they weren't to be ready for nine-thirty either.'

The professional part of his mind felt there was some flaw either of logic or syntax in this statement, but this week-end he was very firmly and very consciously off duty. So he grinned and stepped back from the doorway, craning his neck to spot any signs of activity behind the bedroom curtains.

It was a lovely cottage, just stopping this side of biscuit-tin sentimentality. Tudor, he told himself, half-timbered, doubtless full of wattle-and-daub whatever that was (those were?). A not very successful attempt had been made to train a rambling rose around the doorway. Above the thatched roof a flock of television aerials parted the morning breeze and serenely sang their triumph over charm and Tudory.

'Colin's quite ruthless,' said Ellie, following his gaze. 'If you modernize, modernize. He doesn't see any virtue in pretending that a pair of farm-labourers' cottages was once a desirable sixteenth-century residence.'

'Nor in keeping farming hours, it seems,' said Pascoe,

banging once more on the door and rattling the worn brass handle.

'Though perhaps,' he added thoughtfully, 'they do preserve some old country customs, such as never locking your door.'

He pressed the door-handle right down and pushed. The hinges creaked most satisfactorily as the heavy oak door slowly swung open.

Now it was Ellie's turn to show reluctance.

'We can't just appear at the foot of the bed,' she protested, hanging back.

'Well I'm not going to go and get a warrant,' answered Pascoe. 'At least we can find the wherewithal to make coffee and a lot of noise. Come on!'

The front door opened directly into a nicely proportioned lounge, with furnishings which, though comfortable looking, were antiquated rather than antique. Two or three whisky tumblers stood on a low table in the middle of the room; they were still half full. An empty bottle of Teacher's stood beside them. A Churchillian cigar had been allowed to burn out in a large cut-glass ashtray. Ellie sniffed the air distastefully.

'What a fug! I was right – they must have been having themselves a quiet little ball last night.'

She began drawing curtains back prior to opening a window. Pascoe too was sniffing gently, a faintly puzzled look on his face. He crossed the room to the door in the farthermost wall. It was ajar and he pushed it fully open and stepped through into the next room. It was clearly the dining-room. The round, highly polished mahogany table still bore the debris of a meal.

But it wasn't the table which held his attention.

White-faced he turned to stop Ellie from following him. She had moved to the rear window now and was just drawing the curtains there.

'Ellie,' he said.

12

She froze, her hand on the window-latch, staring incredulously through the pane.

A thin, single-noted scream forced its way from the back of her throat.

Two men were lying on the dining-room floor in the positions indicated in the police photograph 'A1'. They had both received severe gunshot wounds, and had been bleeding copiously. The nature of the wounds and the strong cordite smell I had noticed in the air led me to assume the wounds had been caused by a shotgun fired at close range. The man lying beside the dining-table (position 'X' on the photograph) I recognized as Timothy Mansfield of Grover Court, London, NW2. The other man I was not able to recognize immediately as he had received the greater part of the gun-blast in the neck and lower face, but later I was able to confirm he was Charles Rushworth of the same address. I turned to prevent Miss Soper from following me into the room, but she was clearly disturbed by something she could see from the rear window. I looked out into the garden at the back of the house and saw the figure of a woman lying at the base of the sundial in the centre of the lawn (photograph 'C3') I could not recognize her from the window as her face was pressed to the grass. There had been a great deal of bleeding from the head.

'It's Rose,' said Ellie, not believing herself. 'There's been an accident.'

She made for the dining-room, seeking a way into the garden. Pascoe caught her by the shoulders.

'Telephone,' he said, his voice low, his mind racing. From the dining-room a narrow flight of stairs ran to the next floor. His ears were alert for any slight sound of movement above.

'Yes,' said Ellie. 'Doctor. No, ambulance is better, there was a hospital sign, do you remember?'

There was a telephone on the floor beside one of the two armchairs. She bent over it.

'No,' said Pascoe, taking her arm and pushing her towards the front door. 'We passed a phone box down

13

the road. Use that. And get the police. Tell them they'll need an ambulance and a doctor.'

'Police?' repeated Ellie.

'Hurry,' said Pascoe urgently.

He heard the Riley start as he placed his foot carefully on the first stair. It creaked, the second even more so, and, abandoning stealth, he took the rest at a run, narrowly missing cracking his head against the ceiling cross-beam halfway up.

He went through the nearest door low and fast. A bedroom. Empty. Bed unslept in.

The next the same. Then a bathroom. A tiny junk-room. One more to go. Certain now the first floor was uninhabited, he still took no chances and entered as violently as before.

Looking down at the bed, his heart stood still. A pair of children's handcuffs lay across the two pillows. In one bracelet was a red rose. In the other a young nettle. On the bedhead above was pinned a paper banner.

It read *Eloisa and Abelard, Welcome Home*.

Pascoe felt the carapace of professionality he had withdrawn behind crack across. The room overlooked the rear of the house. He did not look out of the window but descended rapidly. With a great effort of will, he forced himself to confirm by touch what his eyes had told him, that the two men were dead.

Timmy used to play the guitar and when in funds gave presents of charming eccentricity to those he loved. Carlo (it *was* Carlo, the one eye which remained unscathed told him that) had a fiery temper, adored Westerns, demonstrated for civil rights, hated priests.

These were memories he didn't want. Even less did he want to kneel beside this woman, turn her gently over, see the ruin of soft flesh the shotgun blast had made in Rose Hopkins.

She was wearing a long silk evening gown. Even the

14

rain and the dew had not dulled its iridescent sheen of purple and green like a pheasant's plumage. But her eyes were dull.

The sundial against which she lay had an inscription on its pedestal. He read it, desperately trying to rebuild his carapace.

Horas non numero nisi serenas.
I number only the sunny hours.

He was still cradling the dead woman in his arms when Ellie returned, closely followed by the first police car.

Chapter 2

'Dalziel here.'

'Hello, Andy. Derek Blackhouse here.'

'So they said.' Dalziel's voice fell a long way short of enthusiasm. 'It's been a long time. And you must be after a bloody big favour, to be ringing on a Saturday morning.'

'No favour,' said Backhouse. 'I'm ringing from the station at Thornton Lacey. I've got one of your men here. A Sergeant Pascoe.'

'Pascoe!' said Dalziel, livelier now. 'He's not been crapping in the street again, has he?'

'Sorry?'

'Joke,' sighed Dalziel. 'What's the problem?'

'Nothing really. He's down here visiting some old friends.'

'So?'

'So when he arrived this morning, three of the old friends were dead. Shotgun at close range.'

Now there was a long silence.

'Christ,' said Dalziel finally. Another silence.

'That's rough,' said Dalziel. 'I don't think he's got enough old friends left to spare three.'

Backhouse made a moue of distaste at the callousness of the comment, though he thought he detected a hint of real concern in the intonation. But he might have been mistaken.

'Anyway,' said Backhouse, 'I'm just interested in confirming that he and Miss Soper didn't arrive till this morning.'

'She's with him, is she?' grunted Dalziel.

'You know her?'

16

'Vaguely. Hey listen, my lad, you're not thinking Pascoe had anything to do with this, are you?'

'Just checking, Andy. He says he got held up on a case last night.'

'Too true, he did. He wasn't best pleased, but he's a dutiful lad. He was here till about nine-thirty. Then we had a drink till closing. That suit you?'

'I think so. We haven't had the PM yet, but the doctor was very certain it happened last evening. I wasn't really concerned about the sergeant, but I wanted to be sure. He may be a great help to us.'

'Now watch it!' said Dalziel threateningly. 'We've got work to do here too, you know. Nothing glamorous like a multi-murder, but someone's got to catch thieves. And I need Pascoe. He's due back Monday. I'll expect him Monday.'

'We do have experienced detectives of our own,' said Backhouse drily. 'No, the way he can help is with his knowledge of the missing man.'

'Missing man?'

'Didn't I say? We're one light. The host, the man whose cottage it is, Colin Hopkins. Your sergeant's special mate.'

'I see,' said Dalziel. 'You reckon him for it, then?'

'I'd like to talk with him,' said Backhouse cautiously.

'I bet!! Anyway, what you're saying is you want Pascoe to help pin this on his mate? You're asking a bit much, aren't you?'

'It was his friends who died,' said Backhouse quietly.

'Well, he's a good lad. Is he there? I'd better have a word.'

What kind of grudging condolence did he propose? wondered Backhouse.

'He's with Miss Soper at the moment. She is badly shocked.'

17

'Later then. But I want him Monday. Right? I'll look for you on the telly!'

Bloody old woman, thought Dalziel as he replaced the receiver. He scratched the back of his left calf methodically from top to bottom, but derived no relief. *The itches you scratch are internal,* someone senior enough to dare had once told him. He looked with distaste at the mound of files on his desk. Suddenly they seemed trivial. Stupid twats who spent good money on pretty ornaments, then didn't take the trouble to look after them properly. Somewhere in that lot there was a pattern, a flawed system. There was always a flaw. A man lay at the bottom of that pile and they'd find him in the end. But today, this moment, it seemed trivial.

It was a rare feeling for him. He wasn't a man who took his work lightly. But now he stood up and went in search of someone to drink a cup of tea with and talk about football or politics.

The enormity of what had happened had not struck Ellie for some time after her return to the cottage. She had not gone into the building but made her way along the side of the whitewashed garage into the garden. At the bottom of the dew-damp lawn, audible though not visible, ran a stream in a deep cutting, shaded by alders and sallows. The murmuring water, the morning-fresh garden unheated yet by the lemon sunlight, the flight of a white-browed blackbird from a richly laden apple-tree, all helped to make unreal the tableau formed by the man on his knees by the dead woman at the foot of the sundial. Only the gnomon of the dial, cutting the fragrant air like a shark's fin, seemed to be of menace.

Something shone, brighter than dewdrops, in the grass around the body. Pieces of broken glass. Her first concern was intimate, domestic. Pascoe's trousers might be torn or, worse, his knees cut.

18

She knew, and had known since she first looked from the window, that Rose was dead. Calling for an ambulance was a gesture, the drowning swimmer's last clutch at the crest of the wave that will sink him. The ugliness of it, visible now as Pascoe laid the woman on the grass once more, was the greater shock. But even that she assimilated for the moment as she turned back to the cottage, looking for the others. Pascoe stopped her before she went in through the open french window.

But it had been too late to stop her seeing what lay inside.

The police-station at Thornton Lacey was merely the front ground-floor section of the pleasant detached house in which Constable John Crowther and his wife lived and which they would give up with great reluctance when Crowther reached retiring age in a couple of years. Neither he nor his wife was particularly impressed by the arrival of major crime in their little backwater. There was nothing in it for the constable except trouble. At this late stage in his career, not even personal solution of the crime and apprehension of the criminal could bring him promotion. But he was a conscientious man and, unasked, was already preparing for the superintendent a résumé of all local information he felt might be pertinent.

His wife, a craggy woman whose outward semblance belied her good-heartedness, took one look at Ellie on her arrival at the station and led her into the kitchen for tea and sympathy. Ellie had deteriorated rapidly under the treatment (a necessary process, well understood by Mrs Crowther) and by the time Pascoe came away from Backhouse, she had been given a mild sedative by the doctor and removed to a bedroom.

Doctor Hardisty, a rangy, middle-aged man whose unruly grey hair gave him a permanently distraught look, met Pascoe at the kitchen door. They had encountered once already at Brookside Cottage.

'You all right?' he now asked diffidently.

'Fine,' said Pascoe. It wasn't altogether a lie. The act of signing the coolly formulated statement had produced a temporary catharsis. Momentarily the morning's discoveries had been reduced to the status of a 'case'. He even found himself prompted to question the doctor about his examination of the bodies, but decided against it. Hardisty was the local man, living and practising in the village. By now the bodies would be on their way to the mortuary and the probing knife of the pathologist.

By now Timmy and Carlo and Rose would be on their way . . .

He nipped the thought off smartly.

'Miss Soper?' he asked. 'How is she?'

'Resting upstairs. I've given her something.'

'May I see her?'

'If she's awake. It's straight ahead on the landing.'

Pascoe turned and began to climb the stairs.

Ellie opened her eyes as he came through the door. Her dress was draped tidily over a chair and she lay under a patchwork quilt in her slip.

'OK, love?' said Pascoe, taking her hand.

'Doped to the back teeth,' she said. 'I don't want to sleep. It's always worse remembering when you wake up.'

'You've got to sleep,' he said gently. The sight of her lying there so palely moved him almost as deeply as the discovery of the three corpses had done.

She nodded as though he had performed some feat of subtle persuasion, and closed her eyes. But as he opened the door to leave, she spoke again.

'Peter,' she said. 'Where's Colin? He's got to be told.'

'It's all in hand,' he said reassuringly. 'Sleep now.'

On the stairs he felt dizzy and had to pause, leaning

heavily on the banister. It was certainly in hand, the business of finding Colin. But the searchers' motives were far from humane.

'You OK, Sergeant?' said Backhouse from the foot of the stairs. He sounded more concerned than the doctor had done.

'Yes sir,' said Pascoe, descending.

'Miss Soper asleep?'

'I think so.'

Backhouse looked closely at him, his thin scholarly face solicitous, assessing.

'I'm going back to the cottage. The lab. boys should be finished now. I wondered if you felt up to coming with me. I'd appreciate your assistance.'

The ghost of a grin flitted involuntarily over Pascoe's lips at this semi-formal courtesy. Fat Dalziel, his own superintendent, must have missed out on this part of the senior officers' training course.

'Certainly, sir,' he said.

Some minor telepathy must have operated. As they climbed into the waiting car, Backhouse said, 'I've been talking to Mr Dalziel on the phone.'

'Oh.'

'He was naturally sorry to hear what had happened.'

Naturally. But I bet the sod didn't make the normal polite distressed noises. Backhouse was doing a translation job.

'He says you're too important to be spared past the week-end, but I would appreciate what help you can give me in that time.'

Appreciate again. He was being given kid-glove treatment. You didn't have to be a detective to work out why. But let them say it. He was damned if he was going to broach the matter.

Them. With surprise Pascoe realized that he was thinking of the police as *them*.

'Stop here,' said Backhouse to his driver. The car pulled up outside a high-roofed, pebble-dashed building with narrow, church-like windows. A well-kept notice advertised that this was Thornton Lacey Village Hall. Beneath the gold and black lettering a typewritten sheet supplied the menu of activities that could be sampled in the hall during the current week. Last night, for instance, the Village Amenities Committee had met. And tonight the Old Time Dancing Group was scheduled to waltz, fox-trot, two-step, and polka its way down Memory Lane. But the light fantastic would have to be tripped somewhere else, thought Pascoe as he followed Backhouse into the building.

The large musty-smelling room was full of activity. Shirt-sleeved policemen were arranging tables and two Post Office men were fixing up telephones. All the lights were on to supplement the meagre ration of sunlight the windows let in.

'The station's too small,' said Backhouse. 'Especially if this turns into a large scale operation. Which I hope it won't.'

He glanced sideways at Pascoe, then looked quickly away. A uniformed inspector came to meet them.

'Anything new?' Backhouse greeted him.

'Just a couple of things, sir.'

The inspector glanced assessingly at Pascoe, then led Backhouse away to the far end of the hall. Pascoe thought of following. He was desperately keen to discover what was going on but also very conscious of his ambiguous position. He was merely a witness, he had no official standing here.

'What the hell's going on here?'

The interrupter was a big man, barrel-chested and strong-jawed. He was wearing a polo-necked sweater and jodhpurs. Pascoe felt sorry for the horse that would have to carry that bulk which he estimated at fifteen stone. It

22

was all pretty solid stuff. The man was in his forties but still a long way from turning to flab.

'Well? Come on, man. Who's in charge?'

Backhouse's attention had been caught and he came across to meet the man.

'Good morning, sir,' he said. 'I'm Detective-Superintendent Backhouse. And you . . .?'

'Angus Pelman. What the hell are you up to?' asked the man in a rather more moderate tone.

'We're conducting a murder inquiry, sir,' responded Backhouse. 'I'm surprised you haven't heard.'

Yes, that *is* surprising, thought Pascoe. Over two hours had elapsed since the crime had been reported. He had no doubt that shortly – perhaps already – the TV cameras would be rolling and the press-men patrolling around Brookside Cottage. But Angus Pelman had contrived to remain ignorant till he entered the hall.

He was also contriving to look completely taken aback at the news. When Backhouse filled in a few details, he sat down violently on the nearest chair.

'The Hopkinses at Brookside Cottage?' he repeated incredulously.

'You knew them, sir?' asked Backhouse.

'I should do,' Pelman answered. 'I sold them the damned place.'

A memory started up in Pascoe's mind, beautifully clear. The cottage in Eskdale, six (or was it seven?) years ago. The owner had been a farmer who lived half a mile down the valley. He was a big, randy bastard, full of himself, and he took to dropping in from time to time – exercising his right of inspection, he claimed, though his main objects of inspection were clearly the two girls, particularly Rose. They suspected also that he visited the place while they were out walking on the fells. In the end they did something, some kind of joke . . . but the

23

memory faded as quickly as it had come. He would have to ask Ellie.

'Shot, you say? Both shot?' said Pelman.

'Not both the Hopkinses, sir. Mrs Hopkins, and their two guests.'

'And Colin Hopkins?'

'We hope to contact him soon, sir.'

'You mean, he doesn't know? But he was around yesterday evening. I saw him in the village.'

Suspicion dawned, followed by outrage.

'You're not suggesting he had something to do with it, are you? Man, you've got to be mad. I haven't known him long, but it's out of the question!'

Suddenly Pascoe liked him a lot better.

'We've reached no conclusions yet, sir,' answered Backhouse reasonably. 'By the way, if you weren't expecting to find us here, why did you come in?'

Pelman looked puzzled.

'Why did I . . .? Oh, *here* you mean. Simple. I'm the chairman of the Amenities Committee; we had a meeting last night and on the morning after these meetings, the secretary brings the minutes along here. She's got them typed out by then. We check through them together, then pin them up on the notice board so that everybody can see what's been going on.'

'Nice,' said Backhouse approvingly. 'Nice.'

He was looking towards the door as he spoke, and Pascoe, following his gaze, was uncertain whether he was commenting on the democratic process or the woman who stood there.

She *was* nice, if you liked that kind of thing. Early thirties, well groomed brown hair, expensively but quietly dressed, good figure; Pascoe had no objection to any of these. But he felt himself antagonized by her look of amused self-possession as she surveyed the scene.

Upper-middle class, certain of her place in the scheme

24

of things, full of common sense and good works, committee woman, is or will be a magistrate, cardboard cut-out of the good Tory MP's wife, or even the good Tory MP. Complacent bitch.

Pascoe was surprised at the violence of his thoughts. And at the ridiculous speed of his entirely intuitive analysis. There was a spring of rage in him which would have to be tapped with the greatest care. He tried to wipe the slate clean and start again with this woman, but she seemed bent on confirming his conclusions.

'Hello, Angus,' she said in a clear, high-pitched, well-educated voice. 'You're well protected. The minutes aren't *that* explosive, I hope.'

She came forward holding a leather folder in her hand. So this was the secretary of the Amenities Committee. That figured.

'Hello, Marianne. Haven't you heard?'

Pelman briefly told her what had happened. As he spoke, Pascoe observed the woman keenly. Two important members of the village community and neither had heard the news. He would have to revise his ideas about the tribal nature of the English village.

'Would you like a seat, Mrs . . . er . . .?' asked Backhouse politely as Pelman finished.

'Culpepper,' supplied Pelman.

'Thank you,' said the woman. She did not look too overcome to Pascoe's jaundiced eye, but then her upbringing probably laid great stress on the stiffness of upper lips. It worked both ways. She placed the leather folder on a nearby table, but it slipped and fell open to the floor. Pascoe picked it up and stood with it in his hands, glancing down at the neatly typewritten sheets. He took in the topmost of them with the casual ease of a thousand-words-a-minute man. It seemed to have been a lively meeting, mainly centred on the alleged pollution of the stream which ran through the vilage. Downstreamers suspected upstreamers of having inefficient or even extra cesspools. Upstreamers vehemently denied this. The water in question was presumably the brook which ran behind Brookside Cottage. The sundial in the garden rose vividly in his mind. Only the sunny hours . . .

'I'll take that,' said Pelman, seizing the folder from Pascoe's unresisting hand. 'We won't hold you up any more, Superintendent. Come on, Marianne. Let's get you a stiff brandy in the Bird.'

Exit John Wayne with the lady, thought Pascoe as the jodhpured man steered Marianne Culpepper doorwards by the elbow. She gently disengaged herself before passing out into the street.

'Put someone on that door,' said Backhouse mildly, 'before they establish a right of way. I'll be at the cottage.'

He motioned Pascoe to move out before him, and let him wait by the car while he exchanged a few more words with the inspector. The street was surprisingly empty. The sun had grown warm as the morning progressed, but Pascoe shivered from time to time as he waited for Backhouse to come and start the short journey back to Brookside Cottage.

Chapter 3

Their driver parked the car on the grass verge about forty yards from the cottage. The assortment of vehicles scattered in the immediate vicinity prevented a closer approach.

Three or four newspapermen intercepted the superintendent as he walked along the road. Locals mainly, Pascoe assessed. It was still too soon for anyone to have emerged from the chaos of Saturday morning London. But they would do. *Three dead from shotgun wounds* was too big to leave in the hands of a local runner.

Backhouse dealt with them kindly but firmly. No, there were no developments yet. They were looking for a man who might be able to help them with their inquiries. Mr Colin Hopkins, yes, that was him. A photograph and description might be issued if it was felt to be necessary.

Pascoe had dropped behind as the questioning proceeded. When Backhouse and his interrogators stopped in front of the cottage, he found himself, deliberately blank-minded, looking up the side of the building between the garage and the wall. There was activity in the back garden and beyond. They would be looking for the weapon. Everything they found would be carefully scrutinized, of course, but it was the weapon they were hoping for. It made a difference if you knew the man you were searching after *didn't* have a shotgun in his possession.

He doubted if they'd find it so near. Hurled in panic into the woods over the stream, it would have been found by now. Whereas if the killer were cool enough to make a more deliberate attempt to hide it, he would surely wait until his car had taken him a safe distance from the village.

The killer. He tested himself gently from the vantage point of disembodied objectivity he had scrambled on to in the last two hours. Was he ready yet to consider whether Colin . . . why Colin . . .

No. He wasn't quite ready. He walked up to the garage and peered in. What he saw surprised him.

'Sergeant!' Backhouse called authoritatively. Pascoe instinctively obeyed the summons and had joined the superintendent at the threshold before he started wondering about the tone of command. A new step in the psychology of their relationship perhaps. A reminder of his official subordination.

Or perhaps his service with Dalziel had made him too suspicious of all detective-superintendents' motives. Perhaps all Backhouse was doing was using his police rank as a red herring to divert the interest of the newspapermen from him. Clearly, as they moved off in a friendly, almost light-hearted, little group, they had no suspicion that the discoverer of the crime was so close.

In the cottage, much had changed. No effort had been made to tidy up after the rigorous search and finger-printing examination which had taken place. Why bother when there was no chance of an irate householder turning up to complain?

Backhouse thought differently.

'For God's sake, Hamblyn,' he said to the ginger-moustached detective who came to greet him, 'get this place tidied up. And those cars outside. If I want a road-block here, I'll ask for it.'

'Yes, sir,' said Hamblyn unemotionally.

'Anything new?'

'Nothing useful, sir. Not as far as *I* can see. Anything on the car yet, sir?'

'I'm afraid not.'

28

Pascoe spoke lowly, diffidently.

'There's a car in the garage,' he said. It sounded daft as he said it but, hell, he had to say it. Not that it was possible they wouldn't have looked. Was it?

'Yes, yes; I believe there is,' said Backhouse. Then he laughed.

'Oh, I see your dilemma. Yes it's true the Hopkinses' car is in the garage. But it's the other one we're interested in. Royal blue Mini-Cooper according to best report. The one Mr Rushworth and Mr Mansfield arrived in.'

Pascoe was abashed. Hamblyn was looking at him with faint distaste.

'Let's step into the garden,' said Backhouse, like a kindly host desirous of stirring his guest's digestive juices before lunch.

They went through the dining-room, passing the chalked body-outlines and ringed bloodstains, and out of the french window into the garden, halting near the sundial.

I'm really getting the treatment, thought Pascoe. What does he expect from me? Colin's present address?

'The Hopkinses' car was *in* the garage, the visitors' car on the driveway,' said Backhouse. 'This is the arrangement you'd expect and this is what the few people we've found who passed early last evening saw.'

'They couldn't see into the garage,' objected Pascoe.

'True,' said Backhouse. 'Now, here's what happened, or what *possibly* happened supported by a strong scaffolding of what *did* happen. There was a lot of broken glass scattered around here. Did you notice? From a whisky bottle, that was easy enough to establish. Were they hard drinkers, your friends?'

'Only on occasions,' answered Pascoe, recognizing the start of interrogation. 'And the occasion rarely merited the expense of scotch. But that was years ago. Things change.'

29

'Yes. Of course. Well, we've got a thorough house-to-house on now, but the first place my men called was the Eagle and Child, the second the Queen Anne. That's where she bought it.'

'The whisky?'

'That's right,' said Backhouse pensively. 'At about quarter to nine last night. Curious that. The Eagle and Child's nearer. No matter. The landlord's wife, who sold it to her at the off-licence counter, didn't see the car, but heard it drive away. She reckons it sounded more like the Mini-Cooper than the Hopkinses' Cortina.'

'A good ear,' commented Pascoe, watching a pair of thrushes which had decided the policemen were harmless, and were drilling for worms.

'No doubt we'll find someone to corroborate it,' said Backhouse. 'As things stand, it seems likely that they started drinking after dinner. When the scotch began to get low, Mrs Hopkins volunteered to fetch more; she used her visitors' car as it would have to be moved anyway to get her own out. On her return she either walked straight into the garden or went through the front door into the lounge, then the dining-room and out of the french windows.'

'And then she was shot,' said Pascoe.

'It seems likely. Very soon after she came back. She was still holding the full bottle, you see. We found the cap with the seal complete. She must have held the bottle in front of her, either to ward off the shot or to use as a weapon. The blast from the shotgun went right through it. There were splinters of glass embedded deep in the wound. Would any of your friends own a shotgun, do you think?'

'I don't know. I just don't know,' said Pascoe irritably. 'I've told you, Superintendent, this was a kind of reunion. I hadn't seen these people for years. How should I know what they were likely to do now?'

'Do people change that much?'

'They change all right. When someone's put a couple of ounces of lead pellets into your face, you change!'

Pascoe realized he was nearly shouting. Jesus, he thought, I should be back there too, lying on one of Constable Crowther's comfortable beds with some of Doctor Hardisty's comfortable pills inside me.

'Sir!' It was Hamblyn from the french window. Behind him stood two men.

'It's Mr French, the coroner, sir.'

'Hello, Superintendent,' said the taller of the two men who now stepped into the garden. He was over six feet, rather gaunt of feature, well tanned, his nose showing the pale indentations left by a frequent wearing of spectacles. His companion was a good nine inches shorter, less dramatic in every way, but his pale oval face was intelligent and far from weak. Both men wore casual, sporting clothes, French going in for bright colours, his companion much more subdued.

'Sorry to take so long. You must have thought I'd be first on the spot, living on the doorstep so to speak. But I was half-way round the golf-course with Culpepper here. Dreadful business, this. Dreadful. You'd better tell me what I need to know.'

Culpepper, thought Pascoe, as Backhouse and the coroner moved back into the cottage together. The committee secretary – Marianne Culpepper. Her husband?

The man spoke to him and his words seemed to confirm this. His eyes were taking everything in. Despite his air of quiet authority, he felt a need to explain himself.

'Excuse me, could you . . . You are with the police, I'm right?'

'Pascoe, sir. Sergeant Pascoe.'

'It's not just morbid curiosity that brings me here, Sergeant. I live close by. I knew these people, the

31

Hopkinses, I mean. When Mr French told me why he had to come back, I couldn't believe it.'

He fell silent.

'How close do you live, sir?' asked Pascoe. It was easier to fall into the policeman role than explain his true position.

'About half a mile. Round the side of the hill.' He gestured vaguely towards the rising ground which lay to the south of the village.

'What happened here, Sergeant? Is it true they are all dead?'

'Mrs Hopkins is dead, sir,' said Pascoe evenly. 'And Mr Mansfield and Mr Rushworth, two guests who were spending the night with them.'

'Oh, my God. What about Colin, Mr Hopkins? And the other guests?'

'Other guests?' said Pascoe sharply.

'Yes. I ran into Mrs Hopkins in the village yesterday evening when I got back from the office. About five o'clock. It seems impossible . . . anyway, I asked them round for a drink tonight, but she explained they would have a houseful of guests. Four, she said. At least.'

It had been five-thirty when Pascoe had rung to say he and Ellie couldn't make it that evening. If only that case hadn't come up . . . or Dalziel hadn't insisted . . . another two made the odds very strong against anyone trying anything with a double-barrelled shotgun. What an adaptable thing blame was; so easy to shift or attract.

'Had you known Mr and Mrs Hopkins long, sir?' asked Pascoe, evading the question about the guests.

'Not long. Two or three months only, since they bought Brookside, in fact. They have worked so hard on it. The place was not in a good state of repair when they acquired it, you know. And they did wonders, wonders.'

He tailed off into silence.

'Mr Pelman sold them the cottage, I believe,' said Pascoe.

'That's right.'

Something in his tone made Pascoe pursue this line.

'Did he live here himself before he sold the place?'

Culpepper smiled without much humour.

'No. The cottage stands at the boundary of the land he bought when he came here five years ago. His house is the other side of the woods, *his* woods. That's what he really wanted, of course. A place where he could pit his wits against the intelligence of various small beasts and birds. A most uneven contest, I fear.'

Am I supposed to be too thick to get the double irony? wondered Pascoe.

'It's strange, isn't it, that the chairman of the Village Amenities Committee should let such a property fall into disrepair?' murmured Pascoe.

Culpepper raised his eyebrows at him.

'You glean your information fast, Sergeant.'

'We spend our working life amidst the alien corn, sir.'

Culpepper suddenly nodded twice, as though something had been confirmed.

'You're the Hopkinses' policeman friend, aren't you? One of their week-end guests.'

Clever Mr Culpepper.

'Yes. I am. How did you know?'

'Mrs Hopkins, Rose, said something about you, when we talked yesterday.'

So I was an object of interest, worth a special mention. Like a literary lion. Or a two-headed man. What now, Mr Culpepper? wondered Pascoe. Indignation at my mild deceit?

'I'm sorry. I didn't realize. This must be an unbearable situation for you,' said Culpepper with apparently unforced sympathy. 'Were you here when it happened?'

33

'No,' said Pascoe shortly. 'I found them this morning when we arrived.'

'How terrible. You say *we*?'

'A friend. She's resting now. It was a shock.'

'Terrible. Terrible. Such things are a puzzle and a torment to the mind.'

Backhouse and French appeared.

'Are you ready, Hartley?' called the coroner. 'Two-thirty this afternoon then, Superintendent. I hope you find your man quickly.'

He looked sideways at Pascoe and shook his head slightly, but didn't speak. Culpepper held out his hand.

'Goodbye, Mr Pascoe. I'm sorry we had to meet in such circumstances. Your friends were delightful people to have in the village. We counted ourselves lucky that they came here.'

Pascoe shook his hand. There was nothing to say in reply except perhaps that Rose would scarcely have counted herself lucky in coming here; nor Colin, wherever he was.

That was the only thing really worth talking about. Where Colin was. And why. Backhouse must be ready to get round to it now.

He was. French and Culpepper had scarcely disappeared from the garden before Backhouse asked the big question.

'You've had time for reflection now, Sergeant. So tell me. Why should a man like Colin Hopkins take a shotgun and kill his wife and two close friends?'

34

Chapter 4

He had been expecting the question and had felt reserves of angry indignation building up inside him, ready to explode when it was asked. But for some reason the spark did not catch.

'We don't know he did,' he protested weakly.

'You're a policeman,' answered Backhouse. 'Suppose this were your case. What assumption would you be working on?'

'It's all circumstantial. If you knew Colin, you'd know that it's just impossible.'

'I've encountered quite a few murderers,' said Backhouse patiently. 'I dare say you've met one or two yourself. One thing they nearly all had in common was a handful of close friends willing to attest with the most vehement sincerity that the accused was quite incapable of such a crime. Am I right?'

'I suppose so.'

'Good. In any case, as you told me before, a few years can change things. Situations certainly. People as well, though to a lesser extent. So tell me what you know, what you remember. Is he a quick-tempered man?'

'What the hell does it matter?' said Pascoe. If he was going to be questioned as an ordinary witness, he would assume some of the privileges of an ordinary witness. Such as the unnecessity of politeness towards questioning policemen.

'You're going after him anyway. You'll track him down, question him. If there's enough evidence, you'll put him in court. So why waste time talking to me?'

'You know why, Sergeant,' said Backhouse coldly. 'Of

course we're going after him. And of course my men –
your colleagues – will assume it's very likely he has
committed a triple murder. They'll also assume he has a
double-barrelled shotgun which he is willing to use. I want
information, all the information I can get. I want to know
the best way of dealing with him, which way he's likely to
jump. I thought I was lucky when I learnt you were in the
force. A professional first on the scene. It was your bad
luck. I thought it was my good luck.'

'Every point taken,' said Pascoe with tight-lipped
emphasis. 'Only, I cannot believe that he did it.'

'Fair enough. Then why so antagonistic? Tell me things
to prove his innocence. Was he a jealous man, do you
think? Would his wife give him cause?'

'Unlikely,' said Pascoe with a frown. 'At least they
seemed set up for life. Ask Ellie, Miss Soper. She's seen
them much more recently. But we've talked a lot about
them and she would certainly have mentioned any signs of
a rift.'

'There were two single men in the house last night,' said
Backhouse casually. 'Old friends. Going back to before
she married.'

Pascoe laughed now.

'I see it! The triangle. Or even the quadrilateral. It's a
non-starter, Superintendent. Timmy and Carlo were, if
anything, even more devoted than Rose and Colin.'

'I see,' said Backhouse softly. 'I see. But things do
change, as you say. Even . . . tastes. What kind of thing
was it that would put Mr Hopkins into one of his terrible
wraths?'

'I'm sorry?'

'In the letter you showed me,' said Backhouse, 'he says
something about his wrath being terrible if you don't turn
up, and adds that you know just how terrible his wrath can
be. A figure of speech merely?'

Pascoe walked slowly forward and came to a halt on

the edge of the bank which sloped steeply down to the brook. All the police activity was in the woods on the other side now. A slow, methodical and, as yet, completely unproductive search. Despite the warmth of the sun, many of the policemen were wearing waterproof overtrousers as the undergrowth was still soaked from the previous night's torrential rain. It would have obliterated any sign of human passage, but it couldn't wash away a shotgun.

'No, not a figure of speech,' said Pascoe. 'He had a quick temper. Not a violent temper though, it never led him into violence against people. Certainly he never got anywhere near the kind of fury which could make a man pick up a shotgun, kill two of his friends, reload, and shoot his wife. What about the gun, by the way?'

'A 410, we know that from the cartridge cases. But that's it. There's no sign of a licence anywhere in the cottage. Was Hopkins the kind of man to want to do some shooting? Game, I mean.'

'Never knew him express an interest. Though he wasn't an anti, like Carlo and Timmy.'

'And his wife? Was she anti also?'

'Rose? Hell, no. Rose grew up in the country, was used to the idea of birds tumbling from the tree-top straight into the pie-dish.'

'So the presence of this' – Backhouse waved at the woods – 'in his back garden may have been a temptation?'

'Why not ask Pelman? He'd be sure to know who was shooting on his land.'

Backhouse grinned.

'Oh, he's being asked, never fear. And we're checking on all shotgun licences issued locally in the past three months. Mr Dalziel would be proud of us. So you reckon there was no chance of his doing it in a blind rage?'

Pascoe was beginning to adapt to the man's questioning technique. He answered without pause.

'No chance of his doing it. Period.'

'In a blind rage. So, how about doing it in cold blood? What kind of thing might make your high-tempered extrovert friend consider shooting someone dead in cold blood?'

'That's even less likely than the other!'

'So it's more likely he did it in a blind rage?'

'I didn't say that,' protested Pascoe.

'I'm sorry. I thought you said it was *less* likely that he would do it in cold blood?'

'For God's sake! We're not in court!' snapped Pascoe, tiring of this word play.

'It's as well for your friend we are not,' said Backhouse, turning and beginning to walk back to the cottage. Pascoe followed glumly and caught up with the superintendent in the dining-room. Together they stood and looked down at the chalked outlines on the floor.

'These were your friends too,' said Backhouse. 'Innocent, guilty, have you any idea where a man like Colin Hopkins would head for after something like this?'

'The nearest police station,' said Pascoe.

Backhouse shrugged in resignation.

'That's where I'll drop you, Sergeant. Thanks for your help.'

'I'm sorry,' said Pascoe. 'There doesn't seem to be anything I can say. I'm sorry.'

'No matter. Get back to Miss Soper. I'll have another talk with her when she feels up to it. If she's seen your friends more recently, it might help.'

'Yes,' said Pascoe, leading the way to the car. He stepped out of the cottage with a great sense of relief.

'The inquest will be opened in the village school this afternoon,' said Backhouse. 'Just identification and causes of death, I should think. The usual procedure. Two-thirty. We won't need Miss Soper at this stage. I'll send a car for you.'

38

'Yes.'

The rest of the short journey passed in silence. I'm a serious disappointment to him, thought Pascoe. All that kindness wasted.

Ellie was still asleep, so Pascoe went downstairs once more. Mrs Crowther put her head out of the kitchen door and asked how the lady was.

'Sleeping,' said Pascoe. 'But she's got her colour back.'

'Good. It'll do her good. You'll be hungry, I don't doubt. What about a gammon rasher and egg?'

'No, I couldn't put you out,' protested Pascoe, realizing, slightly to his surprise, how hungry he was.

'Not a bit. Crowther'll be in any minute for his, so it's no bother at all.'

It was a well cooked meal, interrupted twice by the telephone.

The first time it was Dalziel.

'You all right?' he asked.

'Fine,' said Pascoe.

'I've got your report on the Cottingley break-in here. You write like a bloody woman's magazine advertiser. When you mean he pissed in the kettle, why the hell don't you write he pissed in the kettle?'

'Sorry.'

'He's a dirty bastard this one. But clever with it. If we don't get him soon, he'll be retiring. How's your girl?'

'Resting. She'll be OK.'

'Good. They're going after your mate, I hear.'

'That's right.'

'Aye. We've had the look-out notice up here. What do you think? Did he do it?'

'It looks bad.'

'But you don't think so? Well, listen. A word of advice. Don't get mixed up more than you have to. Say your piece, sign your statement and get on home. Leave it to Backhouse. He's a bit of an old woman, but he's not a

39

bad jack. And don't be taken in by his good manners. He'll drop you in the cart if he thinks it'll help.'

'Yes, sir. We'll probably get back tomorrow.'

'I should bloody well hope so. You're due in here at eight-thirty on Monday morning. Don't be late. Cheer-oh.'

And up you too, thought Pascoe, looking at the receiver. The fat bastard was probably congratulating himself on his subtle psychological therapy.

The phone rang again as Mrs Crowther reached into the oven for his warming plate. This time to his surprise it was Hartley Culpepper.

'I hoped I'd find you there, Mr Pascoe. Look, it struck me after I left you at the cottage, are you staying in the village tonight?'

'Well, yes,' said Pascoe, surprised. 'Yes, I expect we are.'

'Have you fixed up anything yet?'

'No. Not yet. I haven't really thought,' answered Pascoe. It was true, he hadn't given a thought to what they would do that night. The Crowthers, he suspected, would at a pinch keep Ellie, but it would mean a great deal of inconvenience for them.

'Perhaps one of the pubs,' he mused aloud.

'Nonsense,' said Culpepper firmly. 'We would be delighted if you would stay with us. I was going to ask you and your friend to come to dinner, anyway. So why not bring your bags with you? This must have been a terrible strain for both of you. It'll do you good – it will do us all good – to be in friendly company. Please come.'

'It's very kind of you,' said Pascoe doubtfully.

'Good,' interrupted Culpepper. 'We'll expect you, about tea-time then. The Crowthers will be able to direct you. Goodbye.'

Everyone else is having the last word today, thought Pascoe.

Constable Crowther had arrived home and was taking his place at the other side of the kitchen-table. He nodded an acknowledgement at Pascoe and settled down to eating his meal. Either hunger or some form of diplomacy kept him silent, and Pascoe himself did not speak until he had disposed of his food without further interruption.

'This will mean a lot of work for you,' he said finally.

Crowther nodded.

"A bit. There's a beer in the cupboard behind you if you fancy it.'

'Thanks,' said Pascoe. 'This'll be a quiet patch normally?'

'Quiet enough. Popular for break-ins.'

'Is that so?'

Crowther nodded and chewed his gammon systematically. About thirty chews to the mouthful, Pascoe thought.

'It's mostly business people now, you see,' resumed Crowther. 'Working in the town. There's been a lot of building.'

Another mouthful. Another thirty chews.

'And renovation.'

'Like Brookside Cottage?'

'That's right,' said Crowther, nodding vigorously.

'Was it empty when Mr Pelham decided to sell it?'

'That's right.' Another mouthful. This time Pascoe counted. Twenty-eight, twenty-nine. 'Mr Pelham didn't like that. It was a handy way into his woods from the road for anyone wanting to pot a few birds. And the cottages themselves was always getting broken into. Not that there was anything to take, you understand. Practising for bigger stuff, I reckoned. But they did a lot of damage.'

So. Vandals and poachers all swanning round Brookside Cottage. Homicidal? It was surprising how many people were under the right conditions.

41

Even people you knew quite well.

'Pelman put it on the market then?' mused Pascoe. 'That was quite clever. He'd make a bit of money and have someone there to man his frontier post.'

'Hardly that,' objected Crowther. 'You can get into Pelman's woods at a dozen places. And there's not all that much in there anyhow.'

'No red deer and grizzly bear?'

'No,' answered Crowther, adding, as though in reproach of Pascoe's mild levity, 'just a lot of coppers at the moment.'

Pascoe sipped his beer. Crowther's tastes ran to luke-warm brown ale, it appeared. The thought put him in mind of the two village pubs, in one of which Rose Hopkins had last been seen by anyone alive to tell the tale. Except one person.

'What's the difference between the Eagle and Child and the Queen Anne?' he asked. It sounded like a child's conundrum, but Crowther didn't seem puzzled.

'The Eagle's a free house. Owned by Major Palfrey. The Anne's tied to the brewery. Mr and Mrs Dixon just manage it. Not *just*. They manage it very well, I mean. Nice couple.'

'Who uses which? Or is it just the nearest that people go to?'

Crowther looked at him closely.

'Couldn't say,' he said. 'I use the Anne myself.'

'Just because it's the nearest?' insisted Pascoe. 'I should have thought the local law would have had to preserve a fine show of impartiality towards licensed premises.'

'I do,' said Crowther. 'When I'm on duty. But off, I like to be comfortable where I drink.'

He seemed to make his mind up that Pascoe had a sympathetic ear and leaned over the table confidentially.

'Difference is, and this is just me, mind you,' he went on, 'the Dixons make you feel welcome, the Major always makes me feel he's doing me a favour by pulling me a pint.'

He nodded emphatically and started rolling an absurdly thin cigarette in an ancient machine. Pascoe laughed knowingly.

'Major Palfrey thinks he's the squire rather than the landlord, does he?'

'That's the trouble with this place now,' averred the constable, lighting his cigarette which burnt like a fuse. 'It's full of bloody squires. Trouble is, there aren't enough peasants to go round.'

Constable Crowther, it appeared, invariably took a ten-minute nap after his lunch and could see no reason to interrupt his routine today. Pascoe was sorry about this. The man's conversation interested him and he was still desperately in need of things to interest him. He decided to take a walk, down to the village perhaps, find out what was going on. As he stood up, he realized he hadn't mentioned the arrangements that had been made for the evening.

Mrs Crowther came into the kitchen and bustled around her snoozing husband, clearing the table with no effort at noise-evasion.

'Miss Soper and I are going to spend the night at Mr Culpepper's house,' said Pascoe. 'I'd like to let Miss Soper sleep, though, as long as possible. Is that OK?'

'We could have kept you here,' answered the woman. 'Our lad could have used the camp-bed.'

'Thank you very much. But I didn't want to trouble you. And Mr Culpepper was most insistent.'

Crowther opened his eyes and looked straight at Pascoe.

'Culpepper,' he said. He made it sound like an accusation. Then he went back to sleep.

In Crowther's book, Culpepper was probably one of the self-appointed squires, thought Pascoe as he stood

43

outside the station in the bright sunlight and took his bearings. He wasn't certain if he altogether liked what he saw. Not that it wasn't pretty. In the rememberable past Thornton Lacey must have been a roadside hamlet of a couple of dozen houses plus a church, a shop and a pub which served the numerous farms in the rich surrounding countryside. But things had changed. Over the hill one day, perhaps only a couple of decades ago, had come the first – the first what? He remembered the phrase in Colin's letter. *Pallid cits*. The first pallid cit. Soon there must have been droves of them. And they were still coming. He recalled as he had driven in that morning an arrowed notice on the outskirts of the village had directed their attention to a *High Class Development of Executive Residences*. It had made them laugh to think of Colin and Rose in such company. Many things had made them laugh on the journey.

With an effort of will he returned his attention to the village. Pallid cits had to be catered for. There was a ladies' hairdressing salon very tastefully slotted beneath an awryly-timbered top storey. At least two Gothic-scripted antique shops were visible. Passing pallid cits had to be tempted to stop and invest in the past. But not to stop permanently, he suspected. No one defends the countryside and its traditions more fiercely than he who has just got planning permission for his own half-acre. The Village Amenities Committee didn't sound like a farmworkers' trade union, somehow.

It's that bloody woman again, thought Pascoe gloomily. Why have I taken against her so much so rapidly? And I'm spending the night under her roof.

But why the hell should I? I didn't want to.

That anger which had been bubbling under the surface all morning suddenly broke through again. He had progressed about a quarter of a mile down the long, winding

44

village street and now realized he was opposite the Queen Anne. On an impulse he crossed over and went in.

It wasn't long till closing time and the bar was empty.

'Lager, please,' he said to the attractively solid-fleshed woman who came to take his order.

'Thirsty weather,' she said with a smile.

'Do you put people up?' he asked, sipping his drink.

'Sorry. You might try the Eagle and Child. They have a couple of rooms there they sometimes let.'

'Thanks. Is it Mrs Dixon, by the way?' Pascoe asked.

'That's right,' the woman answered, looking at him with sudden wariness. 'Why?'

'You served Mrs Hopkins, Mrs Rose Hopkins of Brookside Cottage, last night I believe.'

'Yes. Yes, I did.' She glanced through into the other bar.

'Sam. Sam, love. Got a moment?'

A red, jolly-faced man, solid as his wife, stepped through, a smile on his lips. Pascoe could understand how Crowther felt made welcome.

'Lovely day, sir. Yes, my dear?'

'This gentleman's asking about Mrs Hopkins.'

Sam Dixon composed his features to a solemnity they clearly weren't made for.

'A dreadful business. Are you from the Press, sir?'

'No,' said Pascoe. The man looked nonplussed for a moment.

'The thing is,' he said finally, 'it's an upsetting business. Molly – my wife – has spoken to the police already. Now, we don't like talking about our customers at the best of times, but in circumstances like this, especially with friends of the poor woman . . .'

'I'm a friend,' said Pascoe suddenly. He appreciated the man's diplomacy but he couldn't keep the abruptness out of his voice. 'I *was* a friend. I'm not just after a bit of sensational titillation.'

'I never suggested you were, sir,' said Dixon quietly.

'No. Of course you didn't. I'm sorry,' said Pascoe. 'The thing is, well, I found them, you see.'

Absurdly he found himself unable to go on. One part of him was detached, viewing the phenomenon with a sort of professional interest. He had seen this kind of thing a hundred times in his job, had come to watch for it, the moment when a witness to a crime or an accident suddenly *feels* what he has seen. It was a completely unforecastable syndrome. Sometimes it was accompanied by complete collapse. Or mild amnesia. Blind panic. Or, as now, temporary paralysis of the speech organs.

A large brandy appeared under his nose from nowhere. If you had to act like this, his detached portion thought, here was clearly the place to do it.

'Sit down, sir. Drink this up. Nothing like it for clearing the head.'

'I'm sorry,' said Pascoe, suddenly regaining control of his tongue. 'It's ridiculous.'

'Nonsense. Go on, knock that brandy back.'

He did so and felt much better.

'You're very kind,' he said, trying to regain control of the situation. 'I'm sorry. I should have said who I was before I started asking questions.'

'Not at all.' Dixon eyed him with the calculating scrutiny of one long expert at diagnosing the condition of his customers. Pascoe evidently passed muster.

'What did you want to know?'

'Just what happened when Mrs Hopkins came in. What she said. That kind of thing.'

This was silly. It would all be on record. Backhouse might let him see it. Certainly he could arrange unofficially to have a look. What did he expect to do, anyway? Spot some incredibly subtly concealed clue which would reveal precisely what happened last night and prove

46

Colin . . . innocent? He must be innocent! Then where the hell was he?

'There was nothing special about last night,' Molly Dixon was saying. 'We were very busy. You'd expect that at that time on a Friday night, but it was worse than usual as I was on my own with just our barmaid, and she's a bit slow. Sam was at the Amenities Committee Meeting. Rose came to the off-licence counter there.'

She pointed at a small hatch which was visible through a door in the wall joining the two bars.

'There's a bell in there. She rang it. I went through as soon as I could. "A bottle of scotch," she said. "First that comes to hand will do. I can see you're busy." I gave her a bottle. "Will this do?" I asked. "Anything," she said. "They've had so much I could give them cold tea." "I'd try hot coffee if they're that bad," I said. She paid me, took the bottle and went. There should have been a penny change. I shouted, but she didn't hear, and next thing I heard a car starting, so I went back to the fray.'

'The Mini-Cooper? You heard the Mini?' asked Pascoe.

'I'm not that expert! It sounded a bit sporty, that's all.'

'And she said nothing else?'

'Not that I can remember. It was a very busy night.'

'Of course. I'm very grateful to you,' said Pascoe. 'Just one thing. You called Mrs Hopkins "Rose".'

'That's her name, isn't . . . wasn't it?' said Molly, puzzled.

'Yes, of course. What I meant was, you knew her quite well?'

'Oh yes! We got on very well right from the start. I'd only known her and Colin a couple of months, but we soon got on friendly terms. That's why it came as such a shock . . . I still can't believe it.'

'They didn't use the other pub, then? The Eagle and Child.'

He intercepted a quick glance between the man and his wife. Intercepted and, he thought, interpreted.

'They may have done on occasions,' said Dixon in a neutral tone.

'Come on!' said Pascoe. 'Rose is dead and God knows what's happened to Colin. So you can forget professional etiquette for once, can't you?'

Another glance. This time the woman spoke.

'They went there to start with, I think. It was a bit nearer to the cottage. And it's popular with . . .'

She hesitated.

'The squirearchy,' supplied Pascoe. 'What happened?'

'There was a bit of trouble. A row or something.'

'With the Major?'

'I'm not sure. They didn't mention it till we'd got to know them quite well. I mean, they wouldn't come in here right away and start complaining about the other pub. They weren't that kind of people,' protested Molly.

'You're right,' said Pascoe. 'They weren't.'

'They only mentioned it at all as a joke. Saying how lucky it was they had been driven out of the Garden of Eden. *Felix culpa*, Colin called it. He loved to make quotations.'

'Yes, he did,' said Pascoe. 'But whose *culpa*, I wonder.'

He stood up.

'You've been very kind. Colin and Rose were always fortunate in their choice of friends.'

It sounded corny. Or at best vain. But he meant it and the Dixons obviously appreciated it. He left, promising to call back later.

His talk with the Dixons had cheered him and he felt in an almost happy mood as he turned into the Eagle and Child. It was a pleasant room, cool and well wooded. And almost empty. They didn't drink very hard round here. Not at lunch-time anyway. A half-eaten sandwich and half-empty glass on a corner table hinted at someone in the gents. But the only visible customers were seated at the bar. One was a grey-haired, lantern-jawed man in shirt-sleeves. The other was much more colourful. Long auburn hair fell luxuriantly on to shoulders over which was casually draped a soft-leather jacket in pastel yellow. His intelligent face was set in an expression of rapt attentiveness as he listened to the other man.

Pascoe went up to the bar and waited for someone to appear to serve him. He was not impatient. There was a timeless aura about this old room which suited his mood very well. It was comforting somehow to think of Rose and Colin so quickly making friends in the village. Pascoe was used to death bringing out the best in people's memories, but there had been a genuine ring about the Dixon's tributes. And Culpepper's, and even Pelman's for that matter.

Along the bar the lantern-jawed man's voice rose in emphasis and became audible. It was impossible not to hear.

'But if you want the truth about this fella, Hopkins – and don't quote me on this, mind – I would say there's no doubt at all the man is completely unbalanced. Off his chump. I said it from the start.'

Chapter 5

Pascoe's anger broke at last. The professional part of his mind told him he was being very silly, but it didn't slow him down one jot.

He crossed the floor in a couple of strides and seized the lantern-jawed man by the shoulder, dragging him round so forcefully that he half slipped off his stool and only saved himself from falling by dropping his glass and grabbing at the bar.

The leather-jacketed drinker leapt clear with great agility and without spilling a drop of his drink, then settled down to view the situation with interest.

'Who the hell are you?' asked Pascoe in a low, rapid voice. 'Some kind of doctor? A psychiatrist? A trained social worker, perhaps? Or perhaps just specially gifted with superb bloody insight?'

He found he was punctuating his phrases with violent forefinger jabs into the man's midriff. Far from being distressed by the discovery, he found himself contemplating the greater satisfaction he might derive from putting all his pugilistic eggs into one basket and smashing his fist into this fellow's unpleasant, sneering face.

To give him his due, the man did not look frightened, merely taken aback by the unexpectedness of the attack.

'What the hell – look here – you bloody madman!' he expostulated.

Pascoe had almost made up his mind. Even the memory that last time he had thrown a punch in anger the result had been a mild contusion for the recipient and a broken forefinger for himself did not deter him. He clenched his fist.

'Pascoe!'

It was the authentic voice of absolute authority. It might have been Dalziel. He turned. Standing up out of the shadows of the corner near the gents was Backhouse.

A violent push in the back sent Pascoe staggering a few paces forward. His adversary had taken advantage of the interruption to get both feet firmly on the floor and counter-attack. Pascoe looked round at the grey-haired figure crouched in the standard aggressive posture. He looked as if he might in fact know how to handle himself. But this didn't prevent him from seeming faintly ludicrous, and Pascoe felt his anger ebb away as he recognized his own absurdity.

'Go to hell,' he said wearily and pulled out a chair and sat down opposite the superintendent.

Backhouse still looked angry but didn't say anything. Instead he picked up his not quite empty glass and went towards the bar.

'A light ale this time, please, and a scotch.'

'For him? He gets no service here. In fact if he's not out in thirty seconds, I'll get the police to throw him out.'

Pascoe turned, surprised. His late adversary was confronting Backhouse with undiminished aggression. This must be Palfrey, the pub-owning major.

Pascoe groaned inwardly. Even the toughest toughs worked to the principle that if you had to fight in pubs, you never picked on the landlord. Backhouse, he realized, was now in an awkward position. The leather-coated fellow might well be a reporter. Almost certainly was from the tone of Palfrey's remarks to him. He couldn't know yet who the participants in this little drama were, but he would soon find out.

Pascoe rose and made for the door.

'It's all right,' he said to Backhouse as he passed. 'I prefer pubs where the barman sticks to his own side of the counter.'

Thirty yards along the street he paused and waited for Backhouse to overtake him.

'Mr Dalziel never mentioned you were such a violent man,' said the superintendent conversationally.

'He wouldn't,' said Pascoe. 'I wear a heavy disguise whenever I attack him. Will *he* do anything?'

He gestured back towards the pub.

'I don't think so,' said Backhouse. 'For once the publican's well-known reluctance to call in the police could work on our side.'

'He didn't know who you were?' asked Pascoe unnecessarily.

'No. I was just having a quiet sandwich and listening with great interest to the major's reminiscences of your friends to the Press when you so rudely interrupted him.'

'So that thing in the kinky gear *was* a reporter?' asked Pascoe.

'Yes. Not, so far as I could gather, a regular crime man. Some kind of feature writer who happened to be on the spot and is looking for an interesting angle. That's why he's in the Eagle chatting to the major instead of herding with the others at the village school, waiting for the inquest to begin.'

'Already?' Pascoe was surprised. He glanced at his watch. It was just on two.

'Somehow they got the notion it was starting at one-thirty instead of two-thirty. Hence I was able to grab a bite of lunch in peace.'

Backhouse's voice held no irony in either sentence. Superintendents don't need to be ironic, thought Pascoe bitterly.

'What was Palfrey saying about Rose and Colin?' he asked abruptly. 'They had a row, you know. That's why they used the Queen Anne.'

Backhouse sighed deeply.

'You know, Sergeant,' he said, 'you really must try to

break the habit of a lifetime, or however long you've been in the force, and *not* investigate this sorry business. Trust your colleagues. If you don't, it can only lead to grief. You might even end up, heaven forbid, obstructing the police in the execution of their duty.'

'Yes,' said Pascoe, not bothering much to infuse repentant sincerity into his voice. 'Now what was Palfrey saying? Sir.'

'Little enough. I think your friends were a little – what would be the in-character word? – *Bohemian* for his taste. According to his version of the quarrel, he barred his doors to them because their language and behaviour gave offence to many of his old and valued customers. There are, and I quote him now, some words which even in this day and age he would not wish a woman to hear nor expect a lady to use. I think I've got that fine antithesis right. Did Mrs Hopkins swear a lot?'

'When the occasion arose.'

'But not enough to give rise to the occasion?'

'Not when I knew her,' answered Pascoe.

'But that, as you frequently remind me, was some years ago. To continue. Palfrey under the influence of a couple of gins became confidential, said he was not altogether startled that such a household could come to such an end, and had just launched into his attack on your friend's balance of mind when you interrupted him.'

'I should have broken his bloody neck,' said Pascoe dispassionately.

Backhouse sighed once more.

'I suggested to your boss I might like to keep you by me for a while. I was wrong. The sooner you head back to Yorkshire, the better. And don't go near the Eagle and Child again before you go. That's an official warning. Understand?'

'Sir,' said Pascoe. 'What about you?'

'Oh, never fear. I'll see him again and ask him a few

53

questions. It was hardly an opportune moment just now, was it?'

He laughed and burped slightly.

'I won't touch his draught again, though. His pipes must badly need decoking.'

Their conversation had brought them to the village hall. A uniformed constable now stood on duty at the door. He stiffened to attention as the superintendent passed. Pascoe hesitated on the threshold.

'You'd better come in,' said Backhouse. 'Then I can keep an eye on you. We'll go up to the inquest together.'

The hall now contained a neatly deployed and efficient-looking unit, though at a glance Pascoe could tell there was very little happening at this precise moment. There was a slight acceleration of tempo for Backhouse's benefit as he walked the length of the room, but the atmosphere of the place was one of straightforward, almost drowsy routine. A few dust-filled buttresses of sunlight from the narrow window leaned against the shadowy walls. It might have been a summer's afternoon in a Victorian bank.

Backhouse came up, looking at his watch.

'It's about ten minutes' walk to the school. We won't bother with the car, if that's all right with you.'

'Surely.'

'Good. I like to get what exercise I can. There's nothing new by the way. I've brought the men out of the woods. Waste of time. They'll be better on house-to-house.'

Outside they almost ran into the man in the yellow leather jacket. He raised his eyebrows comically as he saw them.

'Hello, darlings,' he said. 'I thought you looked a bit peelerish back in the pub.'

'It was kind of you not to comment, sir,' said Backhouse courteously.

'That's all right. I'm strictly an observer, aren't I? You

54

can reward me, though. How do I get to the village school? I thought I might look in on this inquest thing.'

'We're going there ourselves. Perhaps you'd care to join us?' said Backhouse, somewhat to Pascoe's surprise.

'Well, I suppose it's either that or following you, which might look a trifle odd. This is definitely not a place to look odd in, is it, don't you think? I imagine they stone you if you look odd.'

'You seemed to get on very well with the landlord back there,' remarked Backhouse as they set off up the winding sun-mellow street.

'Yes. Well, I'm Press, you, see, and these village publicans are always hoping for a little puff in the colour mags, if you see what I mean. I've done one or two country-pub gourmet features, you know the kind of thing; horse-brass up your ass, and a beautifully kept pork pie.'

'You must be Anton Davenant,' said Backhouse.

'That's right. How clever. Sounds like a dirty French song, doesn't it? And you . . .?'

'Backhouse. Detective-Superintendent. And this is Sergeant Pascoe.'

'Oh.'

Pascoe felt the man's gaze run swiftly over him as though taking a blueprint and laying it aside for future reference. He recognized the name Davenant faintly. He rarely had time to get as far as the colour supplements on a Sunday, but on some occasion recently he had come across the name.

'How envious all these hard-bitten crime men will be when I turn up in such illustrious company,' said Davenant.

'As a matter of interest,' said Backhouse, 'just what are you doing here among all these hard-bitten crime men?'

'I was fortunate enough to be in the vicinity, that's

55

all. And my current editor, knowing I was hereabouts, instantly got in touch when this dreadful business was bruited abroad. I think he hopes for something rather quaint from me. *A Vintage Murder* perhaps. Or *First Catch Your Killer*. He used words like *atmosphere* and *human interest,* and eventually (and here I capitulated), *money*. But enough of interesting me. What of interesting you? What have your fascinating investigations up-turned?'

'Very little so far, Mr Davenant,' said Backhouse cheerfully, pausing to admire a magnificent dahlia border and being admired in his turn by at least three shadowy figures Pascoe could see behind lace-curtains.

Curiously enough, Davenant seemed satisfied with this answer.

'That must be the old village school at the top of the hill,' he said. 'And over there I spy the old village shop. I must stock up with ciggies. Please don't wait for me. I may find myself compelled to linger, soaking up atmosphere.'

'Don't take too long,' said Backhouse. 'It'll all be over very quickly I should think.'

The journalist disappeared into the tiny shop and the two policemen continued their walk.

'He showed a less than fervent interest in your investigations,' said Pascoe thoughtfully.

'True. Not at all like the mob I'm sure we will meet up here.'

Backhouse was right. There was quite a crowd of reporters waiting outside the school. And an equal crowd of local children had gathered to watch the reporters. Backhouse promised them a statement after the inquest, spoke a few sympathetic words to a television film crew who had got lost on their way to Thornton Lacey and were desperately trying to make themselves operative, then he went inside. Pascoe followed close, still anonymous.

French, the coroner, was there already, his golfing gear exchanged for a grey suit. He and Backhouse exchanged a few words, then very quickly he got the inquest under way.

The superintendent was right about this too. Pascoe was called upon briefly to give evidence of identification and time of discovery; Dr Hardisty gave medical evidence of the cause of death, based partly on his own observation and partly on the pathologist's preliminary report which had just arrived. Death resulted in all three cases from shotgun wounds. The two men had been shot at close quarters with one cartridge apiece. Timothy Mansfield had received his shot full in the chest and had died as a result of the damage inflicted on his lungs and heart. Charles Rushworth had been shot in the neck and lower face. His windpipe had been severed. Rose Hopkins had been shot from a greater distance than the other two, but both barrels of the gun had been used on her. No vital organ had been hit, but her jugular vein had been severed and she had bled to death as she lay unconscious from the shock of the onslaught.

Pascoe put his head in his hands and stared desperately at the floor. The wood was old and tending to splinter. Dangerous that for children.

Time of death was between eight and eleven pm. The full autopsy results might be more precise, but the coroner would appreciate that with three bodies to work on, it had not yet been possible to deal fully with them all.

The coroner appreciated this, spoke briefly of the horror of the event, wished the police inquiries an early success, and declared the inquest adjourned.

Pascoe had had enough to do with inquests to know what this meant. An early arrest was expected. No attempt would be made to resume the inquest if this happened and someone was charged. The coroner would wait until the criminal court proceedings were over, then make his return to the registrar of deaths on the basis of that court's verdict.

And if an early arrest was looked for, there could only be one person they had in mind.

As he rose to leave, he found himself surrounded by newspapermen. From being just an anonymous policeman, he had been pitched into the current star role. For the discoverer of the deaths to be a detective himself, *and* an old friend of both the murdered trio and the chief suspect, was a splendid bit of gilt for this lily of a murder. They were as decent and compassionate as it is possible to be when a dozen or more people are all trying to have their questions answered at the same time. To Pascoe it felt like having his head in a cloud of amplified midges. He tried to answer their questions for a few minutes, then, trailing them with him, he pushed his way to the door.

Backhouse's car was parked by the school-gate. Pascoe opened the door and climbed in.

'The super says to take me back to the station,' he told the driver, who set off without hesitation.

A piece of mind-reading rather than a lie, thought Pascoe as he settled back in his seat.

As the car passed the little shop on the hill, he saw the colourful figure of Davenant just coming out. The man gave a cheery wave, apparently little disturbed at having missed the inquest. Pascoe ignored him. You didn't wave at people from police cars.

The main street traffic had suddenly become very heavy and they had to wait a few minutes at the intersection.

'It's been on the news,' said the driver knowledgeably.

'What?' said Pascoe.

'The murders. That's what this lot are after. It's better than *Grandstand* on a nice afternoon.'

It was a phenomenon that Pascoe was not unused to. The *spectator syndrome* he had once called it to Dalziel,

58

who had shrugged and said that it was better than watching cock-fighting and cheaper than watching strippers and what the hell kind of word was *syndrome* anyway? Before today it had often fascinated him as a sociologist and sometimes annoyed him as a policeman. But now it made him sick and angry. It did no good to tell himself that most of the shirt-sleeved drivers and their family-packed cars were probably going about their legitimate Saturday afternoon business. The thought that any of them had driven out of their way especially to look at the cottage where last night three people were shot to death filled him with an indiscriminate loathing.

At Crowther's house he stepped from the car with the curtest of nods to the driver and went quickly inside.

To his surprise Ellie was up and dressed. She looked pale but alert and warded off his attempt at a comforting embrace.

'Have they found Colin?' was her first question.

He shook his head.

'What happened at the inquest?'

'It was adjourned.'

'I asked you what happened. They didn't just open the thing and adjourn it, did they?'

'No. They took evidence of identification and cause of death.'

'Tell me.'

At first he demurred, but she pressed him hard and his own powers of resistance were so low that in the end it was easier to answer her questions than evade them.

'So it happened between eight and eleven?'

'Yes. They reckon so.'

'And Rose bled to death, lying there unconscious?'

'Yes.' He spoke very low. He knew what was coming, didn't want her to say it, but knew no way of preventing it.

'So then. If it hadn't been for you and your bloody job,

we'd have got there last night. We might have got there in time to stop all of this happening. We'd certainly have got there in time to help Rose. Is that right?'

'I suppose so. Yes. I've thought of it too.'

'Have you now? I should hope you have. What I wonder, Peter, is how the hell are you ever going to stop thinking about it?'

She turned from the window at which she had been standing and faced him accusingly.

'Have you thought about *that*?'

Chapter 6

'What I should like from you, Miss Soper, if you feel up to it,' said Backhouse sympathetically, 'is background information. Anything at all you can tell us about Rose and Colin Hopkins. And the other two as well, of course.'

He had turned up midway through the bitter quarrel which had followed Ellie's accusations. The news that Ellie had recovered sufficiently to leave her bed had been given him by Crowther and he had come as quickly as possible. Not that there was any real urgency about interviewing the woman. The trouble was that now the machine had been started and was running smoothly, there was no real urgency about anything. It had been decided to issue photographs of Hopkins to the Press and television services. He was still being described as 'a man the police wish to interview'. At the same time, the public were being warned that if they saw him or his car, they should make no approach themselves but call the nearest police station.

So now it was mainly a matter of sitting back and waiting for the reported sightings to start flowing in.

He looked impassively at the photograph in his hand. It wasn't bad. The police photographer had had a good selection to choose from. The Hopkinses had been hoarders of snapshots. There had even been a couple with a very youthful but instantly recognizable Peter Pascoe grinning merrily at the camera. But this he held in his hand was the face they were after. An intelligent face. Wide-eyed, a humorous mouth easily pulled into a smile or opened for laughter, yet something restless haunted those features. The picture of his wife gave a much greater impression of calm reliability. Perhaps he needed this in her. Had needed it. Was without it now.

'You'll have to ask me questions,' said Ellie. 'I don't know where to start.'

'Of course. It's difficult, I understand. I'll put the big question first. Have you any idea where Colin Hopkins might be?'

'No, I haven't. I'm sorry, but . . .' she looked from Backhouse to Pascoe who sat, pale and withdrawn, staring through the window. She hasn't caught on yet, thought Backhouse suddenly. She thinks Hopkins was called away unexpectedly last night, is going to appear full of horrified amazement at what's happened, will need to be calmed, comforted, consoled. For God's sake, what the devil has Pascoe been saying to her?

He remembered the atmosphere when he arrived. Strained, tense, there had been great hostility in the air. Any minute now, some of it was coming his way. He might as well get it over with.

'Miss Soper,' he said gently, 'I think you should understand the position. Mr Hopkins was almost certainly with his wife and friends last night. He had had dinner with them. He had been drinking with them after dinner. We know this. There was a half-filled glass with his fingerprints on in the lounge.'

'What are you saying, Superintendent?' asked Ellie, pushing her hair back from her brow.

Pascoe interrupted from the window.

'He's saying that they're not searching for Colin so they can give him the bad news. They want him as the chief – in fact, the only – suspect,' he said.

Ellie froze, her hand still at her brow.

'Of course,' she said after a while. 'I've been silly. It must be those bloody pills they gave me. That's what you would think, isn't it? It's nonsense, of course, but that's how your minds would work.'

At least she's taking it quietly, thought Backhouse. Too soon. She turned towards Pascoe.

'So while I've been sleeping, you've been helping them hunt down Colin?' she uttered vituperatively. 'And now they've pumped you dry, they want to see if I can put them on to any other scents!'

'For a would-be novelist you do mix your metaphors,' said Pascoe coldly.

'Please, please,' said Backhouse soothingly. 'Let's keep things calm. Miss Soper, if it's any consolation to you – though, as an intelligent and no doubt public-spirited woman, I don't see why it should be – Sergeant Pascoe has been most unco-operative, even antagonistic, with regard to our search for Mr Hopkins. In fact, I had to intervene to prevent him from physically assaulting one man who talked critically of your friend. Such loyalty, I hasten to add, I do not find touching but foolish. The circumstantial evidence against your friend is strong. But now if it turns out to be misleading, he's got to be found. Now, will you help?'

Ellie nodded, her eyes on Pascoe.

'Yes. If I can,' she said quietly.

'Right. Tell me about Colin Hopkins then.'

'We were all at university together,' she began. 'Colin, Rose, Timmy, Carlo. And Peter and me. We were pretty close. There were plenty of others, of course, but we were close.'

'You all went on holiday together,' prompted Backhouse.

'That's right. So we did. In Eskdale.' She smiled at the memory. 'Life seemed fairly cut and dried then. In the nicest way. Rose and Colin. Peter and me. And . . .'

'The other two men were homosexual,' said Backhouse neutrally.

'Yes. That's right,' said Ellie challengingly. Backhouse ignored the challenge.

'Things seem to have worked out as you anticipated,' he said. 'But you seem uncertain?'

'I didn't anticipate this,' she snapped, relenting instantly. 'Sorry. No, after we all finished, it was only Colin and Rose who stuck together. They got married about a year later. I don't think they'd have bothered, but Colin had joined a publishing house and they thought it was worthwhile observing the conventions till he got stinking rich. Timmy was a linguist and got a job in the Common Market HQ in Brussels. Carlo went to work for some firm in Glasgow. I finished my research.'

'Research?' interrupted Backhouse.

'That's right. I was a graduate research student. I just condescended to mingle with the children. I'm a couple of years older than the others,' she added defiantly.

Backhouse studied her slim figure, held the gaze of the grey eyes set in the finely-sculpted head with its close-cut jet black hair.

'You carry your burden of years very well,' he murmured.

'Thanks.' She smiled, the first time he had seen her do so. 'I got an assistant lectureship in the Midlands. And Peter, of course, put on the helmet of salvation and became a policeman. I think the only time we all met together again was at Colin and Rose's wedding.'

'Not Timmy,' interjected Pascoe. 'He couldn't make it.'

'That's right. He couldn't. Well, we all kept intermittently in touch and saw something of each other. Except Peter. Within a couple of years or so he'd fallen almost completely from sight.'

'I was very busy. Besides being poorly paid with very limited vacation periods,' said Pascoe.

'A policeman's lot,' said Backhouse.

'Of course, he got a bit of a complex too. Felt that he would be a bit of a nuisance, perhaps even a butt, in the liberal academic and cultural circles his friends inhabited,' said Ellie mockingly. But her tone was light.

'But you saw the others?'

'Sometimes. A couple of years ago, Timmy returned from the Continent. I think Carlo had already been working in London for six months or so. They took a flat together. Colin meanwhile had been going from strength to strength and had become the darling of his bosses to such an extent that he got them persuaded a few months ago to give him a year's sabbatical so that he could write *his* book which would make everybody's fortune. Brookside Cottage was where he decided to settle for the period. And he planned to keep it on as a week-end retreat after his triumphal return to London.'

'I see,' said Backhouse thoughtfully. 'And did you know all this before you met him in London recently?'

Ellie shot a quick glance at Pascoe.

'It was in the letter of invitation which the sergeant showed me,' explained Backhouse.

'I knew vaguely about it,' said Ellie. 'But it wasn't till I met him that I got all the details.'

'A chance meeting, was it?'

'That's right. Chance. Oh hell, no. Not chance. I've been trying to flog a book of my own, a novel. Without much success. I laid an ambush for Colin. I thought he might be able to help.'

'You never told me that,' said Pascoe, surprised.

'No,' said Ellie sheepishly.

'Peter had told me to get in touch with Colin from the start,' she added to Backhouse. 'But I was too proud. And I don't like putting my friends on the spot. But when things didn't go too well with the book . . .'

'You laid an ambush,' said Backhouse. 'Any luck?'

'I didn't even mention it,' sighed Ellie. 'He'd just got everything organized for his own move and was bubbling over. It didn't seem fair to take advantage. And when I told him that Peter and I had re-established contact, he was genuinely delighted, took his address, said we'd be the first to sample his rural hospitality. Here we are.'

'So he was a man who had everything going for him at the moment?'

'Everything,' echoed Ellie.

There was a knock at the door which opened almost simultaneously.

'Cup of tea,' said Mrs Crowther, coming into the room with a tray and the expression of one with whom superintendents cut very little ice.

She put the tray down in front of Ellie and took a small bundle of typewritten sheets out of her capacious apron pocket.

'Here. These are for you,' she said to Backhouse. 'I've been typing them for Crowther. If you take them now, it'll save him a journey later. Not that I'd pay them all that much attention. It's his job to hear things, but they were a nice young couple, the Hopkinses. That's what counts, not a lot of malicious gossip.'

She left with the shadow of a wink at Ellie.

'Interesting woman,' commented Backhouse, riffling through the papers. 'We could do with her on the strength.'

'I think you've got her,' said Pascoe drily.

Backhouse folded Crowther's report carefully and slipped it into his pocket.

'To get back to business,' he said. 'Can either of you think of anything at all which might cause stress and strain in the relationships between these four?'

'Not really,' said Ellie. 'Rose and Colin always talked most affectionately of the other two. And vice-versa as far as I know.'

She glanced across at Pascoe. Backhouse could not read her expression.

'You talked to Mrs Hopkins on the phone last night,'

he said. 'Did she say anything specific about their plans for the evening?'

'Well, she may have done. We talked for about ten minutes. But nothing's stuck, nothing specific. I'm sorry.'

She looked bewildered. Backhouse patted her hand where it rested on the arm of the sofa.

'Never mind. If anything comes to mind, you can let me know. Anything new from you, Sergeant?'

Pascoe shook his head.

'I'd better get back to work then,' said the superintendent, standing up. 'What are your plans for tonight?'

'We've been asked to stay with the Culpeppers,' said Pascoe, recalling his earlier decision to find somewhere else. It didn't seem worth the bother now. And if the Eagle was the only place in the village which let rooms, his chances of success were slim.

'Culpeppers? I remember. The committee secretary woman?'

'And the man who came to the cottage with the coroner. I'm sure they'll be in Crowther's dossiers.'

'No doubt. I'll know where to find you, then. Thank you, Miss Soper. You've been most helpful. Please believe me when I say you have my deepest sympathy.'

He did it better than Dalziel. Not that Dalziel wasn't good when he wanted, but good in the style of the old actor-managers. There was always a sense of performance. Backhouse was more natural. There was even a chance that he was sincere.

'Just one thing more,' he said, pausing at the door. 'What was Mr Hopkins writing his book about?'

'His book? Poverty! He laughed when he told me. Coming to Thornton Lacey to write a book about poverty in modern Britain was like hunting polar bears in Africa, he said.'

'It doesn't sound a best-selling subject,' opined Backhouse cautiously.

'I don't know. Full of case histories, hard-luck stories, people driven to crime, the effect of inadequate diets on sexual performance, that kind of thing. It's the kind of pop sociology that could sell.'

'You sound disapproving.'

'Not at all. Envious perhaps. Until this morning.'

'Yes. Not much cause for envy now. Goodbye.'

They sat in silence for a while after he had gone. Ellie spoke first.

'I'm sorry,' she said.

'What for?'

'For before, what I said. Grief's a selfish emotion really. I had forgotten they were your friends too.'

'Yes. And Colin still is.'

'Do you think he did it, Peter?'

Pascoe made a hopeless gesture.

'I don't know. I can't believe it, but I've got to admit the possibility. People kill those they love all the time.'

'But you were willing to attack some poor bloody stranger because *he* accepted the possibility? Odd behaviour for a policeman,' she mocked affectionately.

'I'm an odd policeman,' he said, kissing her gently.

'Thanks,' she said. 'Now I'm going to pull myself together and face the world. Whatever the truth, Colin will need friends when they catch up with him.'

She stood up and stretched her arms as though newly roused from sleep.

'Do I gather you've got us invited somewhere for the night?'

Pascoe explained briefly about the Culpeppers, concealing his own irrational dislike of Marianne.

'I see,' said Ellie. 'Sounds all sweet sherry and sympathy. I'll go and freshen up, then I wouldn't mind sampling the country air for half an hour or so before we present ourselves to our hosts.'

'A good idea. There's plenty of time,' said Pascoe.

The door opened and Mrs Crowther reappeared.

'He's gone then,' she grunted. Her gaze fell on the tea-tray.

'And no one wants my tea?'

'Oh, I'm sorry,' exclaimed Ellie. 'It's my fault. I just forgot.'

'Look,' said Pascoe. 'Why don't you two sit down and have a cup? It should still be hot. I just want to pop out and check the car. It seems to be eating oil lately.'

Ellie shot him a curious look, but he left quickly before she could say anything. As he had expected, the office section of the house was empty. Crowther would be very busy about the village this afternoon. He made straight for the table which carried the solid old Imperial type-writer, and saw what he was looking for straightaway. In the wooden tray by the machine were Crowther's notes on local colour plus the carbon of the typewritten version given to Backhouse. He ignored the original in the constable's crabbed hand and picked up the copy.

He had just started on the first of the five quarto sheets when a voice spoke behind him.

'Excuse me.'

Pascoe started so violently that his leg twitched and cracked painfully against the rim of the desk. Christ! he thought, your nerve ends really have been exposed today, my boy.

Instinctively he let the sheets of paper slide out of his hands into the tray before he turned.

Standing behind the small counter across which the public could seek audience with their local guardian of the law was a rather frail old lady who seemed to be wearing a military uniform of sorts. WVS? wondered Pascoe.

'Yes?' he said.

'I was hoping to find Mr Crowther.' She had a slow, gentle voice. Definitely good works, he decided. Moral

69

samplers and nourishing broth round the farmworkers' hovels.

'I'm afraid he's not here at the moment. I don't know when he'll be back. Is it urgent?'

'I'm not sure.'

She stared hard at him and asked dubiously, 'Are *you* a policeman?'

'Well, yes. Yes, I am,' said Pascoe. 'Sergeant Pascoe.'

'Sergeant? That ought to be all right then. I am Alicia Langdale.' She paused. For effect? thought Pascoe. Is she the lady of the manor? Should I be impressed?

'Yes?' he prompted.

'And it's connected with my job, you see. That's what makes it so delicate.'

'What *is* your job, Mrs Langdale?'

'Miss. Can't you see? I'm a postman.'

Oh my God! thought Pascoe. That's what the gear is! He could see he had lost what little ground the revelation of his rank had gained him.

'Of course,' he said with a smile.

'My sister, Anthea, and I keep the post office. She takes care of the internal business and I look after deliveries. Normally what happens, of course, is that people post their letters, they are collected in a van and taken to the main post office in town where they are sorted.'

'I see,' said Pascoe.

'But sometimes, if it's a matter of *local* mail – things that I'm going to have to deliver anyway, you understand – some people just leave them on the counter or push them through our letter-box.'

She raised her chin and looked defiantly at Pascoe, who suddenly knew what this was all about. He took the letter Miss Langdale produced from her large pocket and stared down at Colin's distinctive handwriting. J. K. Palfrey, Esq., The Eagle and Child, Thornton Lacey.

70

A flock of thoughts rose and fluttered around Pascoe's mind. The proper course of action was clear. Take the letter to Backhouse who would then take it to Palfrey and require it to be opened in his presence. If it was not relevant to the inquiry that would be an end to it. But if it was . . .! Pascoe did not feel somehow that Backhouse would be keen to let him read it.

He realized with a start that Miss Langdale was still speaking.

'I was almost at the Eagle and Child this morning when I met Mrs Anderson who told me the news. She picks up everything very quickly, I'm afraid. Normally I pay no heed, but this was different. This was dreadful, dreadful. So I finished my round but kept this letter. Anthea and I have been discussing all day what we ought to do. It's our duty to deliver the Queen's mail, you see. But if, as seemed possible in the circumstances, it might cause distress . . . and in a sense, it had not in fact been *posted*, had it? So here I am. Will you give me a receipt, please?'

Her voice was suddenly brisk, businesslike. Pascoe looked round for a piece of paper and a pen. He had made up his mind to open the letter and damn the consequences. Every instinct in his body warned him against it, but told him at the same time how important the letter was. He had to see. This might be his only chance.

'Receipt book's in the top drawer, Sergeant.'

It was Crowther, standing quietly in the doorway. His chance had gone.

'Interesting, this,' said the constable, holding the letter before him after he had efficiently disposed of Miss Langdale. 'I'd better let the super have it right away. Thanks for taking care of things.'

He put the letter in his tunic pocket, tidied up the papers on his desk, stared a long moment at the disturbed

71

carbon copy of his notes but did not remove them, and left.

'Damn! damn! damn!' said Pascoe. But he shuddered to think of the dangerous course he had been about to steer on. The sooner he got back to Dalziel and other people's losses, the better.

He went back into the living-room to collect Ellie and take her to the Culpeppers'.

Chapter 7

The Culpeppers' house was an impressive structure. Built in traditional Cotswold stone, its lines and proportions were unequivocally though unobtrusively modern.

The gardens consisted principally of herbaceous borders and lawns running down to an encirclement of trees. Whether the Culpepper estate extended into the woods was not clear. The lawns themselves were beautifully kept. Only one of them, hooped for croquet, showed any signs of wear. Coming up the drive, Pascoe had glimpsed a bent figure in a bright orange coat slowly brushing away the leaves which the autumn wind had laid on one of the side lawns. A fluorescent gardener, he thought, and prepared himself for anything from a parlourmaid to a full-dress butler when he rang the bell. But it had been Culpepper himself, features etched with well-bred solicitude, who opened the door.

Pascoe could see that Ellie disliked him at once. He recalled his own reaction to Marianne Culpepper and groaned inwardly at the thought of the evening ahead. Not that much social intercourse would be expected of them, surely. Or sexual either, he added to himself as they were shown into separate bedrooms. The bed at Brookside Cottage with its ornamental pillow came into his mind. Half the local police-force would have seen it. It was a good job he hadn't been having a bit on the side with the chief constable's wife.

The frivolity of the thought touched him with guilt. This was the way grief worked. It could only achieve complete victory for a comparatively short time. But it filled the mind with snares of guilt and self-disgust to catch at all thoughts and emotions fighting against it.

Ellie felt the same. She had raised her eyebrows humorously at his as Culpepper opened her bedroom door. But it was a brief flicker of light in dark sky.

The evening's prospects did not improve when Marianne Culpepper returned. Pascoe heard a car arrive as he was unpacking his over-night case and when he left his room a minute later to collect Ellie, he found her standing at the head of the stairs, unashamedly eavesdropping on a conversation below.

Culpepper's neutral tones were audible only as an indecipherable murmur, but his wife's elegantly vowelled voice carried perfectly. Pascoe was reminded of teenage visits to the local repertory theatre (now declined to bingo) where hopeful young actresses projected their lines to the most distant 'gods'.

Even half a conversation was enough to reveal that Marianne Culpepper had no knowledge whatsoever of her husband's invitation to Pascoe and Ellie. They exchanged rueful glances on the landing. Pascoe moved to the nearest door, opened it and slammed it shut. It might have been more politic to retreat for a while, but Pascoe found himself looking forward to putting all that good breeding below to the test.

'Let's go down, shall we?' he said in an exaggeratedly loud voice.

The Culpeppers presented a fairly united front as introductions took place.

'Didn't I see you in the village hall this morning?' asked Marianne of Pascoe. 'I didn't realize then. I thought you were just one of the policemen.'

Oh, I am, I am, thought Pascoe.

'Look,' the woman went on, 'I'm terrible sorry about your friends. I hardly knew them, the Hopkinses I mean, but they seemed very nice people.'

74

Everyone speaks as if we've lost them both, thought Pascoe. Perhaps we have.

'You'll be tired of expressions of sympathy I know. They become very wearing.' She paused as though communicating with herself only, then continued. 'Which brings me to this evening. You are very welcome indeed to our house, but Hartley and I have got our lines crossed somewhere. I've asked a couple of friends along to dinner and a few more people may drop in for drinks later. Please, it's up to you. If you'd rather duck out, have your meal early, and generally avoid the madding crowd, just say so. Don't be silly about it.'

The crossed lines cut both ways, Pascoe mixed his metaphors. Hartley knew as little of his wife's evening invitations as she did of his. Or did he?

'I think we'd like to join in,' said Ellie, rather to Pascoe's surprise, though it confirmed his own reaction. The reasons must be very different, however. 'If we're not going to be spectres at the feast, that is.'

'Not at all. Good, that's settled. It's just a cold collation on Saturdays, but I'd better go and get things organized before I change.'

She was wearing slacks and a chunky sweater and looked wind-blown, as if she had just returned from some fairly active outdoor activity.

'May I help?' asked Ellie.

'Why not?' she said with a smile. 'How are you at carving? Hartley's a near-vegetarian and doesn't take kindly to sawing up chunks of dead animals.'

'Are you interested in porcelain?' asked Culpepper when the two men were alone.

'I know little about it,' answered Pascoe cautiously. More therapy? he wondered. From Dalziel's burglars to Culpepper's culture. I must appear all things to all men.

'My own knowledge is very limited,' said Culpepper modestly. 'Come and see my few pieces.'

He rose, led Pascoe across the entrance hall and unlocked a solid-looking oak door. When he opened it, Pascoe was surprised to see a metal grille, rather like the expanding doors used in old-fashioned lifts. Culpepper inserted another key and the grille slid back of its own accord.

Whether the value of the collection justified these elaborate precautions Pascoe could not say. The pieces were magnificently displayed. There were no windows in the room and the walls were broken by a series of different sized niches which held the porcelain. Each niche had its own light, controlled separately so that it was possible to centre the attention completely on each of the pieces in turn. The only free-standing pieces were two large capped urns which occupied plinths in the middle of the room. They were decorated in the Chinese style but Culpepper assured Pascoe that they were late eighteenth-century English imitations.

'Out of place here, really,' he said. 'But they were the first things I ever bought when I discovered I had enough money to start buying.'

'How much is it all worth?' was all Pascoe could find to say.

'Oh, several thousands,' said Culpepper vaguely. 'Much of it is not what the experts might call first-rate. But to me it is irreplacable and therefore invaluable.'

He led the way out, crashing the grille door locked behind him.

'Valuable or not, I wish more people would take the precautions you do with their property,' said Pascoe, thinking of the ease with which his current burglar had been helping himself to small fortune. This time last night he had been working on the case. It seemed barely credible.

Dinner went quite well. Ellie and Marianne seemed to have taken to each other, though Pascoe would not have seen either as the other's 'type'. The guests, John and Sandra Bell, were a pleasant enough couple in their mid-thirties, he extrovert, outspoken, nearly hearty; she pretty, much quieter but far from subdued. The name touched a chord in Pascoe's mind. But it was only when the conversation, carefully vetted and censored for his and Ellie's benefit, came round to the local water pollution controversy that he recalled noticing Bell's name in the Amenities Committee minutes. He was a staunch down-streamer, and complained bitterly that the village brook was being polluted upstream by careless management of the cesspool drainage which many of the local properties still relied on. Culpepper, eating an egg mayonnaise with green salad, pushed his plate away from him with an expression of distaste.

'John, please,' said Mrs Bell. 'You're making Hartley nauseous and must be boring his visitors stiff.'

'I'm sorry,' said Bell, grinning at Ellie. 'Forgive me. It's all right for the idle rich on this side of the village. They can be objective. But that stream runs at the bottom of my garden and I've got a young son. He catches enough without getting typhoid. But never fear. I have a plan. The next Amenities Committee meeting may get a surprise.'

He winked conspiratorially as Marianne began clearing away the plates.

The first after-dinner guest arrived as they were drinking their coffee. Marianne let him in. There was a perceptible interval before she returned with Angus Pelman. Pascoe assumed the time was spent in warning the man about the strangers in the house.

Pelman made no attempt to avoid the subject of the killings.

'Any news of Hopkins?' he asked brusquely after being introduced.

'I think not,' intervened Culpepper diplomatically. 'I

77

wonder, Miss Soper, if you would care to see my collection of porcelain?'

'Oh, blast your porcelain, Hartley. Miss Soper isn't a child to have her mind diverted by a bag of sweets.'

Culpepper turned away and busied himself removing the foil cap from a fresh bottle of scotch. One two-thirds full stood in full view on the sideboard. Marianne glanced over at him with a faint pucker of worry between the eyes.

'We're all shocked by what's happened,' Pelman continued. 'They were nice people, our neighbours, members of our community.'

'Which not everybody made them particularly welcome to,' murmured Culpepper. 'Let me freshen your drink, Mr Pascoe.'

'Meaning?' demanded Pelman.

'That business at the Eagle, for a start,' replied Culpepper.

'That was between JP and the Hopkinses,' intervened Bell. 'Nothing to do with anyone else. They were well out of it. It's a much better pint at the Anne, and cheaper too.'

He grinned amiably, the pourer of oil on troubled waters.

'Who's JP?' asked Ellie.

'Palfrey, the owner of the Eagle and Child,' said Marianne Culpepper.

'Who, blameworthy though he is, should not be allowed all the blame,' said her husband blandly. 'And there were other things besides. Eh, Pelman?'

There was a ring at the front door bell.

'Hartley, would you answer that?' said Marianne, separating the antagonists. She tried to consolidate the forced armistice by changing the conversation and Pelman seemed much readier to accept this from her.

78

'If this weather keeps up, we'll get some good riding tomorrow. Are you going out, John?'

'No such luck. I haven't reached Hartley's stage of executive elevation yet. I still have to bring my work home with me. Besides, Sandra says riding gives you a big bum.'

'John!' protested his wife. But she met Marianne's quizzical gaze with the unruffled smile of one whose own buttocks were as compact as a boy's.

'What is your job, Mr Bell?' asked Pascoe, trying to sound unlike a policeman. Nowadays he was never sure when he succeeded.

'I'm sales director of Nuplax, the kitchen utensil people. In Banbury.'

'That sounds very high-powered.'

'Oh, it'll do. But it's small time compared with Hartley. He's a top finance man with the Nordrill group.'

Pascoe looked impressed to conceal his ignorance. Nordrill he had heard of. An up-and-coming oil and mining consortium often in the news. But just what such a job meant in terms of responsibility and reward he could not conceive.

'That must be worth a few bob,' he said knowingly.

'It keeps him comfortable. Eh, Marianne?'

Bell's gesture included the woman as well as the unostentatious luxury of the room. Marianne smiled, but with little humour.

'I didn't realize Nordrill were centred in the Midlands,' said Ellie.

'Oh, they're not. But London's no distance with a decent car and a *pied-à-terre* if you don't fancy the drive back.'

Lucky old Hartley, thought Pascoe.

Lucky old Hartley re-entered accompanied by Dr Hardisty who, from the length of time they had taken, must have been giving as well as receiving information. With him was his wife, either younger or better preserved, with the brisk movements and reassuring smile that Pascoe associated with the nursing profession. It seemed a probable guess.

They hardly had time to express anxiety over Ellie's well-being and regret over Rose's death, at the same time studiously avoiding any reference to Colin, before the bell rang once more. This time Marianne went and after the inevitable delay, reappeared by herself.

'Hartley,' she said quietly. 'Do you have a moment?'

Culpepper left the room. Pascoe wandered over to the sideboard and freshened his drink generously. He was a firm believer in the social maxim *from each according to his ability* and there was evidence of a great deal of ability here.

Bell joined him.

'Does Palfrey do most of the social liquor trade round here?' Pascoe asked, holding the bottle of scotch like a conversation piece.

'Christ, no!' said Bell with his likeable grin. 'The odd bottle when you're stuck, perhaps. But who's going to pay his prices when you can get the same stuff for 15p less in town? Don't let our outward affluence deceive you, Mr Pascoe. Hartley may have an antique superior wine-merchant tucked away in the City, but the rest of us still push trolleys round the supermarkets.'

'Big of you to refuse to take advantage of your wealth,' said Pascoe, softening the comment with his own likeable grin. He had no desire to antagonize Bell. And he did want to talk about Palfrey. Why, he wasn't sure. Personal antipathy? Well, he had no official standing in this case, so the presence of personal prejudice could for once be ignored.

'How does Palfrey fit into the local scheme of things?' he went on. But his policeman's voice must have sounded through.

'You're very interested in old JP,' commented Bell curiously. 'Is it because of the row? If so, I really don't think I should comment. Not during a casual chat in a friend's house.'

Being without official standing clearly cut both ways. Pascoe tried another smile. It didn't feel quite as likeable as the last.

'Why JP?' he asked. 'Just his initials?'

Or is there some bloody masonic oath which prevents you from answering that?

Bell laughed.

'Yes, they are his initials.' He glanced around and dropped his voice. 'But they do service for other things besides. He's got ambitions to get on to the bench. God help all petty offenders if that happens! But they really stem from our vicar. He's a nice little Welshman, just one step out of the coalmine. He recalls in the old days in his village, a local copper-smelting firm hired a man to go around the streets every morning with two great buckets on a yoke. Everyone would empty their jerries into them!'

He laughed so heartily that the others stopped talking and turned to look. Like a disturbance at a funeral, thought Pascoe, surprised to find himself feeling embarrassed.

'They used the stuff in some process at the copper-works,' explained Bell. 'Anyway, this man was known familiarly as Jim Piss! And the vicar, after his first taste of the bitter at the Eagle when Palfrey took over, told the story. The name stuck, but for politeness's sake, it became JP.'

Very droll, thought Pascoe. But it took him no further forward. He wasn't even very sure in which direction *forward* lay.

The Culpeppers were in the room again, he observed.

But there had been no noticeable addition to the company. Which might or might not be odd.

Ellie was talking to the Hardistys and looking desperate. Pascoe could see why. Medical solicitude emanated from them almost visibly. He appproached to effect a rescue, but it proved unnecessary.

'Please excuse me,' she said to the medical twosome. 'I think I'll have an early night.'

Simple as that, thought Pascoe, smiling ruefully at his loss of role. In times of stress, the weakness of others is a useful source of strength. Ellie's self-possession was throwing him more and more into a confrontation with his own emotions, making him more and more of a policeman in order to retain his equilibrium.

But what the hell was there to investigate here? He looked hopefully around the room.

Ellie was at the door, reassuring Marianne that all her needs were catered for. She caught his eye and smiled briefly, then was gone. He felt a sense of relief, edged with guilt. With Ellie out of the way, there might be a chance to provoke some reactions. Pelman seemed the best bet. He had seemed much in favour of plain speaking on his arrival, though now he seemed content to turn the treadmill of social trivia with the rest. At the moment he was complaining about the cost of estate management.

'You're a working member of the community then?' asked Pascoe brightly. 'You don't just sleep here.'

The Bells and Hardistys exchanged a glance which told Pascoe he had been inept in his choice of words. John Bell seemed very amused, the others less so.

'Yes, Mr Pascoe. I have a dairy herd and one of the biggest hen batteries in this part of the world. I work for my living.'

A hint of sneering stress on 'work'? Pascoe wasn't sure.

'So do we all,' smiled Dr Hardisty, perhaps having felt it also. Pelman grunted and sipped his drink.

'If you like what you're doing, it's not work,' said Bell with mock sanctimoniousness.

'Do you like *your* job?' asked Sandra Bell suddenly. 'What is it you do, Mr Pascoe?'

Doesn't she know? Or is she just trying out her claws? She seemed a nice woman, but Pascoe felt far from competent to judge.

'I'm a policeman, Mrs Bell,' he said.

'Oh.' Collapse of thin woman.

'CID, aren't you?' said Pelman. 'Tell me, what's your professional prognosis in this case?'

'Angus!' protested Marianne.

'He needn't answer if he'd rather not,' said Pelman, staring hard at Pascoe.

'Another drink, anyone?' said Hartley Culpepper.

'Police procedure is quite simple in such matters,' said Pascoe. 'Three things mainly. The weapon is looked for. Absent persons who may be able to help are looked for. And a great number of people are interviewed, statements taken, information amassed. That's about it. Nothing very dramatic. In the majority of murder cases, the police know who did it within twenty-four hours of being called in. Often sooner.'

He scanned the group, poker-faced.

'And in this case?' asked Pelman, softly.

'Who knows? I'm not on the investigating team,' said Pascoe. 'I'm just a witness. Like the rest of you perhaps.'

'How important will finding the weapon be?' asked Mrs Hardisty to fill the ensuing silence.

'It's finding who it belongs to that's important in the case of a gun,' explained Pascoe.

Pelman laughed explosively, unhumorously.

'That's no problem. It belongs to me.'

No one rushed to fill the silence this produced. But Pascoe had no doubts about, the thoughts swimming goldfish-like behind the surprised eyes. A joke in bad

83

taste? Some kind of confession? A simple misunderstanding?

'Didn't Backhouse tell you?' asked Pelman.

'I said I'm not one of the investigating team,' said Pascoe.

'No. Of course not. But it's not a secret, is it? The thing is, when the superintendent spoke to me, one of the things he was interested in was my guns. Naturally. It had gone from my mind till I looked.'

'What had?' asked Marianne impatiently. 'For God's sake, this is serious, Angus. Don't make a golf-club anecdote out of it.'

Pelman took his scolding meekly and went on.

'One of my guns was missing. I had lent it to Colin Hopkins a week or so ago and he hadn't let me have it back. Not that there was any hurry. It wasn't up to much and I have plenty of others.'

'No doubt,' said Culpepper.

'So you think it was your gun that was used . . .?' Mrs Hardisty saw no need to finish her sentence.

'It seems probable.'

'Why did Colin want the gun?' asked Pascoe, listening carefully to the timbre of his own voice. It was light, steady. He was doing remarkably well. The control was there. Fat Dalziel would be proud of him.

The lounge door burst open and he whirled like a startled cat, slopping his whisky over the rim of his glass.

In the door stood a tall, angular woman of some considerable age. Her skin was brown and creased like a tortoise's neck, but her eyes were bright and alert. The nylon overall she wore was the luminous orange of a road-worker's safety jacket, clashing horridly with her dark violet slacks and fluffy red slippers. This, thought Pascoe with surprise, must be the gardener.

'There's a man upstairs,' she said in a flat south Lancashire accent.

84

'It's all right, Mother,' said Culpepper in a reassuring tone. 'We have guests.'

'I'm not blind,' said the old woman scornfully.

'To stay, I mean. Mr Pascoe here. Pascoe, I'd like you to meet my mother, who does us the honour of living with us.'

'You could put it like that,' said the woman, staring at Pascoe with a marked lack of enthusiasm. 'It wasn't him.'

'Wasn't . . .?'

'Upstairs.'

'Then it was probably Miss Soper, our other guest,' said Culpepper triumphantly.

'It was a man,' she insisted.

Marianne Culpepper slid open a panel in an elegant walnut cabinet to reveal the contents of an expensive-looking hi-fi system.

'The new Drew Spade album came this morning,' she said brightly. 'Shall we listen? I haven't heard it myself yet, so I can't say what it's like.'

Another diversionary tactic. What a snarled-up lot of people they were! And the sound which began to thump out of the speakers was hardly music-for-the-bereaved, either. But it wasn't quite loud enough to prevent Pascoe from hearing the rest of the exchange between Culpepper and his mother.

'No, it must have been Miss Soper,' said Hartley.

'Please your bloody self,' answered the old woman, shrugging her still broad shoulders. 'I'm off to my bed. I only hope I'm not murdered in it.'

The remark acted on Pascoe like an electrical impulse. He handed his glass to Culpepper, pushed between the man and his mother without apology and ran lightly up the stairs.

It was absurd. Probably the old woman had indeed just caught a glimpse of Ellie. But she seemed sensible enough. Something of a burden, perhaps, to Culpepper and his wife, but that was none of his business. To an investigating officer, *everything* is his business. One of Dalziel's dicta.

He pushed open Ellie's door quietly. She was sitting up in bed with the lights on, smoking a cigarette.

'Hi,' she said, unsurprised.

'Hi,' he said. 'Back in a sec.'

His own door was slightly ajar. The room was in darkness. The door moved easily at his touch and he stepped swiftly inside, trying to recall where the light-switch was.

His groping hand could not make contact with it, but he knew someone was there in the room with him. The image of a shotgun rose suddenly in his mind and he abandoned his search for the switch, moving noiselessly away from the line of light spilling in from the landing. As he dropped on one knee beside the wardrobe, he heard a noise. The curtains moved and the clear autumn sky leaned its pinholes of light against the glass till a figure blotted them out. Everything went still again.

Pascoe spoke.

'Colin?' he said uncertainly.

He stood up.

'Colin? It's Peter, Peter Pascoe. Is that you, Colin?'

He was by the small bedside table now. His hands plunged down on the lamp which stood there. The ball of his thumb caught the switch and the soft light blossomed into the room.

The figure by the window spoke.

'No, I'm sorry, Mr Pascoe,' he said compassionately. 'It's not Colin.'

'So I see,' said Pascoe, looking steadily at the man before him. 'What are you doing in my room, Mr Davenant?'

86

Chapter 8

'Oh, there you are, Anton,' said Marianne Culpepper from the doorway. 'What on earth are you doing in here?'

'Forgive me, darlings,' said Davenant moving away from the window. 'I am quite, quite lost. That little room you put me in downstairs was super, Marianne, except that it didn't seem to contain a loo. And while I'm sure a house of such distinction has loos all over the place, I could find none downstairs, though I did peer through a kind of grid thing at a room full of po-shaped objects.'

'You mistook my room for a bathroom?' said Pascoe with carefully measured incredulity.

'Not in the least. I tried the door in my search, though, peered in, realized my mistake of course and then forgot all else as across the window, outlined against the evening sky, swooped *Asio otus.*'

'What?' said Marianne.

'The long-eared owl, my dear. I may have been mistaken, but I think not. Those ears! I forgot everything. One call of nature gave way to a greater, and I darted across the room to watch his flight. Glorious! Then someone approached. I froze into quietness, but alas! I was discovered. Forgive us our trespasses, I pray you.'

He smiled sweetly at Pascoe, who put on the all-is-explained face he often used when faced with a blatant liar.

'You've got him then,' said Mrs Culpepper, senior, in a triumphant tone. She peered curiously over her daughter-in-law's shoulder. 'He's a funny-looking devil.'

'Hush!' said Marianne. 'This is Mr Davenant, Mother. An old friend of mine.'

The plot thickens, thought Pascoe. And with the dramatic metaphor came a sense of staging, of something being not quite real.

'From London, is it?' said the old woman, as if wanting the worst to be confirmed.

'That's right,' said Marianne.

'I thought so.' She left, nodding triumphantly.

'Darling,' cried Culpepper up the stairs. 'John and Sandra are going.'

'Sorry to rush, but Eric's got a chill and we don't like to leave the sitter too long,' came Sandra Bell's voice.

Marianne looked uncertainly at Pascoe and Davenant, then turned and went down. Davenant made to follow her.

'I didn't realize you had friends in the neighbourhood,' said Pascoe, sitting on the bed.

'Why should you? I didn't realize you had either. What I mean is, I didn't understand your odd behaviour in the pub till I found out later who you were.'

'Oh. Have you known the Culpeppers long?' asked Pascoe.

'Not long. In fact, hardly at all. Dear Marianne was putting it on a bit, for the old dragon's sake, I fancy, when she called me an old friend! No. In fact . . .' he hesitated and peered assessingly at Pascoe.

'In fact,' he went on, 'if I'm an old friend of anyone, it's of your old friends.'

'I'm sorry?' said Pascoe. Then, amazed, 'You mean of Colin and Rose's?'

'Yes. Well, more of Timmy and Carlo's really,' answered Davenant. 'Though I knew Rose and Colin well also.'

Pascoe stood up and closed the bedroom door.

'You'd better tell me exactly what you're doing here,

Mr Davenant,' he said. Despite all his efforts he could not keep a threat out of his voice.

Davenant's story was simple. In Oxford, collecting material for an article on English provincial cooking, he had heard the news of the murders at mid-morning. As soon as he recognized the names, he had set out for Thornton Lacey.

'I was all of a tremble, I promise you. I could hardly point the car straight. But I had to come, you understand. By the time I got here, I'd settled down a trifle. It struck me that I would be foolish to appear as a friend of those murdered.'

'What made you think that?' demanded Pascoe.

'You're involved in the grief then. People don't talk to you as they would otherwise. You must have found that too.'

'I suppose so,' admitted Pascoe grudgingly.

'I wanted to be able to ask questions. Poke my nose in. Be a journalist. Just as you must be dying to be a policeman. I wanted to find out everything I could about this awful business. So I invented that silly story about my editor putting me on the job.'

'You did it very well,' murmured Pascoe.

'Thank you kindly. I decided I'd like to talk with you when I found out who you were. They told me you were staying up here. As soon as they mentioned the name Culpepper, I thought, Good Lord! Hartley! I've met him several times in town at mutual acquaintances', and I knew he lived in the country out here somewhere, but I'd quite forgotten it was Thornton Lacey. In other circumstances, a delicious coincidence.'

'Delicious. So they shut you away downstairs?'

'Until the other guests had gone, yes. It seemed easier. These villages are full of eagle eyes and tattle-tales.'

'And long-eared owls.'

'What? Oh yes. I wonder where the chappie's gone.'

89

He turned to the window once more and stared out into the star-filled night.

'Autumn,' he said. 'Always a sad time. I'm sorry now that I came and disturbed you. Perhaps I should go.'

'Where are you staying?'

'With your late pugilistic opponent,' said Davenant, turning and smiling. 'At the Eagle. If I start walking now, I'll be in time for a nightcap in the bar.'

'You walked here? Let me drive you back,' offered Pascoe.

'How kind you are. But no. I really like to walk. And perhaps *Asio otus* will appear for me again.'

'Then I'll walk with you,' said Pascoe. 'The air will help me to sleep. And I too would like a sight of your owl.'

To his surprise Pascoe found that he really was enjoying the walk after the first few minutes. There were things about his companion which he did not yet understand and a large part of his purpose in accompanying him had been to probe deeper. But the night was not made for chatter, idle or serious, and even the sound of their footsteps in the gravel of Culpepper's drive seemed an intrusion. It ran before them, white as an Alaskan river, and when they finally stepped off it on to the darker surface of the lane which led down to the road, they both hesitated as though uncertain of their footing. The night sounds gradually took control: a breeze in the trees; something rustling through the grass; a distant chatter, suddenly ending, then a long, wavering note which caught at the nerve-ends.

'There!' said Davenant. 'That's him.'

'Your owl?'

'Probably. Or it may just be a tawny owl. They're more common. Listen.'

The note came again. Pascoe felt as if the Indians might be about to attack.

'I think it is a tawny,' said Davenant. 'Sweet things in their way, but not the same.'

They set off walking again.

'Tell me,' said Pascoe when they reached the road, 'what did Palfrey have to say about Colin before I interrupted him? Or after.'

They had turned right towards the village. Left would have taken them towards Brookside Cottage.

'Now you're interested!' said Davenant. 'Well now, he was far from complimentary, you understand. I had met Colin through Timmy and Carlo and was not so deeply involved with him as you. Also, of course, I had set out to make him talk. So I didn't react like you.'

'No need to apologize,' said Pascoe. 'I was stupid.'

'Perhaps. Our emotions deserve an outing from time to time. Things had started going wrong fairly early in his acquaintance with the Hopkinses. According to his highly coloured version, very attractive, alas, to some of my fellows of the Press, Colin was an unbalanced, exhibition-istic Marxist. *Marxist,* by the way, is something pretty ultimate in the Palfrey insult book. He would rather put his handsome teenage son into the tender care of someone like myself than entrust him to a Marxist.'

'Specifically, what did he tell you?' inquired Pascoe.

'Little enough, though I've gleaned a much more detailed version of the story from other sources. It seems that he tried the public-school-and-Sandhurst condescen-sion bit first of all with the parvenus. When this didn't wash and he saw that Rose and Colin were accepted by those he, Palfrey, liked to be accepted by, he tried the all-chums-in-the-jolly-old-mess line. They didn't take all that kindly to that either, but being nice they tolerated it until one night he turned out a couple of rather noisy kids who'd strayed in by accident. He made the mistake

91

of appealing to Rose for moral support. She stood up, declared that she'd always thought the beer was off but now she knew the full reason why he was called Jim Piss, and marched out. Palfrey said something about an ill-bred bitch; Colin – on his way after Rose – stopped long enough to pour the remnants of his drink over Palfrey's head. They never came back. After such a splendid exit, who could?'

'But that wasn't an end to it,' surmised Pascoe.

'By no means. Absence made the heart grow harder. Palfrey pursued them with calumny and slander and tried to spread rumours about their immorality, political extremism and, worst of all to the middle-class ear, economic unsoundness. Colin and Rose had plenty of friends, but there are always ears willing to listen in a place like this.'

'And . . .?' inquired Pascoe after they had walked another fifty yards in silence.

'And nothing. There's an end. Though I am told that Colin was seen coming out of the Eagle just before opening time on Friday morning and that Palfrey was rather quieter than usual with his lunch-time regulars.'

And Colin wrote a letter to Palfrey that afternoon. What the hell could have been in it? Backhouse would know. But would he know the background? Of course he would! Just as he, Pascoe, would have done if he'd managed to read all Crowther's notes!

They reached the village without saying much more. Outside the Eagle and Child they paused.

'Drink?' said Davenant.

'I don't think so,' said Pascoe. 'Not in there anyway.'

'No, of course not. Let's try the other place then.'

They made it just in time for 'last orders'. The place was crowded and Molly Dixon was under heavy pressure. Her quality as an inn-keeper was clearly demonstrated by the way she was coping, and she acknowledged Pascoe's arrival with a welcoming smile and a quick but genuinely concerned, 'OK?'

'Fine,' he answered.

'Mr Dixon not here?' he asked when she'd drawn his drinks.

'No,' she replied. 'It's the annual dinner of his bowls club. A stag do, very conveniently! Last orders, gentlemen, please! Come along now. Quickly as you can. Is there anyone without?'

She made it sound as if she were genuinely distressed at having to stop the flow. An admirable quality, thought Pascoe. Particularly when managing alone.

Looking round, he became aware that several eyes were focused in his direction. Reporters rather than locals, he surmised quickly. They had an air of alertness at variance with the closing-time conviviality of the rest.

He sipped his beer pensively and looked at his companion, wondering whether he'd act as a buffer against his colleagues. More likely his company would egg them on for fear they were missing something.

'How long have you been in journalism?' he asked.

'Centuries, sweetie,' answered Davenant. 'Don't let my aristocratic profile deceive you. I come of a poor when honest family who thrust me out to earn a living at the earliest opportunity. But tell me, how does it feel for a policeman suddenly to have a murder investigation come so close to him? A bit like Torquemada getting accidentally trapped in the Iron Maiden, I dare say.'

'You ought to know.'

'Feeling and knowing are not the same.'

Pascoe was saved from further cryptic conversation by the distant clanging of a fire-engine bell. Conversation died as it rapidly came near, so rapidly that by the time those sufficiently curious had got to the door, the tintinnabulation had soared to its climax and the fast-receding tail-lights were all there was to be seen.

'A sad time for a fire,' said Davenant.

'Sorry?'

'Autumn. Hay-stacks high and granaries full. I wonder if the nice lady behind the bar is open to suggestion. For more drink, I mean.'

'She's called last orders.'

'Which is what I mean to make.'

Davenant emptied his glass and made for the bar. The moment he moved, a tall, greying man presented himself before Pascoe.

'Mr Pascoe? I'm from the *Echo*. Could I have a quick word?'

'No,' said Pascoe.

'Just very quickly. Please.'

Others were drifting in his direction, Pascoe noted with irritation.

'Shove off,' he said.

'Oh, come on, Sergeant!'

His rank was used like a threat. Pascoe quietly put down his glass on a nearby table. He felt in perfect control but did not discount the possibility of pushing in this man's leering, insinuating face. But he didn't want to be holding a fistful of glass when he did it. Not that he was going to do it. Of course not.

'This must have been a terrible shock to you, Sergeant,' said the reporter.

Pascoe changed his mind, made a fist, changed his mind again and thrust it deep into his pocket.

'Go away,' he said.

The door of the bar was pushed open. An excited-looking rustic entered and spoke to some near acquaintance. Other people looked up, listened. The words danced through the assembled drinkers like dryads in a moonlit forest. Tantalizing. Hard to grasp.

'Brookside . . . Fire . . . Cottage . . . Fire . . . Brookside Cottage is on fire!'

94

The reporter went away.

By the time Pascoe reached Brookside, the fire was out. There seemed to have been some kind of explosion in the kitchen and the blast, though causing a great deal of damage, had probably almost extinguished the flame that caused it.

A uniformed constable, left on duty to watch the property overnight, had decided it was foolish to patrol outside all the time and had entered the living-room just as the explosion occurred. He was badly cut about the face, but had managed to phone for assistance.

Backhouse was on the scene but seemed disinclined to allow Pascoe any special privileges. Pascoe felt he could not really blame him, and hung around the fringe of the little knot of newspapermen whom Backhouse addressed in a friendly, conciliatory manner. Certainly he was a different breed from Dalziel!

'It seems there was an escape of gas in the kitchen probably ignited by a pilot-light in the cooker. The kitchen itself has been extensively damaged, but only superficial damage has been done to the other rooms.'

'An accident you would say, Superintendent?'

'What else?' asked Backhouse blandly.

What indeed? wondered Pascoe. He did not trust coincidences.

The firemen began to pack up their gear. A Gas Board van arrived and a couple of men went into the cottage to deal with the fractured pipes.

The group of onlookers broke up and began to drift away. Pascoe watched them go. When most of them had got into their cars, he noticed a vaguely familiar figure step out of the shadows on the other side of the road and make his way briskly along the road away from the village. Pascoe had to puzzle at his memory to work out who it was.

Sam Dixon, he realized suddenly. He must be on his way back from the bowls club dinner.

It wasn't till he was making his way up the lane towards Culpepper's house that another thought struck him. Dixon had been out of the pub the previous night too.

But it did not seem a very important thought, not as important at this moment as his concern about who was following him through the trees which stretched out on either side of the lane.

'Nerves,' suggested Ellie. 'Or that thing that Davenant claimed to have seen, *Anus mirabilis.*'

'*Asio otus.* No, this was no owl. More like a Hammer Films sound effect. Cracking twigs and rustling undergrowth. I was glad to get back.'

The party had broken up when he returned. Culpepper let him in, explained that the guests had gone and offered him a nightcap.

'Marianne has gone to bed,' he added. 'I hope you will forgive her, but we had no idea how long you would be in returning and she's had a tiring day.'

'I hope I haven't kept you up,' apologized Pascoe.

'Not at all. I need very little sleep. It will be three or four hours before I go up. Sometimes I don't bother at all, just take a cat-nap in my chair.'

He did not press when Pascoe turned down a second drink, and they said good night. Pascoe heard the grille-door of the porcelain room opening as he went up the stairs.

He thought of looking into Ellie's room, decided not to risk disturbing her, and found her sitting by the window in his own room when he put the light on.

'Christ,' he said. 'This is doing my nerves no good.'

'What's new?' she said.

Briefly he filled her in on events since he had left the house.

96

'I heard the fire-engine,' said Ellie. 'I wondered what was going on.'

'Of course you would hear it up here,' said Pascoe. 'Curious. Culpepper never mentioned it.'

'He's probably got other things to worry about. Maid Marianne, for instance.'

'Meaning?'

Ellie pointed at the window.

'I haven't been sitting here like stout Cortez for nothing. If he thinks Marianne's in bed, he's sadly mistaken. Fifteen minutes after the last guest went, she tripped smartly across the drive and disappeared into the trees.'

Pascoe whistled.

'Risky.'

'Not as much as you'd think. They don't share a bedroom.'

'Nosey old you! Who was the last guest?'

'You've guessed.'

'Pelman. That figures.'

'If you put out the light, we could watch for her coming back.'

Pascoe switched off and joined Ellie at the window.

'Perhaps it was Marianne I heard as I came up the drive,' he mused.

Ellie leaned back against him, soft and warm in her nightdress.

'Not the last of the Zombies?' she said sleepily. 'A pity.'

They watched in silence for a few moments.

'I've had it,' said Ellie. 'I'm off; to bed. All this watching.'

She turned away from him and climbed into bed.

'Hey,' he said. 'That's my bed.'

'You don't think I'm going back to mine with things rustling through the undergrowth, do you?'

She spoke lightly, but Pascoe knew better than to

97

take her lightly. The day's events were waiting patiently for darkness and loneliness to let them take shape and substance in their minds. He realized that to be alone tonight would have been unbearable.

Quickly he undressed and joined Ellie in the narrow bed.

'Peter,' she said.

'Yes.'

'Let's go home in the morning. Straightaway. As early as we can.'

'Yes,' he answered. 'Sleep now. We'll go home in the morning.'

PART TWO

Chapter 1

'You look as if you've been shagging a sheep,' said Dalziel with distaste.

Thus spoke the last of the dandies, thought Pascoe, glancing at his superior's shapeless trousers and the military-issue braces, strained dangerously taut over a parabolic waist. But he had to admit that he had brought back with him a lot of white hairs.

'Funny how some dogs lose them but never go bald,' he said brushing ineffectually at his trouser legs.

Dalziel grinned humourlessly and scratched one of the shining deltas on his grey, stubbly pate.

'Not much of a guard-dog,' he said.

'It's a pom,' Pascoe said patiently. 'And they don't leave it in the house when they're on holiday. Not for a fortnight. The RSPCA object.'

'Silly twats,' said Dalziel. 'He'd be two thousand quid better off if there'd been a hungry dog in the house.'

'The insurance will pay,' said Pascoe indifferently.

'You're not suggesting anything?'

'What? No. Christ, why would he want to try a fiddle like this? Twenty thousand, yes. But this is pin money. You've seen the house?'

'No. But you can't always tell. Still, you're right. It's almost certainly our lad, *your* lad. I can't see Mr Stan Cottingley piddling in his own kettle.'

The thought amused him and he laughed himself into a fit of coughing into his outsize khaki handkerchief.

He's not well, thought Pascoe suddenly.

I'm not well, thought Dalziel for the tenth time that

morning. There was a pain across his chest. It was a broad chest, so it was a broad pain. If there had been anyone to mop his fevered brow and ladle out the nourishing broth, he might have stayed in bed that Monday morning. More probably he would have dismissed such solicitude with his customary brusqueness and come in to work anyway.

He looked at Pascoe gloomily and wondered if he should tell him that his promotion was as good as confirmed. Once again he decided against it. Promotion should mean something, be marked by a drink and a bit of jollity. In present circumstances he doubted if Pascoe would react at all. It would be a pity to waste what was a minor triumph. Pascoe could have achieved inspector status at least twelve months earlier if he had stayed in, or been willing to return to, uniformed duties. But the lad had been adamant. The career of administrator and ideas-man his background seemed to equip him for had not appealed. He wanted to be a detective.

And he wasn't making a bad job of it, thought Dalziel with a creator's pride, as he examined again the meticulously prepared file on the string of burglaries which was the sergeant's main case at present. His own interest was twofold. A single break-in at a private house was rarely enough to involve the majesty of a detective-superintendent. But a long sequence – eleven now, almost certainly all by the same man – began to achieve the status of a major crime. Especially when there was reason to believe the perpetrator would resort to extreme violence if interrupted. At the fifth house a pensioner who did odd-jobs in the neighbourhood had been contracted by the owner to keep an eye on the garden while the family were away. Conscientiously, the old man had turned up late one summer evening to water the borders out of the heat of the sun. A man had emerged from the kitchen door as he passed, almost bumping into him. Without hesitation, the intruder had launched into a violent attack. Only the fact that the old man rode a moped and had not yet removed the crash-helmet he always wore saved him from serious damage. But the force of the blow from what was probably a crowbar left deep indentations in the helmet and was sufficient to stun the wearer.

This was the only sighting of the man there had been and the description was almost useless. But the incident was deeply worrying. All the break-ins had taken place when the houses were empty, usually when the owners were on holiday. If this pattern continued, interruption was unlikely. But if it did happen again, there might be no protective headgear next time.

He tossed aside the file with another string of coughs. Meticulousness was not enough. There was nothing there which turned him in any particular direction. Perhaps Pascoe's mind would be programmed by it to some effect. Himself, he needed something more animal; a scent. He sniffed in unconscious acknowledgement of the thought.

Pascoe, he decided, needed chivvying. It would take his mind off things.

'It's more than twelve thousand now with Cottingley's bits and pieces.'

'Thirteen thousand one hundred and thirty-five,' said Pascoe. 'According to the insurance count, that is.'

He glanced at his watch. He had promised to phone Ellie at lunch-time. It was a necessary contact. It might not prove possible to meet at night. Too often in the past he had had to cancel engagements at the last moment. Last Friday, for instance.

'He must be getting rid of the stuff somewhere.'

'The thought had crossed my mind,' sneered Pascoe.

Dalziel rose and stared down at him, removing the thick-rimmed spectacles he wore for reading. It was a menacing gesture.

'That's far enough, Sergeant,' he said. 'It's been a bad

101

week-end for you. But there hasn't been a civil word from you since you came in this morning. I hope to God you spoke to Cottingley a bit fairer.'

By Dalziel's standards, it was a mildly expressed rebuke, but Pascoe felt a touch of shame.

'I'm sorry,' he said. 'Sir. I have this feeling of – well – frustration . . . as if . . .'

But Dalziel had no desire for a heart-to-heart talk. His pain was worse. Indigestion, he decided with desperate optimism. Too much stodge, not enough exercise. A brisk walk to the chemist's would do him good.

'Get your finger out, Sergeant,' he said wearily. 'There's some good descriptions there. He can't just be filling his bottom drawer with what he takes. It must turn up somewhere.'

He left. Pascoe should have felt indignant, hurt even. But oddly enough he felt almost affectionate as the sound of coughing receded down the corridor.

'Hello, love. You all right?'

'Fine. Lots of sympathy concealing academic ghoulish-ness. No reaction from my students, though. They don't believe we have lives separate from them. How was the Fat Man?'

'A bit under the weather, I think. But pretty consider-ate for him. We're very busy.'

'That's good. At the moment anyway. But is it late-busy?'

'I don't know. I'll ring when I do.'

'Please. Peter, I dreamt about them last night.'

'Oh, love.'

'We were back in Eskdale. Remember? Only it was Brookside Cottage, not that old grey farmhouse. A thought struck me. Colin might have gone back there.'

'Why?'

102

'I don't know. Just a thought. It was where my mind took me to get away from them being dead. Understand?'

'I think so.' He was silent for a moment. 'Look, I've got to go now. Sooner I get started, more chance of seeing you tonight.'

'Right. I'll hear from you later. 'Bye.'

''Bye.'

The trouble with most of the stuff Pascoe's burglar got hold of was that it was valuable without being unique. The kind of houses he chose had enough good china, brass, bronze, silver and, occasionally, gold, lying around in one form or another to make his visit worthwhile. Bits of jewellery, cash even, generally quite inadequately locked away, were a frequent perk.

His technique as reconstructed by Pascoe was simple. He chose houses with gardens large enough to provide some kind of seclusion; drove up in his car (they had some completely unhelpful tyre marks); parked out of sight of the road, in the garage sometimes; smashed a window to get in (noise was no object where there was seclusion; on one occasion he had simply chopped down a kitchen door); examined the interior at leisure; filled a suitcase or two with whatever he evaluated highest; and left.

At first the break-ins had been straightforward. The first couple of houses looked as if they hadn't been touched. But an element of despoliation had crept in. Walls were defaced, carpets stained, furniture scarred. At Cottingley's house, the latest in the series, perhaps in acknowledgement of the value of his haul, he had merely left a kettle full of urine. Or perhaps, thought Pascoe, this marked a new direction. Defacation, masturbation even, during thefts of this kind were not uncommon elements in a certain criminal syndrome, frequently

103

associated with great mental and emotional instability. He recalled uneasily the attack on the old man.

None of the stuff had turned up, not locally anyway, so there must be an efficient distribution system. Not that a great deal of it would be clearly identifiable in any case. The latest haul had been typical. A small amount of silver, as valuable melted down as in its present form. Some valuable but not unique glass. Ornaments. Some jewellery. An old clock. And Mrs Cottingley's collection of stones and pebbles, picked up all over the world, as she accompanied her husband on his frequent business trips. Only the clock offered them any real chance.

What he needed was a lead. At the moment there was not a useful thought in his head.

'Stuff it,' he said, and picked up his morning newspaper which he had not yet had time to open.

Colin peered out at him from near the bottom of the front page. For a moment he thought it meant they had found him, but it was only an appeal for public help. The short piece on the killings contained nothing new. There were a couple of meaningless quotations from Backhouse and, more surprisingly, a little harangue about the public weal from French, the coroner. Clearly he was a man who liked to be noticed.

He turned the pages to escape the photograph. Other people's troubles seemed to start from every column. Explosions, revolution, unemployment, a couple of strikes; a trade union leader in Bradford was accused of corruption; an international footballer had been suspended; a mineral mining company was accused of despoiling bonny Scotland. He looked at the last item more closely. The company was Nordrill; Culpepper's firm he recalled. Suddenly he was back in Thornton Lacey.

He crumpled the newspaper in his hands and dropped

it into the waste bin. There was a knock at the door and a young head peered cheerfully round.

'Excuse me, Sarge, but there's a Mr Sturgeon here. Says you'll be glad to see him.'

'Will I?' said Pascoe. 'OK. Show him in.'

Edgar Sturgeon had been number five in the list of victims. Pascoe remembered him well, partly because he had lost a stamp collection valued at just under a thousand pounds and partly because he hadn't seemed particularly distressed to find his house burgled on return from holiday. In some people this would have been suspicious but Pascoe couldn't find it in him to suspect the old man of being bent. They had almost instantly taken a liking to each other – not the kind of reason for quieting suspicion that Dalziel liked, but, in any case, Sturgeon was too comfortably placed to need an insurance fiddle. A self-made man, he had recently retired, having sold out his interest in the local timber-yard he had built up from nothing over forty years. Perhaps he was not quite ready for the life of easy retirement his comfortable wife and her three tortoiseshell cats had planned for him, and Pascoe had suspected from his lively demeanour that he was still putting his business acumen to some profitable use.

'Hello, Mr Sturgeon. Come on in,' he said with a smile.

'Hello, Sergeant Pascoe,' said the grizzle-haired, thick-set man who slowly entered.

He looks older, thought Pascoe. And his demeanour was now far from lively.

'What can I do for you?' he asked.

Sturgeon sat down and took an envelope out of his breast-pocket.

'I've got some of my stamps back,' he said flatly.

'Have you indeed? That's great. Where from?'

'A friend of mine. I saw him at the club on Saturday and he told me he'd bought some stamps for his nephew's birthday. Coronation set 1953. Couple of quids' worth. He asked me to take a look to tell him if he'd been done or not.'

Pascoe looked with interest at the block of four stamps he had shaken carefully out of the envelope. They were unfranked.

'How can you be sure these are yours?' he asked, after vainly trying to spot any distinguishing feature.

'Them's mine all right,' asserted Sturgeon. 'Give us some credit, lad! I did a little repair job on the big 'un. You can hardly see it, but it means it's worth precious little. My mate was done! And if you look at the back you can see how they've been mounted. They don't do that nowadays but when I started, you stuck 'em in.'

'I'll take your word,' said Pascoe, glad to see the old man a little more lively. 'This friend, where'd he get them?'

'Etherege and Burne–Jones. Out at Birkham.'

'Birkham? Yes, I know it.'

Birkham was a village a few miles to the east. It made a useful half-way meeting point for Ellie and Pascoe, particularly as it possessed in the Jockey a very pleasant pub which provided excellent steaks. The only trouble was that, as always, excellence and beauty attracted crowds and Birkham was a fashionable place both to visit and to inhabit. The architectural and gastronomical delights of the place had been examined in a colour supplement article about a year previously and this had naturally increased its popularity.

It was, thought Pascoe with a small shock of recognition, a kind of Yorkshire Thornton Lacey.

He shook his mind free from the thought and concentrated on Messrs Etherege and Burne-Jones. He knew their shop, a converted barn, by sight but had never been inside. To a policeman's eyes, all second-hand shops, whether claiming to deal in 'antiques' or 'junk', were

106

suspect. They provided the best and most obvious outlet for stolen property. But in his experience, a fashionable establishment like the one at Birkham was less likely to be used for this than its urban counterpart. The opportunities for legal dishonesty in the selling of 'antiques' were too great to make fencing a worthwhile risk.

'What will you do?' asked Sturgeon.

'We'll take a look, of course. See if there's anything else of yours there. You say you were shown the stamps on Saturday night? Why didn't you get in touch yesterday?'

Sturgeon shrugged.

'It didn't seem worth spoiling your week-end,' he said.

Pascoe stood up and crossed to a filing cabinet which he opened and peered into.

'That was kind of you,' he said after a while. If his voice sounded strange, Sturgeon obviously did not notice. He sat staring dully at the desk before him.

He's not interested in the stamps, thought Pascoe suddenly. There's something else.

He extracted a file from the open drawer.

'We have an inventory of your stuff here, Mr Sturgeon,' he said. 'Now this would be item 27, wouldn't it?'

Sturgeon looked and nodded. Quickly and efficiently Pascoe drafted out a statement for the man to sign. But when he had done so, he seemed reluctant to leave.

'Sergeant,' he said. 'Could you do something for me?'

'Depends what is,' said Pascoe.

Sturgeon produced a piece of paper. It had a name and address written on it. He passed it to Pascoe who read it without enlightenment.

Archie Selkirk, Strath Farm, Lochart, Nr Callander.

'Lochart's a village in Perthshire,' said Sturgeon, speaking quickly as if eager to get the words out. 'There's a police-sergeant stationed there. It'll be like it is in the villages round here – everyone knowing everyone else's business. Could you ring this sergeant and ask him what he knows about that man?'

'Archie Selkirk?' said Pascoe thoughtfully. 'I'm not sure, Mr Sturgeon. What is it you want to find out?'

'Nothing,' said Sturgeon. 'Nothing in particular. Just anything that might be known. Can you help?'

'Well, I'll see what can be done. But people have got a right to privacy, you know, Mr Sturgeon. The police force can't just be used as an information centre. We've got to have some reason for making inquiries.'

Sturgeon stood up, pushing his chair back angrily.

'If you can't help, you can't help,' he snapped and made for the door.

'Hold on!' said Pascoe. 'I said I'd see what I could do.'

'Please yourself,' said Sturgeon stonily and left, closing the door forcefully behind him.

Pascoe took a couple of steps after him, then 'Shit!' he said and sat down. His business was crime. Today he would stick to it and leave the social therapy to others.

He thrust Sturgeon's piece of paper into his breast pocket and went down to the canteen for lunch.

He had a hard but totally unproductive afternoon. Paperwork seemed to come at him from all sides and his one excursion into the outside world proved fruitless too. The 'closed' sign was up in the premises of Etherege and Burne-Jones at Birkham and he had a flat tyre on the journey back. He changed the wheel in record time, determined that at least the evening was going to remain unspoilt.

His haste turned out to be unnecessary. When he rang Ellie at five-thirty to say it looked as if he was going to be able to get away that evening, she answered in a voice distant with fatigue.

'I'm whacked, Peter,' she said. 'It just came on this

108

afternoon. I had to send a class away. They probably reckon I'm pregnant. Or at the menopause, more likely.'

Her effort at lightness failed miserably.

'Have you seen a doctor?' asked Pascoe anxiously.

'Hell, no. I got some pills from the college sick-bay. Guaranteed to knock me out.'

'Pills? Don't you think you should . . .'

'Oh, stop fussing!' she snapped in irritation. 'We've got a trained nurse here and she only doles out two of these things at a time, so there's not much risk of an overdose.'

'I didn't mean . . . all I said was . . .'

'OK, Peter. I'm sorry, love. I'm beat. All I want is a dose of oblivion, a nice, effective, SRN-measured dose. Would you mind if we scrubbed round this evening? Hell, we'd just sit and look miserably at each other anyway. What can you talk about when there's only one thing to talk about? No news yet?'

'Nothing.'

'Well. No news is . . .'

'. . . no news. That's all.'

'Yes. Ring me tomorrow, will you?'

'Yes. Look, Ellie, let's have lunch together. I'm going to be out at Birkham in the morning. It's not so far for you to come. We'll have a bowl of soup at the Jockey.'

'OK. About one; that suit? Good. 'Bye.'

'Bye, love.'

He replaced the receiver thoughtfully.

'What's the attraction at Birkham? Apart from the soup.'

Dalziel was standing at the door. You had to admire the way the man made no effort to conceal his eavesdropping. Or perhaps you didn't have to admire it at all. It was no use protesting about it, that was certain.

Quickly he filled him in on the day's events.

'Precious bloody little,' he grunted. 'If we got paid by results, there'd be a lot of hungry buggers in this building tonight.' He coughed ferociously into his large khaki handkerchief.

'I'd see about that cough, sir,' suggested Pascoe diffidently.

'Would you now?' said Dalziel. 'Well, Sergeant, as you seem to be at a loose end tonight, you can stroll me quietly down to the Black Eagle and buy me some medicine. George, you coming?'

The inspector thus addressed as he moved past the door in his raincoat didn't pause in his stride.

'Not tonight, thanks, sir,' his voice receded. 'Urgently expected at home.'

Pascoe admired him. It took a good man to keep going when Dalziel spoke. Perhaps that was the quality he lacked, which would keep him a sergeant all his days.

'The girl, she's all right?' asked Dalziel as they stepped out into the cool evening air.

'Yes, thanks.'

'Good. She seemed tough enough.'

Dalziel had met Ellie during an investigation at the college where she lectured, the same investigation which had brought Ellie and Pascoe almost reluctantly together again after years without contact. Pascoe was still not certain about the depth and strength of their relationship. They met regularly, slept together when they felt like it (which meant when Ellie felt like it: Pascoe nearly always did), but their intimate talk was always of the shared past, never a shared future. The week-end at Thornton Lacey had seemed in prospect something of a proving ground. It might still turn out to have been so.

But the relationship between Dalziel and Ellie was clear enough. They did not like each other. Each was the other's bogeyman, monstrous and against nature – Dalziel the brute with power and Ellie the woman with brains. Pascoe sometimes felt it would be very easy to find himself crushed to death between them.

110

'I had a word with Backhouse earlier. He was cagey, but he's no further forward.'

Dalziel made it sound as if in Backhouse's place he would have been a great deal further forward.

'There's not much he can do, sir,' said Pascoe, deciding he might as well go along with this we-can-discuss-the-case-coolly therapy. 'Not until they find Colin.'

'If he did it. Which seems likely. What seems likely is usually what happened. Though there is one thing.'

What the one thing consisted of was not to be immediately revealed. They passed through the saloon bar door of the Black Eagle as Dalziel spoke. The barman stood with the telephone to his ear.

'Just a minute,' he said. 'For you, Mr Dalziel.'

Dalziel listened with nothing more than a couple of grunts and one long cough.

'Right,' he said finally. 'Send a car.'

He replaced the receiver firmly. Pascoe looked at him expectantly.

'Just in time for a drink,' said Dalziel. 'Two scotches, Tommy. Quick as you like.'

'We're going out,' stated Pascoe.

'Right. Good job your bit of fluff's tired. Cheers.'

He downed his scotch in one.

'Laddo's been at it again,' he continued. 'Only this time he was interrupted.

'You, mean we've got a witness?' asked Pascoe hopefully.

'No. From the sound of it we've got a corpse.'

Chapter 2

It was one-thirty when Pascoe arrived at the Jockey at Birkham. The pub was situated alongside a boarding kennels and the resident dogs howled accusingly at him as he parked his car.

Ellie had finished her soup and was tearing the heart out of a steak pie, signs of a good appetite which pleased him as he made his apologies and refilled her glass.

'I thought you said you were going to be in Birkham this morning,' she complained.

'Something came up.'

Dropping his voice, he quickly sketched out what had happened the previous evening. Matthew Lewis, forty-three, senior partner in a firm of estate agents, had been called back from a late holiday in Scotland to attend to some urgent business. He had finished at his office at four-thirty. Deciding he was too exhausted to face the long drive north that evening, he made for home.

A neighbour had seen him turn in to the drive of his handsome ranch-style bungalow at ten past five. At five-thirty, the neighbour, Mrs Celia Turvey, had gone to the front door of Lewis's house with a parcel she had taken in for him from the postman. The front door was open. No one answered her calls. She went into the house and discovered Lewis lying dead in the lounge.

Pascoe talked calmly, objectively, about the case, keeping a close eye on Ellie's reactions. It was a good thing to have her interest like this. But it would be easy to let this new act of violence spill over into the emotional area of their own week-end. The momentum of the case had carried him unquestioningly along for most of the previous evening. But when Mrs Lewis, travel-weary and pale beyond despair, had arrived with her two young children, he had turned away and left rather than run the risk of having to speak to her.

He did not tell Ellie this. Nor did he tell her that Matthew Lewis's head had been beaten so badly that slivers of bone from his fractured skull were found buried deep inside his brain. He kept the affair at the level of a problem, as much for his own sake as for hers. But the targetless anger he had felt in Thornton Lacey was beginning to scratch demandingly at whatever cellar-door of his being contained it.

Ellie too had sombre-coloured news. She had been in touch with Rose's parents in Worksop and discovered that the body had been released to them and the funeral was taking place the following day.

'That's quick,' commented Pascoe.

'It's not something to be put off,' said Ellie. 'With the funeral done, there's some chance of starting to live again. Can you, go? It's not that far.'

'I'll try,' said Pascoe. 'Of course, we're very busy.'

'Oh, stuff your precious bloody job!' said Ellie, standing up. 'Are you finished? Let's get some air.'

They strolled in silence along the road outside the pub, arriving eventually at the old barn which bore the sign *David Burne-Jones and Jonathan Etherege – Antiques*. This had been his original reason for meeting Ellie in Birkham, but there had been no time that morning to visit the shop. He had intended to call there later, after Ellie had departed, but now, as she stopped and peered through the open doorway, he said nothing but waited to see what she would do.

'Fancy a browse?' she asked.

'Anything you say.'

They went in. Sitting, and managing to look comfortable, on a Victorian chaise-longue was a man who seemed just to have finished a picnic lunch and was cleaning his teeth on an apple. About forty-two or -three, he had a round, cheerful face which matched his general shape. Fat if you disliked him, otherwise just chubby, thought Pascoe, leaving his own judgement still in the balance.

'Afternoon,' he said. 'Anything in particular you want?'

'Just browsing,' said Ellie.

'Be my guest. Let me know if you come across anything half decent among the junk.'

The shop was divided into three sections. The largest contained furniture, the next local craft-work, and third and smallest, a mere couple of display cabinets, stamps and coins.

Pascoe peered closely at these, laboriously trying to set them against a mental check list.

'I didn't know you were interested in stamps?' said Ellie, appearing at his shoulder.

'There's a lot you don't know about me,' murmured Pascoe. And vice versa.

They wandered back into the craft section. He picked up an ashtray thrown by some local potter.

'You can steal better at the Jockey,' he said.

'I've often thought of it,' said the apple-eater, who had wandered up behind them unnoticed.

'Sorry,' said Pascoe, putting down the ashtray hastily.

'No need,' grinned the man. Pascoe grinned back, making up his mind. Anyone who could laugh at his own business deserved to be chubby.

'These are nice,' said Ellie. She was looking at a selection of pendants and brooches made up from small stones, some polished, some not, all described as 'Real Yorkshire Stones' as if this gave them special value.

'You won't find those in the Jockey,' said the dealer.

114

'But all good local work. Very local. Me, in fact. Keep your local craftsmen happy.'

'And rich,' said Pascoe drily, looking at the price tag of the red-flecked green stone pendant Ellie seemed to be taking most interest in.

'All right,' said the man. 'Instant reduction of twenty-five p. just to test the sincerity of your interest.'

Ellie looked at Pascoe, grinning broadly at his predicament. He reached for his wallet and paid up. The grin alone was worth it.

'Thanks,' she said. 'Now I've got what I want, I'm going to rush off. I have a class at two-thirty. Ring me about tomorrow, will you?'

'OK,' said Pascoe. 'I'll just hang on here a bit.'

He watched her go, then turned to the dealer.

'Mr Burne-Jones?' he asked.

'Nearly right. Etherege,' said the man.

He looked unperturbed when Pascoe introduced himself and blank when he was shown the stamps.

'Sorry,' he said. 'They're just bits of paper to me. Never been able to see it, myself. My partner looks after that side of things. There's nothing in it for us, really, but he's interested.'

'That would be Mr Burne-Jones? Could I speak to him?'

'Not for a few days. He went off to Corsica for his hols this very morning.'

'Damn,' said Pascoe. He produced a copy of the complete list of stolen articles.

'You'll have seen this?'

'Yes,' said Etherege. 'They keep on coming round, but as you can see, it's mainly furniture we deal in here. A bit bulky for your cat-burglar and in any case I buy most of it in myself at the sales, so we know where it's come from.'

'What about the stamps?'

115

'God knows. I sometimes think David, my partner, hangs around school playgrounds and does swops. Look, if you like, why don't you sort out anything from our stock which matches any of the stamps on your list and take them away for a closer check.'

'That's very generous of you,' said Pascoe who had been about to do just that. But it was nice for a change not to have a fuss.

'Not really,' said Etherege. 'Nothing there's marked at more than a few quid. No penny blacks, I'm afraid.'

There were one or two items, not of any great value or rarity, which corresponded with entries on Sturgeon's catalogue. Pascoe gave Etherege a receipt for them.

'If there's no identification, you'll get them back, of course.'

'And if there is?'

Pascoe shrugged.

'Never mind. I'll take it out of David's profits,' smiled Etherege. 'Cheerio, Sergeant. Come again and do some browsing. Bring the young lady. She seems able to get you to spend rather than just confiscate! Is she in the force too, by the way?'

'No such luck,' said Pascoe. 'Goodbye.'

He walked back to the pub car-park. It had not so far been a very productive day. As he approached his car which was parked up against the fence surrounding the kennels, he heard the dogs howl again, forlorn, wanting their owners.

Dalziel's pain, dissipated or forgotten in the activity of organizing a murder hunt, had returned after lunch. The timing supported his own diagnosis of indigestion, but having worked his way in vain through a variety of pharmaceutical and folk cures, he reluctantly made an appointment to see his doctor. This produced an immediate improvement in his condition and the optimistic

116

reaction was still in evidence as he talked about the Lewis case with Pascoe.

'We need this one. This boy's mad.'

'Sir?'

'You saw Lewis. There was no need for that. The first blow would have stunned him, the next put him out cold. He must have been flat out on the floor for the next half-dozen, the ones that killed him.'

'Panic?' suggested Pascoe.

'I don't think so. You run when you panic. Hit anything in the way, perhaps, but mainly just run. There was no sign of this boy running. He beat an orderly retreat, didn't waste any time, but left in good order. It all points to a nutcase. We'd seen the signs.'

'Killing a man's not quite like peeing in a kettle,' protested Pascoe.

'I don't know. You leave him lying there in the middle of the room. Like a heap of garbage. That's all a dead man is, after all.'

Pascoe looked doubtful. He was used to playing Dalziel's straight man. It was an exercise which often produced results.

'We're not even absolutely certain it's the same fellow,' he said.

Dalziel snorted with magnificent scorn.

'We've got a villain who does medium large detached houses while the owners are away on holiday. He has shown himself ready to use violence. The owner of a medium large detached house . . .'

'Bungalow.'

'. . . who should have been on holiday gets beaten to death by someone he catches in the act. Therefore . . .'

'He was done to death by a disgruntled client who helped himself to some bits and pieces to make it look like a robbery.'

'Fine. Except that no one knew he was going to be at

117

home that day. He was supposed to be on holiday. Remember?'

'He did come back for a meeting, sir,' replied Pascoe. 'Someone must have known.'

Dalziel sighed as if Pascoe had taken all the joy out of his life.

'All right. Talk to the people at his office if you like. Let's leave no stone unturned. Or uncast, for that matter. We've got to get at this boy somehow. And if he is our thief, then we've only got two starting points. The break-ins themselves, or disposal of the loot. Which so far means a few bloody stamps. Was Etherege any good?'

'No. Oh, he'll know a few ways to make a quick bob or two, but I can't see anything there for us. I brought some stamps for Sturgeon to look at.'

'Which leaves your actual crimes,' said Dalziel, setting in train a long spiral scratch which began at his calf and gave promise of attaining to his crotch.

Pascoe was silent. Everyone on the case had worked long and hard in the search for a common denominator which might lead somewhere. But such a thing was hard to come by. In only two cases did they even know the day of the week and the time of day the crime had taken place. The first, when the old gardener had been attacked, was a Thursday at seven-thirty pm. The second, when Lewis was killed, was a Monday at five-fifteen pm. Early, but that meant nothing. Given a choice, most thieves preferred daylight for a housebreaking job. There was no worry about lights, less risk of being asked to explain your presence on the streets by a casual policeman.

The only real potentially useful link between the crimes was that the house-owners had all been on holiday. The thief must have some source of information.

The trouble was there were any number of ways in which a professional thief could unearth the fact that a house was empty. Thought just how much of a real

118

professional their man was, Pascoe wasn't sure. Certainly it was doubtful whether he was known to the police. Every likely villain in the area had been descended on with great force and alacrity in the two cases where the time of the job was known. The results had been negative.

And the deliberate slaying of Lewis (if it had been their man in his house) bothered Pascoe considerably. Your thief had a great instinct for self-preservation. He might smash what lay in the way of his escape, but would probably see no reason to hang around to make a job of it.

'I still don't think he's a nutcase,' he averred as he left Dalziel groaning his satisfaction as he reached the vertex of his scratch.

In the corridor he met Detective-Inspector George Headingley, the man with the strength of will to resist Dalziel's drinking invitations. He held a sheet of paper in his hand.

'There's more in piss than meets the eye,' said the inspector sagely.

'What?'

'It was your idea to send the contents of Cottingley's kettle to forensic, wasn't it? Take a house-point. Our lad's a diabetic.'

'A what?'

'He's got diabetes, which might narrow things down a bit. I'm just on my way in to tell the super. Come along. He might kiss you on both cheeks if you're not nippy on your feet.'

Together they went back into Dalziel's room. The fat man had the telephone to his ear. After a moment he put it down and looked glumly at Pascoe.

'You ought to know,' he said. 'I asked them to keep me posted on your spot of trouble. There's a man at Nottingham helping with enquiries. Backhouse has gone off to see him, so he looks good for your mate, Hopkins. I don't know what I'm sorry for, but I'm sorry.'

Chapter 3

'A false alarm,' said Backhouse. 'They had just about established this by the time I arrived. He was a very good prospect – looked just right and wouldn't say a word.'

He laughed shortly.

'Turned out to be a Pole whose English was practically nil and whose previous experience with authority had taught him that silence was golden. I spent the night in Nottingham, saw a nice bit of Pinter at the Playhouse, and being handy, decided to come on here today.'

Here was the small village outside Worksop where Rose Hopkins had been born and where just a few minutes previously she had been lowered into the earth.

Pascoe wondered what Dalziel would make of Pinter.

He had been surprised by the number of people at the funeral, and by one or two unexpected faces in particular. Backhouse's interest must, of course, be mainly professional though he disguised this well. And it was perhaps not too surprising to see Anton Davenant there, whether as friend or journalist he couldn't say. His most unfunereal clothing had won some curious glances and deprecating mutters from the locals.

But the most surprising sight had been of Marianne Culpepper and Angus Pelman among the mourners. Some atavistic puritanism stirred in Pascoe at what appeared so blatant and unseemly an advertisement of their relationship. They were all in the saloon bar of the village pub, having politely turned down an invitation to share the funeral meats offered by Rose's parents. Ellie was sitting with Pelman, Davenant and Marianne, while the two policemen carried on what probably appeared their very conspiratorial conversation at the bar.

The beer, drawn from the wood, was cloudy but they drank it without complaint.

'Are things no further forward, sir?' asked Pascoe cautiously.

'Afraid not,' said Backhouse. 'Since *you* left, things have been very quiet in Thornton Lacey.'

'I'm sorry if I was a trouble to you.'

'No trouble, Sergeant. No; what troubles me is the place itself. There are things happening there, tensions, probably nothing whatsoever to do with the crime, but they muddy the water. Or perhaps they are something to do with the crime. Let's accept the most obvious solution. Hopkins killed his wife and two friends. No, hang on a minute. It's a hypothesis which forces itself upon us, even upon you, I suspect.

'So. He did it. He is the murderer. But what is it that made such a man do such a thing? It must have been a pressure beyond anything I have ever experienced. Yet I have a feeling that such pressures as these are never so far away in a place like Thornton Lacey unless you keep on the move, on the alert, and never let them build up.'

'But he'd hardly been there any time!' protested Pascoe. 'What the hell could have happened so quickly?'

'He managed to make at least one good enemy that we know of.'

'Palfrey?' said Pascoe.

Backhouse nodded.

'What was in the letter?' Pascoe asked, not really expecting an answer.

Backhouse looked at him assessingly.

'Why not?' he said, almost to himself. 'Palfrey was becoming an annoyance to your friend. He decided to strike back and hit on the ingenious idea of checking the so-called major's military background. To his probable delight he discovered that no such creature as 'Major' Palfrey existed, though his alleged regiment did once have in its number a catering sergeant of that name. Evidently Hopkins called on Palfrey on Friday morning, put this to him and warned him against continuing his alleged slanders.'

'And the letter?'

'The lettter merely enlarged upon this, setting down coldly what had obviously been uttered in extremely warm terms earlier the same day. A kind of blackmail note, I suppose.'

'Which is a very old and very popular murder motive,' said Pascoe thoughtfully.

'True,' said Backhouse. 'Palfrey claims he was serving cloudy pints in his pub all Friday night. Surprisingly difficult to check. I wonder if he's got some connection with this place?'

He examined his beer sadly then pushed it aside and stood up.

'I'm sure I'll see you again, Sergeant. Soon, perhaps. Mr French, the coroner, is uncommonly keen to exercise his few powers in this case.'

He shook his head in disapproval. Pascoe could understand why. A coroner who would not be led by the police could still prove an irritation.

'Goodbye, Mrs Culpepper, Miss Soper.'

With a nod at Pelman and Davenant, Backhouse left and Pascoe joined the others. They stopped talking as he did so.

To make a solid silence, he thought, just add one policeman.

'Another drink anyone?' he asked.

There were no takers.

'How's Mr Culpepper?' he said to Marianne, suddenly feeling a bit aggressive.

'Very well,' she answered in her cool, clear tones.

'He would have come today, but something came up. Business.'

Unlike her type to volunteer an explanation to my type, thought Pascoe. But it could be true.

'Is there some trouble?' he asked. 'I saw in this morning's paper that Nordrill say they are going to abandon their explorations in Scotland.'

Pelman and Marianne exchanged an unreadable glance.

'Bully for the conservationists, say I,' said Davenant. 'It's been lovely seeing you all once more, despite sad circumstance. Mr Pascoe, would you care to walk me to my car?'

They left and made their way towards the bright red Citroën GS which seemed to mirror Davenant's personality somehow.

'I just wanted to ask if there was anything new. I ask as a friend, not a journalist, you understand.'

'No. Nothing as far as I know.'

'I see. I wondered if dear Mr Backhouse had unearthed anything startling perhaps.'

'He's not showing it to me if he has.'

'Ah well. I hope things do not drag on for ever.' He climbed into his car. 'Nice to have seen you again. And to meet Miss Soper. An intellectual gem in the constabulary crown! Ciao!'

'He seemed to have taken a fancy to you,' said Pascoe on the way home.

'I hope not!' said Ellie. 'He seemed rather patronizingly surprised to discover that I, a lecturer, hob-nobbed with the fuzz. *Did* Backhouse tell you anything?'

'No,' Pascoe lied. Policemen sometimes had to lie to their woman. It was an occupational hazard.

'And there's no sign of Colin.'

'No. Wherever he is, he's lying very low.'

The skies, unpromising all morning, went frighteningly dark as they turned off the dual carriageways of the A1.

The pathetic fallacy, thought Pascoe. Something dreadful is about to happen. But, please God, not to me. Don't let it happen to me.

A white Rover passed them in the opposite direction and turned south on the A1. Pascoe did not even notice it pass.

Chapter 4

Back at the office Pascoe found a message on his desk. Sturgeon had rung several times that morning. 'Sounded urgent,' said the note cryptically, 'but wouldn't say what.'

Silly old sod! thought Pascoe. Does he think I've nothing better to do than make stupid bloody telephone calls to Scotland?

But he reached for the phone, at the same time digging into his breast pocket for Sturgeon's scrap of paper. He sorted it out with some difficulty from the large collection of frayed and folded stationery the pocket contained. It was a kind of portable (and permanent) filing cabinet. A sergeant's pay did not encourage the wearing of any great variety of clothes.

The phone rang for more than a minute before it was answered.

'Can you no' wait?' demanded a Scots voice, the owner of which then apparently dropped the receiver to the floor and went back to whatever business had been interrupted. It seemed to involve drawing a metal edge down a sheet of glass.

Eventually he returned and after some coaxing revealed himself as Sergeant Lauder. He was even more reluctant to accept that Pascoe was, in fact, Pascoe; and only an exasperated invitation to him to replace the receiver and make further investigations at Mid-Yorkshire HQ persuaded him to concede the point. As soon as Pascoe mentioned Archie Selkirk of Strath Farm, Lauder's doubts seemed to reassert themselves.

'Is that you?' he demanded. 'Is it you again, man?'

'It's me. Sergeant Pascoe. For God's sake! Can't you understand?'

'No need to blaspheme, whomever you are. Then you're no' the one who phoned yesterday?'

'No, I'm not. If I'd phoned yesterday, I wouldn't be . . . oh, forget it! What about Archie Selkirk?'

'Ay, well, Archie Selkirk, is it? That's what the one yesterday was asking about too.'

'What?' Pascoe was suddenly interested. 'Didn't he give a name?'

'No. No name.'

'Yorkshire accent?'

'Perhaps. Perhaps. But you all sound much the same to me.'

'Well, what did you tell him?' demanded Pascoe.

'Just the same as I'm going to tell you, Sergeant Pascoe,' answered Lauder, still by his intonation managing to infuse a great deal of incredulity into the last two words.

'And what's that.'

'Simply, there's no such man. Not farming round here, that is.'

'You're sure?'

Lauder indicated by his heavily scornful silence that he was sure.

'And Strath Farm?'

'No.'

'No such farm.'

'Aye.'

'And you told this to the man yesterday.'

'Aye.'

The pips went.

'This must be costing the ratepayers a mint of money,' said Lauder, stung out of monosyllables.

'Aye,' said Pascoe. 'Thanks.'

126

He pressed the rest, got the dialling tone, and dialled Sturgeon's number.

The old sod must have got impatient and decided to do it himself, thought Pascoe. Why he couldn't do it in the first place, God knows. And why had he rung so urgently that morning?

The phone was still ringing. He glanced at his watch and groaned. Time was marching by and there was work to be done. Sturgeon would have to wait. In any case, he almost certainly knew what Pascoe had to tell him. Though what it could mean teased the mind. But there was a murder waiting to be solved.

He replaced the receiver and set off for the late Matthew Lewis's office.

Dalziel came from behind the screen with all the demureness and probably the total volume of Gilbert's three little maids from school. He pulled himself together as he caught the glint of amusement in the eyes of the solitary witness and removed his instinctively modest hand from his crotch.

'You'd think someone as rich as you could keep this bloody place warm!' he snapped, blowing into his hands. 'Let's get it over with before I freeze to death.'

'Now you know how it feels to be one of those poor bastards you torture in your cells,' grunted Grainger, the doctor.

He and Dalziel were old acquaintances. Each affected to believe the other embodied all the public misconceptions and suspicions of his profession. Secretly they were not altogether convinced this was not in fact true.

Grainger began his examination. It had seemed an excellent opportunity to give Dalziel a thorough overhaul when the other man had made this, his first appointment in half a dozen years. Now, ignoring Dalziel's impatient

127

protests, he took his time as he moved from one part of the test-sequence to the next.

'Do they pay you by the hour?' grumbled the superintendent. 'Look, while I'm here, you might as well make yourself useful. What can you tell me about diabetes? Or didn't they discover it till after you graduated from the barber's shop?'

'You don't think you've got diabetes, do you?' asked Grainger. 'You haven't. God knows what else is wrong with you, but you're not diabetic.'

'Thanks. No. There's someone we're anxious to see and he's got diabetes.'

'How do you know?' asked Grainger. 'Turn over, will you, if you can manage without a lever.'

'He left a kettleful of piss behind him.'

'Jesus!' said Grainger, pausing with his stethoscope poised. 'I thought *my* job brought me life in the raw.'

'You don't know you're living. Come on them. Diabetes. What can you, tell me about our man?'

'It's not as simple as that,' answered Grainger, 'as I'm sure your police-surgeon would be only too pleased to tell you. There are three types of diabetes for a start, Type A, Type B . . .'

'And Type C. Christ, is that what you spend five years learning? The bloody alphabet?'

'. . . and Type AB,' continued Grainger, unperturbed. 'Type A's the most popularly known form, though by no means the commonest. If you've got type A it means you're dependent on insulin injections for the rest of your life. It usually manifests itself in young people. Classified symptoms are excessive hunger and thirst and frequent urination.'

'In a kettle,' said Dalziel, interested.

'That might be a symptom of something to a psychologist, not to me,' said the doctor. 'Sit up. My God, what a gut you've got, Andy. If you were going to get diabetes,

128

it'd be type B. It usually doesn't strike till middle-age and the victims are nearly always overweight. It's the most common form of the disease and is usually treated orally rather than through insulin injections.'

'You mean they drink the stuff?'

'No! Insulin's got to be injected. They take something else, a hypoglycaemic agent – that means something which lowers the amount of sugar in the blood.'

'And Type AB?'

'Stress diabetes. This is a form bought on by an undue emotional or physical stress. People in their thirties or forties get it. Symptoms in its mild form are much for Type B, only the victim's not overweight. On the contrary, he's often underweight. But violent stress can bring on a violent reaction and make the patient insulin-dependent, for a while at least. Stand up now.'

Dalziel obeyed, groaning.

'Well, you've been a great help. We're looking for a thin man of thirty or forty, or a fat man of forty or fifty, or a thin or fat man of almost any age at all.'

'It could be a woman,' suggested the doctor.

'Get stuffed. Look, for God's sake, how long are you going to be? I've got work to do.'

'Another twenty minutes. Here, that is,' answered Grainger. 'Then I've fixed up for you to be X-rayed at the hospital. You'll be done by tea-time.'

'What the hell do you think I've got?' demanded Dalziel with an aggression meant to be comic.

But he heard in his voice the frightened plea of the suspect demanding to be told the nature of the charge.

Lewis and Cowley Estates was the kind of firm which did not put the prices of its property in the window. Rare for Yorkshire, thought Pascoe. They generally liked a price-tag on everything. Brass was a matter of general public concern.

The 'closed' sign was up in the velvet-curtained window, but he could see movement inside. He rapped sharply on the door. And again after a few seconds.

A thin-faced man appeared, stared assessingly at Pascoe for a moment, decided rightly that as a potential customer he did not promise much, and gesticulated at the 'closed' sign.

For answer Pascoe produced his warrant-card, pressed it to the glass and imitated the man's gesture.

The man stepped back, turned and seemed to be saying something to whoever was in the office with him. Then he opened the door.

'Mr Cowley?' asked Pascoe.

'Yes?'

'Detective-Sergeant Pascoe, sir. May I come in?'

Cowley was in his early thirties. He was excessively lean and hungry-looking and he carried his head thrust forward aggressively, putting Pascoe in mind of a beef-eater's pike.

'Is it about Matthew? I talked to some of your people yesterday, you know. At length.'

Pascoe stepped by him into the front-office. No vulgar counter here, but a scattering of comfortable chairs and low tables on which gleamed copies of *Country Life* and *Vogue*. Three doors opened off this area, one marked *Mr Lewis*, another *Mr Cowley*, while the third, the central one, was unmarked and presumably led to their secretary's office.

'I won't take long,' said Pascoe. 'Shall we sit down?'

Cowley glanced towards the door of his room which was slightly ajar. Pascoe courteously suspended his buttocks six inches above the nearest chair and looked up expectantly. Like a dog waiting for a biscuit.

'Oh, all right,' said Cowley.

With an audible sigh of relief, Pascoe sank into the soft leather.

'But make it quick, will you? I do have a client with me at the moment.'

Pascoe felt slightly disappointed the man had admitted someone else was here. Part of the joy of being a detective was having something to detect.

'Business goes on?' he murmured sadly. 'Of course; it must. I'll try not to keep you, sir. Now, as I understand it, Mr Lewis drove down from Scotland on Monday to attend a business conference?'

'That's right.'

'I see. Now, at the conference there were yourself, and Mr Lewis and . . .?'

'And no one. That was it.'

'Really?' said Pascoe, infusing just a touch of polite surprise into his voice. 'Your secretary, perhaps?'

'No.'

'No. I see. But she would be here . . . somewhere?'

He waved his hand vaguely towards the central office. He always enjoyed this vague-young-man-from-the-Foreign-Office role.

'No. Monday's our staff half-day. We don't fit in with the shops. That way our girls can go shopping.'

'And shopkeepers can go house-hunting? Convenient. So there were the two of you only?'

'I've told you,' said Cowley, exasperated. 'What's the difficulty?'

'No difficulty. I merely wondered, if just the two of you were involved, why not conduct your conference on the phone? Why break into Mr Lewis's holiday like this? I know how much I value my two weeks' peace and quiet, ho ho.'

'Do you? Well, Matt liked to work. In any case, he was up and down to Scotland half a dozen times a year. He owns – owned – a cottage there, so it was no skin off his nose coming back.'

131

'A cottage. Nice. Well, I take your point, Mr Cowley, but it still must have been a fairly important matter.'

'Not very. It needed a quick decision, that was all.'

'A business matter?'

'Of course.'

'Routine, but urgent? Timewise, I mean.'

'That's it. You've got it. Now, please, Sergeant, could we get on?'

'Of course. Just another minute, sir.'

Another minute spread to ten. Pascoe could not really say why he was trying to niggle this man, except that his air of chronic impatience seemed to invite such treatment, just as some people look so self-effacing and humble, it is difficult not to tread on them.

But after ten minutes, all Pascoe had was the mixture as before, and Cowley's annoyance was reaching legitimately large proportions. At last Pascoe beat a strategic retreat, feeling he had wasted his time. Despite this, he wasted another fifteen minutes sitting in his car thirty yards up the road until Cowley too came out accompanied by a grey-haired, stocky man in an old tweed suit. Pascoe had never seen him before. It didn't seem very likely he would ever see him again. He glanced at his notebook which held the names and addresses of Lewis and Cowley's two secretary/typists. Doubtless they would be enjoying their unexpected day off, perhaps a little worried about the job now with half their employers dead.

He shut the notebook with a snap and leaned his head hard against the cool glass of the windscreen. It was so easy. So easy to forget what a death could mean to other people. For all he knew, there could have been a close relationship between Lewis and his secretary. Sexual perhaps; such things were commonplace. Or perhaps she just liked him, admired him, shared jokes with him. What did it matter? What did matter was that he, Detective-Sergeant Peter Pascoe, should not so easily brutalize in his mind people he had not met.

He glanced at his book once more. Marjory Clayton, 13 Woodview Drive. Not far from old Sturgeon's place, if his geography were right. He ought to look in and have a word with Sturgeon while he was out that way.

But first things first. He let in the clutch and set off for Woodview Drive.

Sturgeon had been heading steadily south for the past half-hour. He knew he wasn't going fast enough, but his right foot seemed weightless, not able to cope with the job of depressing the accelerator. Ferrybridge and its great cooling towers, the Age of Industry's version of Stonehenge, had moved slowly by a few minutes earlier. The Doncaster bypass was not far ahead, and then the road would split, giving a choice between the A1 and the M1, two great alimentary tracts via which the north voided its products into London. London still had a sinful sound to him. True, in his sixty-eight years he had been there a couple of dozen times, perhaps more; but always it was the first time he recalled, and his old grandmother who had never been farther south than Newark sewing his purse to his woollen vest as a precaution against pickpockets.

But now the days of such precautions were by. He smiled at the double irony of the thought and glanced at his watch. Mavis, his wife, would be getting home soon. She was rarely late back from shopping because she did not like to leave the cats. Though of course she would not think the house would be empty. But it wouldn't perturb her, not Mavis. Not at first. She'd set about making his tea with swift, deft, long-practised movement. He owed her much. She'd married beneath her, so her relatives had said or plainly hinted. There'd been a bit of brass there. But he'd never taken any; he had shown them; by his own efforts with his own hands. He had shown them.

It had started raining, a fine misty rain out of which a slow lorry suddenly appeared ahead, snapping him back to the present. He swung out sharply to overtake. Behind him a blue van, breaking the speed-limit on the outside lane, bore down on him relentlessly, flashing its lights.

He stamped on the accelerator now, finding his strenth. The Rover leapt forward, the loose seat-belt buckle swinging noisily against the door. In a few seconds his speed had doubled.

It was all a question of timing really. He suddenly felt optimistic. It was the right thing to do, there was no alternative. The thing was to do it right. He opened his mouth in triumphant song. The road glistened damply.

Behind him, the driver of the blue van watched in dis-believing horror the beginnings of the skid. This couldn't be happening just because he had flashed his lights. It couldn't be!

The road here was slightly raised above the level of the surrounding countryside. The car slid gracefully off the hard surface, struck the grass-verge, then flipped sideways and over down the embankment.

By the time the van-driver halted and made his way to the car, everything was quite, quite still.

The royal-blue Mini-Cooper, backed deep into a tunnel of hawthorn and briar, was still too. The small boy approached it carefully. He had been observing it just as carefully from his hiding-place for the past ten minutes. At last he was satisfied that it was just as unoccupied as it had been the first time he noticed it two days earlier.

The boy had very good reason for not wishing to be observed. Of all the places his kill-joy parents proscribed, this was placed under their most severe proscription. To be found here would be to risk the most dreadful punishments. The reason lay fifteen yards or so behind him where the sheer walls of the old clay-pit, rimmed now with a double thickness of barbed-wire, fell fifty feet to the opaque waters below.

Hed reached the car and peered in. It was, as expected, empty. But the key was in the ignition which meant that whoever owned it might not be far away. Yet he was certain its position had not changed since he first spotted it. All in all, it was worth taking the risk of looking inside.

Disappointingly it contained little of interest. A sheet of paper had been left on the passenger seat with a lot of writing on it. But he couldn't make a great deal of sense of it.

Rain spattered on the windscreen. It was time to go. He walked back towards the clay-pit and through the gap in the wire to peer down once more at the water. If the rain really got going again, would the surface of the water ever reach the top? It was an interesting speculation, but the growing co-operation of the rain-clouds made him cut it short and retreat. It was a useful gap, this. Eventually someone would notice and repair it, but not many people came this way.

Like the car, it was his secret for the moment.

Wet but happy, he began to make his way home to the village.

Chapter 5

There was a police-car outside Sturgeon's house when Pascoe arrived.

Marjory Clayton had not been much help. Aged about twenty, she was a plain girl, rather anaemic in complexion and wearing a shapeless cardigan which looked as if it had been woven round a sack of potatoes. She seemed genuinely upset at her employer's death and Pascoe treated her gently. Monday had been her half-day and she had been nowhere near the office after midday. Nothing unusual had occurred during the morning. In fact practically nothing at all. No customers, few calls. Business, it seemed, was very, very slack. No, she had not known that Mr Lewis was returning from Scotland that afternoon, though it didn't surprise her. He spent a lot of time up there and seemed quite happy to drive back and forth at fairly frequent intervals.

The other secretary, Jane Collinwood, lived at the far side of town. She would have to wait till later. It was beginning to feel like a wasted day.

But the scene that met him when he stepped through the open front door of Sturgeon's house drove his own troubles out of his mind. Mavis Sturgeon, aged from a sprightly sixty to a parchment-like ninety, was being helped into her coat by an awkward-looking constable. She was clearly in a state of shock and showed no sign of recognition.

'What's up?'

'Are you a friend, sir?' asked the constable hopefully.

'I'm a detective-sergeant, son. Come on, what's happened?'

'It's Mr Sturgeon, Sergeant. There's been an accident, and I was sent . . .'

'Yes.' Pascoe put his arm round the woman's shoulders. 'Have you sent for a doctor?'

'Well, no. She wouldn't . . . she just insisted on going straight to the hospital,' the constable answered helplessly.

'For God's sake, man! She's in no state, can't you see?'

Pascoe's anger drained quickly away. Being a messenger of death and disaster was no job for a young man. He pointed at the leather-bound address book by the telephone in the hallway.

'You'll find her doctor's number in that, probably. It's Andrews, I think. Ring him. Tell him to get out here at once. Then go next door, dig out a neighbour and bring her round.'

'Please, I must go to Edgar,' said Mrs Sturgeon piteously.

'Yes, love. Soon. Come and sit down a moment,' answered Pascoe, leading her gently into the lounge.

'He's been so worried lately. So worried. He wouldn't tell me why. I should have been harder. I should have tried harder.'

She began to weep and the trio of cats which had been viewing the scene suspiciously from the darkest corner of the room now advanced, mewing piteously, and jumped up on her knees. She buried her fingers in their fur, crying still.

A few minutes later the constable arrived with a neighbour, a sensible middle-aged woman who took control with the brisk efficiency of a Women's Institute president. Pascoe retired to the hall and spoke to the constable.

'Yes, Sarge, pretty serious, I believe. He was still alive when they got him to hospital, but at that age . . .'

'Do you, know how it happened?'

137

'No. Not the faintest. Nothing else involved, that's all I know.'

'And he was down the A1?'

'Nearly at Doncaster. That's where they've taken him.'

Pascoe turned to the phone, first making sure the lounge door was firmly shut. He had to wait a few moments for the operator to answer and his eyes ran over the opened telephone book. One number caught his eye. A Lochart number, but the name next to it meant nothing.

Finally the operator replied and with compensatory swiftness put him through to the Doncaster Royal Infirmary. He identified himself and inquired after Sturgeon. The old man was very ill, he was told. Face cut, ribs broken, left kneecap shattered, no serious internal injuries as far as they knew yet, but he had lost a great deal of blood and was in a serious condition. Anyone wanting to see him might be well advised to move as quickly as possible.

'Thanks,' said Pascoe, putting down the phone.

Hospital, doctors; blood, violence, death.

'It's a hell of way to make a living,' he said to the fresh-faced constable. 'You'll hang on here till the doctor comes?'

'Yes, Sarge. You going now?'

'There's work to do,' said Pascoe.

Dalziel had decided to skip tea, partly as a result of Grainger's suggestion that he should try to lose a pound or two and partly because the medical examination had taken the edge off his usually ferocious appetite. He had left samples of just about everything extractable or removable from his body. It had made him very conscious of himself as a scaffolding of bone with flesh, blood and gut packed into the interstices. The thought of ham sandwiches or sausage rolls had no immediate appeal.

138

But neither his mind not his body could find anything wrong with the thought of a large stiff scotch (pure malt, drunk with a large dash of gusto) and accordingly he settled down in his room with the aforesaid medication and tried to think about the work in hand.

He was disturbed to find how little it interested him. When a man had devoted his life to something – even, some might say, destroyed it for that something – the least that something could do in return was not bore him.

The telephone rang. It was the duty sergeant.

'Sorry to bother you, sir, but I was just wondering if you knew when Sergeant Pascoe would be back. I know he's out doing something for you and . . .'

'I am not Pascoe's bloody keeper! Nor am I a bloody answering service. What do you want him for?'

'It's not me, sir. It's the young lady, Miss Soper, the one who was with him, at the week-end, you know. And she's very insistent on getting in touch with him, so I thought in the circumstances I would ask . . .'

Heart. There's a nasty outbreak of heart about this bloody place, thought Dalziel. The usual symptoms. Swellings of sympathy, failure of the proprieties. He drank the rest of his whisky.

'Put her through to me,' he said on impulse.

'Hello?'

'Hello, Miss Soper. Dalziel here.'

'Oh.'

'Sergeant Pascoe's not here at present, but I hope to be seeing him later. Was it urgent?'

'No. No, not really.'

'Forgive me asking, Miss Soper, but is it a private matter? Or is it police business?'

'I didn't realize you drew a distinction, Superintendent.'

That's better, thought Dalziel. That's the authentic liberal radical left-wing pinko Dalziel-hating note.

'If it's police business, Miss Soper, I'm sure the sergeant would want you to tell me.'

'What kind of police business had you in mind?'

Dalziel poured himself another scotch with his free hand.

'You are linked with a current inquiry, Miss Soper. Please accept my sincere condolences on what happened at the week-end. It must have been very trying for you.'

'Oh yes. I was very tried. Very tried indeed.'

Dalziel sighed and drank deeply.

'But, please, if any pertinent information should come your way, think carefully before you burden Pascoe with the weight of it. It's wrong to put overmuch strain on a man's loyalties. Wrong for everyone.'

'Let's chuck the circumlocutions, shall we? What're you trying to say, Superintendent?'

'I'm trying to suggest,' said Dalziel, his voice rising in spite of himself, 'that if for instance the man, Hopkins, should get in touch with you, it's your plain duty to inform the authorities. It would be wrong, and stupid, and bloody selfish to tell Pascoe and then try to get him to conceal the information. That's what I'm trying to tell you, Miss Soper. Not that you ought to need to be told, you're supposed to be so damn clever. Pascoe's a good lad, he's got a fine career in front of him if no one starts screwing him up. You stick to giving him soldiers' comforts in the night and leave him to do the job he's paid for. *That's* what I'm trying to tell you.'

He stopped and listened, waiting for a verbal explosion in reply or the sound of the phone being hammered down. Instead of either, he heard a soft rhythmic sound like a broken humming. It might have been either weeping or laughter.

'Miss Soper?' he said. 'Miss Soper.'

The line went dead.

He poured another inch of whisky. As usual, he had

been right, he thought, staring down into the glass. This outbreak of heart was spreading widely. It was going to be difficult to avoid the contagion.

'Hello, Eric, or little by little,' said Angus Pelman, smiling through the Land-Rover window at the very damp boy on the grass verge.

Eric Bell was unamused by the facetious form of address. He hadn't been amused the first time he'd heard it and since then had found no reason to adjust his reaction.

'Hello, Mr Pelman,' he said politely. The man after all was a friend of his parents, though the word 'friend' seemed to have a rather odd meaning in the adult world. His mother and father always seemed delighted with Mr Pelman's company, made much of him, plied him with drink. But after his departure, the things they said about him though not always comprehensible were clearly far from complimentary.

'You'd better get in,' said Pelman. 'Though you couldn't get much wetter.'

Eric climbed in.

'No school today?' asked Pelman.

'No. The teachers are having a meeting.'

'Oh? With the holidays they get, you'd think they could meet in their own time. Don't you think so, Eric?'

Eric didn't bother to answer, ignoring his number one dictum, *it pays to be polite to adults*. He was going to pay the price he realized almost immediately.

'Was that you I saw earlier going up Poplar Ridge?' said Pelman casually.

'Up Poplar Ridge?'

'That's right.'

'It might have been.'

'Oh. There's not a great deal up there, is there?'

'Not much.'

141

'No,' said Pelman. 'Except the clay-pit.'

Eric fixed his eyes on the rain-pustuled glass in front of him. The windscreen-wiper was defunct on the passenger side and could only flick spasmodically like the broken wing of a shot bird.

His mind worked quickly. He saw no reason at all to trust Pelman. He hadn't laughed at his jokes, which is the biggest of anti-male sins. Therefore Pelman was almost certain to put the idea of the pit in his mother's mind. And that would be that. When it came to extracting information, Chinese inquisitors were mere unsubtle blockheads by comparison with his mother.

The best hope was to create a diversion.

'Yes,' he said. 'The clay-pit is up there. But that wasn't why I went. I went to look at the car.'

'The car?'

'Yes. There's a car up there. I went to see if it was still there.'

'What kind of car?' asked Pelman, slowing down.

'A blue car. A Mini.'

The Land-Rover came to a gentle halt by the roadside. Pelman peered closely at the boy.

'A blue Mini, Eric. Did you find it, or did somebody tell you about it?'

Eric thought quickly. It sounded better for him if he'd merely gone to investigate someone else's report, he decided.

'Someone told me,' he said, adding virtuously, 'I wouldn't have gone up there.'

'That's very interesting,' said Pelman, setting the Land-Rover in motion again. 'Then we'd better tell somebody else, hadn't we?'

On the surface, Jane Collinwood was even more upset at the loss of her employer than her fellow secretary had been, but Pascoe suspected she was thoroughly enjoying the thrill of being so closely connected with a real life murder. She was a pretty girl, except for rather crooked teeth, not much more than seventeen, and full of the careless vigour of youth which overflowed even into the little bouts of weeping she thought the fitting punctuation of her speech.

He asked the obvious questions without much hope. Anything odd she'd noticed? Any reason to think someone might want to hurt Lewis? Everything she replied discouraged him more and more in his theory that there might have been something personal in this killing. Dalziel was right, as always. The house-breaker had been disturbed and lashed out in panic. Tough on Lewis.

'Do you know why Mr Lewis came back on Monday?' he asked finally, preparatory to leaving.

'Oh no. Not exactly.'

'Not *exactly*? But you've got *some* idea?' asked Pascoe, suddenly interested. 'You heard something in the morning?'

'No, I didn't hear anything. I'd no idea he was coming back. It was just later when I heard . . . the news . . .'

'Blow your nose,' said Pascoe with headmistressly firmness. It seemed to work.

'I presume it was something to do with Mr Atkinson.'

'Who's he?' said Pascoe puzzled. The name rang some kind of bell, but not one connected with Lewis.

'I don't really know,' said the girl.

Pascoe was beginning to feel irritated, but he kept it in check. The girl's blether was far too near her eyeballs, as he had heard Dalziel say in one of his more Scottish moments.

'Then why do you say . . . well, whatever it is you *do* say?'

He thought he'd done it again, but she recovered. It was very hard being sympathetic for long, he suddenly realized. Grief was so anti-life. It is a relationship with the dead, emotional necrophilia.

'Mr Atkinson and Mr James and Mr Matt . . .'

'Who?'

'Mr Cowley and Mr Lewis. I always called them . . .'

'All right. Go on.'

'Well, they had been doing some business together for a long time. It seemed to be private, I mean there wasn't any correspondence, not that I was asked to do anyway.'

'Miss Clayton perhaps?'

'Perhaps. She was senior.'

She made seniority sound like a disease thought Pascoe.

'Anyway, I knew Mr Atkinson by sight. He always said hello when he came into the office.'

'And what makes you think that it was this business that brought Mr Lewis back on Monday?'

She looked at him in exasperation.

'I'm telling you. Mr Atkinson went along to the office that afternoon. *That's* why it was probably about their business. Why else should he go to the office when it was closed?'

Pascoe restrained himself with difficulty from shaking her till her crooked teeth rattled.

'*You* weren't at the office on Monday afternoon though?'

'No. But I was in the High Street shopping and I saw Mr Atkinson and Mr James going into the office.'

'Ah.'

There didn't seem much else to say for a moment.

'What time was this?' he managed finally.

'About three. A bit later perhaps.'

'But you didn't see Mr Lewis?'

'No.'

'Sure?'

'Of course I am! I'd have noticed, wouldn't I, especially as he was meant to be in Scotland?'

144

'I suppose you would. This Mr Atkinson now . . .'

He paused. Suddenly he recalled where he had seen the name. *John Atkinson. Lochart 269.* In Sturgeon's telephone book. It was an absurd coincidence.

'What does he look like?'

'Look like. Well, I don't know.'

'Tall? Tall as me?'

'Oh no. A bit shorter, I'd say. But broader across the shoulders. And he's older too. He's got grey hair. And a nice smile.'

'Thank you, Miss Collinwood,' said Pascoe. 'You've been very helpful. Just one more thing.'

It was absurd. But he might as well ask.

'Just where in Scotland is Mr Lewis's cottage?'

'Where? It's in a villge somewhere. Near a place called Callander.'

'Lochart?'

'That's right. How did you know? It sounded very nice. He once said I could stay there some time. When he and his family weren't there, of course.'

'Of course,' said Pascoe, not even noticing the imminence of tears this time. His mind was too occupied elsewhere.

His indifference seemed to be therapeutic, for suddenly the girl brightened and smiled sweetly at him.

'Are you driving through town? You couldn't give me a lift, could you? I want to make a hair appointment. It's my birthday on Saturday.'

'Certainly,' said Pascoe. When she smiled she looked extremely pretty. She should smile more often. Perhaps everybody should.

But he could not feel that any possible development in this particular case was going to cause much amusement.

145

Chapter 6

'Don't be daft,' said Dalziel more from habit than conviction. 'What kind of connection could there be?'

'I don't know, sir,' said Pascoe. 'All I know is the
conection that already exists.'

'Lewis has a cottage in a village called Lochart where
Sturgeon appears to know somebody? It's not much!'

'Where Sturgeon appears *not* to know somebody.
Remember that Harry Lauder, or whatever his name
was, denied the existence of an Archie Selkirk.'

Dalziel whistled a few bars of 'Roamin' in the Gloamin',
ending with a scornful discord.

'And there was the other man, Atkinson, also with a
Lochart number.'

'Oh? Have you tried ringing it?'

'Not yet. I thought I'd check with Lauder first.'

'Go ahead,' commanded Dalziel waving at the phone
on his desk.

He's hooked, thought Pascoe. It's a bit early yet for
him to admit he likes the taste, but the bait's been
swallowed.

'And there's another connection,' said Pascoe as he
waited for his call to be put through.

'Yes?' said Dalziel, who had removed his left shoe and
was scratching the sole of his foot on the corner of his
desk.

'They were both burgled.'

'So they were. But so were a dozen others. You're not
seriously suggesting that Lewis wasn't killed by laddo,
but by someone else who had it in for him personally?'

'I don't know, sir.'

'You realize there's only one guy to date who might connect the two things. And that's your mate, Sturgeon. What's the theory then? He wants to do for Lewis, so lies in wait for him at his home, beats him to death, then makes it look like a housebreaking along the same lines as happened to him? Did he strike you as being the super-criminal type?'

'On the contrary,' said Pascoe. 'But men do strange things when . . . hello! Sergeant Lauder? Look, it's Sergeant Pascoe again, Mid-York . . . PASCOE, yes. We spoke earlier. No, it's not about Archie Selkirk again. No. John Atkinson. What's that you say?'

Some impediment on the line suddenly cleared and Lauder's voice came through loud and as clear as his accent would permit.

'No. There's nae such creature, Sergeant Pascoe. What is it that's making ye think all the missing persons in Yorkshire are coming here to Lochart? We're just a wee village, ye ken. Are ye no' mistaking us for Glasgow, mebbe?'

Dalziel took the phone from Pascoe and held it close to his lips.

'This is Detective-Superintendent Dalziel here, Sergeant. Let's not waste public money. Just answer the questions. Right? Lochart 269, whose number's that?'

'Good evening to ye, Superintendent Dalziel. You're no' from these parts, are ye? If it was a Dalziel you were seeking after, I could lay my hands on a dozen. They seem to be very thick about here.'

Too true anywhere, thought Pascoe, keeping a straight face with difficulty.

'Now, 269. Well, that's easy. It's the hotel. The Lochart Hotel. It's very comfortable, I believe.'

'I'm not bloody well going to stay there!' roared Dalziel. 'Listen, I'm interested in a man called Atkinson, John Atkinson, who may have stayed there in the recent

147

past. I don't know how recent. Now if without causing too much disturbance you could find out when he was there, how long, and (if possible) why, I'd be very grateful.'

Description, mouthed Pascoe, trying to make it look somehow accidental.

'Shall I try for a description also?' asked Lauder. 'To make sure it's the right man?'

'Please,' murmured Dalziel with a self-restraint which Pascoe would not have believed he possessed. 'Soon as you can, eh.'

He gave Lauder his telephone number, replaced the receiver, and picked it up again straightaway.

'Get me the infirmary at Doncaster, will you?' he said. 'I want someone who knows something about the condition of Mr Edgar Sturgeon. I *don't* want some little brown man who doesn't know a thermometer from a banana.'

If they could expel Dalziel from the Commonwealth, thought Pascoe, there might be hope for peace in our time.

'Your girl-friend called, Sergeant,' said Dalziel suddenly.

'What?'

'I spoke to her.'

'*What!* I mean, what did she want, sir?'

'How should I know? She said bugger all to me.'

A tiny, tinny voice was coming out of the ear-piece with which Dalziel was massaging his bald spot. Finally he became aware of it.

'Hello!' he roared, reducing it to silence. But after introducing himself, he settled down to listen.

'Well, there's no help there,' he said when he had finished. 'It seems to me as if Sturgeon and Lewis are soon going to have something else in common. They're both going to be dead.'

* * *

The men searched the ground thoroughly for over an hour. Then they searched it again, this time with a metal detector. Only after this second search and after as comprehensive a photographing of the area as was possible outside Hollywood did Backhouse send the order to tow the blue Mini-Cooper away. There was no question of driving it away. The ignition had been left on, the engine was sodden wet and the wheels had buried themselves deep in a morass caused by the recent rains.

Backhouse walked through the gap in the wire and peered down into the clay-pit.

'I wouldn't go too near the edge, sir,' said Constable Crowther, practising what he preached and standing a good two yards back. Always sensitive to local expertise, Backhouse retreated before asking why.

'If you look over to the other side, sir, you'll see there's quite an overhang. Well, that continues all the way round. They gouged deep into the sides before they decided the place was played out.'

'When was that?'

'Oh, when I was just a lad, sir. I'm from these parts, as you know. There was always trouble with the drainage, I believe. Water coming in, but not finding a way out very easily. Finally they struck an underground stream and that was that. Once they stopped pumping it away, the place just filled up.'

'It's deep then?'

'It is, especially after the rain we've been having. Deep and dangerous. Bits of the overhang drop in from time to time. That's why they've got this wire round it. But what's wire to kids? Or anyone determined to get through?'

'What indeed?' said Backhouse staring at the neatly cut gap in the fence. 'Any fatalities?'

'Three, sir, that I know of.'

'Children?'

'That's what you'd expect, sir, but the answer's no. If

149

they'd all been kids, something would have been done about the place long ago. Only one was anything like a child. Boy of sixteen, skylarking with friends round the edge, slipped and fell in. He couldn't swim.'

'And the others?'

'A man and woman, sir. Suicide pact. They were having an affair, but there were difficulties. They both wanted divorces but there was little chance of that. So they talked it over, it seems, then strolled up here one night and jumped in.'

'Good Lord! Yes, I seem to remember something. About twelve years ago?'

'That's right, sir.'

'I wasn't in this area then, of course, but it was in the national Press. Wait now, wasn't one of them called . . .'

'Yes, sir. Mary Pelman. She was married to Mr Angus Pelman.'

'Well now. There is a thing, Crowther,' said Backhouse. It was difficult to know whether he was commenting on Crowther's information or the arrival of the breakdown vehicle which came grinding up the long, wet track from the distant road.

'We found her almost at once,' Crowther continued. 'She came up to the surface. He stopped down in the mud. It took nearly three weeks before they got him out.'

'Who does it belong to, Crowther?' asked Backhouse, watching the breakdown truck negotiate itself into position before the Mini.

'No one, really,' said Crowther. 'Mr Pelman owns most of the land on this side, the south. His house is at the back of that ridge over there. Then the land drops away, woodland mainly, down to the village.'

'The woods behind Brookside Cottage?' said Backhouse.

'That's right. But there's no direct route. Not for a car.

150

It'd have to come round by the road and up the old track. Three miles about.'

'Something seems to have come this way pretty regularly,' said Backhouse, examining the ground carefully. 'I wonder why? And who would want to cut a gap in the wire?'

'Can't say, sir,' said Crowther. 'Do you think Hopkins is in there, sir?'

'I don't know yet. I'm not even sure if I'd like him to be. It'd be neat, certainly. But I don't know.'

Forgetting Crowther's injunction, he strolled back towards the edge, thinking of the odd, enigmatic note found in the car. It was back at HQ now undergoing the most rigorous examination. Fingerprints, handwriting, type of paper, all would be subjected to the closest scrutiny. But the state of mind of the writer was what interested Backhouse. Could it be read as a confession and the last desperate cry of a man about to drown himself? It might well be. Hopkins seemed to have been something of an original. Perhaps the opinion of that other highly individual young man, Sergeant Pascoe, might be worth seeking. If it could be obtained without sparking off some kind of explosion.

The breakdown truck was advancing from the bosky tunnel into which the Mini had reversed. He turned to watch it. It wasn't possible for the truck to turn towards the track until the car was clear of the undergrowth. Therefore it came straight towards him. For a frightening second he thought it wasn't going to stop, but the driver began to spin the wheel round a good twenty feet away. In any case, it could hardly come through the small gap in the wire.

One of the truck's wheels lost its grip on the soft ground momentarily and began to spin. Foolishly the driver revved up and the next minute both were spinning wildly.

151

Half-wit, thought Backhouse, staggering slightly for some reason. Fainting fit? he wondered. The first warnings of a stroke? It was frightening, as if the ground were moving under him.

'Superintendent!' yelled Crowther.

Backhouse, still surprised, stepped towards him, then turned his step into a leap, as beyond all dispute the ground moved.

Crowther seized him by the hand and dragged him violently away from the quarry. Quite unnecessary, Backhouse thought, as he turned and looked back. It was a goood two seconds before a long section of earth, including the bit on which he had been standing, slid undramatically out of sight into the depths below. It was difficult to see any difference. If it hadn't been for the posts supporting the wire leaning drunkenly out into space it would have been impossible to detect that anything had happened.

'Get this thing out of here before it causes any more damage!' commanded Backhouse, pointing at the truck.

'If he's under that little pile, sir, he'll be hard to find,' said Crowther.

'We'll find him, never fear,' said Backhouse. 'If he was buried under a mountain, we'd find him.'

'Hello! Peter?' said Ellie uncertainly, standing at the open front door.

'Hello, love,' said Pascoe, stepping into the hallway. 'Come on in.'

Ellie entered, still looking puzzled, and followed him into a comfortable sitting-room furnished in a period-less old-fashioned style.

'What are you doing here?' she asked. 'Or more important, what are *we* doing here? This isn't a subtle way of setting the scene for a marriage-proposal, is it? Because if this is your idea of home, I refuse!'

'It's not bad,' protested Pascoe. 'Very cosy.'

'So it's cosy! It also reeks of a-woman's-place-is-in-the-home. You've got a very Victorian paterfamilias look about you.'

'There are worse fates,' said Pascoe.

'What *are* we doing here, Peter?'

'Looking for cats. Or rather *a* cat. I've got the other two locked in the kitchen. Let me explain.'

'I wish you would.'

Pascoe had called to see Mavis Sturgeon in hospital. She was confined to bed, but much more alert now. Her main concern had naturally been for her husband, but she seemed ready to accept assurances that he was all right, but too weak to be visited even had she been fit. Pascoe had delicately probed to see if there were anything she could tell him, but the names of Cowley and Atkinson meant nothing to her. Lewis she had read about in the paper and she had an idea he was a member of the Liberal Club which Edgar had belonged to for more than forty years. She confirmed that her husband had been withdrawn and irritable for the past week or more, following a period of unexplained high spirits and excitement.

'I was worried about his retirement at first,' she said. 'He missed the business a lot. But then he seemed to come round, start taking an interest in things. I thought that . . . I thought . . .'

She blinked back tears. Pascoe intervened swiftly.

'Do you know where he might have been going today?' he asked.

'No. That's what makes it so odd. He'd no reason at all to be on that road. I've never liked that road, never. Always accidents, always something.'

Pascoe had risen to go, making an automatic promise to do anything he could to help and being surprised to find himself instantly put to the test.

153

'It's her cats. The neighbours will feed them, she knows, but she'd be happier if they went into their usual kennels. So I said I'd take them. And as it's no job for a singlehanded man, I left the message for you.'

'Thanks a lot.'

'Why did you ring me earlier?' asked Pascoe casually.

'Oh, nothing. I just felt like a chat,' she replied.

'I gather you had one with Dalziel.'

'We talked.'

'What did he say?'

'He advised me of my constitutional rights. And duties. And suggested strongly that a woman's place *was* around the home. Particularly the bedroom.'

'Did he?'

'Yes.'

'Let's find that cat, shall we?'

Ellie took a china ashtray from the mantelpiece and rattled it energetically against the wall. Ten seconds later a sleek ginger shape slid casually from beneath the chair on the arm of which Pascoe was squatting. The animal purred as Ellie picked him up.

'Well done, St Francis. What's the secret?'

'Make a sound like a rattling food-dish and these creatures will come from miles away. Otherwise, if they don't feel like it, you, can coax and threaten all night without results.'

'They remind me of you.'

'That'll cost you a steak.'

'See what I mean?'

This slightly unreal, consciously superficial relationship was maintained all the way to the kennels which conveniently turned out to be the ones behind the Jockey at Birkham.

A man was unloading trays of meat and made-up pet food from a blue van as they came out of the office. His

154

van proclaimed that he was Jim Jones, Purveyor of High Class Pet Food.

'Does it make you hungry?' asked Pascoe.

'No. But I am.'

He glanced at his watch. It was just on six-thirty.

'Not too early? Then let's be first in the Jockey. You don't deliver there as well, do you?' he added jocularly to the petfood man who had stood aside to let them past.

He didn't answer, but merely stared unblinkingly at Pascoe and shook his head. Take a joke seriously and you take the wind out of anybody's sails, thought Pascoe, disconcerted. It was one of Dalziel's favourite tricks.

They weren't the first in the pub, but were the first to order their steaks. Ellie drank her lager thirstily, then sat toying with the pebble pendant Pascoe had bought her.

'Peter,' she said, 'when I talked to Dalziel he warned me about putting you on the spot.'

'He did *what*?'

'You know. He said that I should be careful about sharing information with you as a friend that might possibly cause you difficulties as a policeman. If Colin got in touch with me, for instance, wanting help.'

'Has he?' asked Pascoe flatly, staring into his glass.

'No, he hasn't. But it made me think, what he said. I've been worrying at it ever since. He's wrong, you know. I've just decided that. Fat Dalziel is wrong.'

'Put it in writing,' said Pascoe with a smile.

'Hell, I'm not gone on the complete honesty bit. Some things are better kept quiet. But not for the reasons that Dalziel gave. Not so that you can grow up into a nice fat superintendent like he is.'

'I agree,' said Pascoe. 'That's not at all a good reason for not telling me something. Though I'll want to look more closely at these other things that are better kept quiet.'

'You might be shocked!' she said lightly. 'The real

155

reason I rang you this afternoon was something rather odd. After you dropped me in town I didn't make straight back to college. I had nothing on there and anyway I felt like being among a lot of people after this morning. So I shopped for a couple of hours. Then, about four it must have been, I set off back. I came through Birkham, of course, and stopped to have another wander round the antique shop. But it was shut.'

'Not a very keen trader, our Mr Etherege,' commented Pascoe. 'Who, by the way, has just come into the bar.'

Etherege seemed to be well known and entered immediately into a cheerful exchange of greetings with the landlord and other drinkers.

'Anyway,' said Ellie, 'I was just getting back into the car, when another car pulled up behind me. I thought I recognized it, bright red Citroën. Out jumps Anton Davenant, greets me warmly and says he is just on his way to see me at college.'

'Interesting,' said Pascoe. 'What the hell did he want that he couldn't have got when we met him this morning?'

'I wondered that too. The only thing I could think of was your absence!'

'Flattering. OK. What did he say?'

'I'm not really sure. He seemed to be feeling his way, if you know what I mean. He talked about Colin and the others, particularly Timmy. Evidently he met him when Timmy was working at the Common Market HQ in Brussels and Davenant was doing some kind of gastronomic architectural Grand Tour.'

'Then Timmy comes back and takes up with Carlo again. Interesting.'

'I thought so too. I began to wonder whether he was in fact in the district completely by accident.'

'That,' said Pascoe, 'is the kind of nasty thought only policemen are supposed to have.'

'Dalziel would be pleased. But I did begin to wonder

after a while if Colin might have been in touch with him and he was sounding me out to see whether a policeman's paramour was to be trusted.'

'And was she?'

'Evidently not. He said nothing anyway. He did seem very interested in the book Colin was working on, but I couldn't tell him a thing about that. Perhaps Colin's worried about his manuscript and notes?'

'Wherever Colin is,' said Pascoe unemotionally, 'he'll have a lot more to worry him than the health of his manuscript. So you rang me to chat?'

'That's right. Davenant was still with me, he'd just popped into the loo. I thought you'd like to know.'

Their steaks arrived and with them Etherege. He didn't sit down but stood looking down at them, a gin in one hand and a small bottle of tonic in the other.

'Hello again,' he said with a smile. 'Sorry to interrupt, but I just wondered about those stamps.'

'We haven't been able to have them examined yet, I'm afraid,' said Pascoe, thinking of poor old Sturgeon, critically ill, perhaps by now even dead.

'Not to worry. No hurry. Pop in and buy the lady another present some time! Cheers.'

He turned and left them.

'Not a bad idea,' said Ellie.

'At his prices?' Pascoe sampled his steak and nodded appreciatively.

'Careful,' warned Ellie. 'Jones the Cat Meats has just come in.'

He glanced at the bar. She was right. The po-faced man had just entered.

Pascoe grinned.

'Well, if they use him here,' he said, 'all I can say is how nice to be one of Mrs Sturgeon's cats!'

* * *

Dalziel meanwhile was still in his room, sipping a cup of tea with only half his usual quantity of sugar and unenthusiastically contemplating an evening without potatoes.

The phone rang.

'I'm sorry to have been so long, Superintendent, but there was some urgent business came up.'

'Trouble in the glen?' said Dalziel sourly.

'Aye. Something of that. Now, the man Atkinson at the hotel, he's your man surely, fits the description to a "t".'

'Good. Anything else?'

'Well, no address, I regret to say. They let him put just "London" in the registration book, I'm afraid. I've had a wee word with the manager, and things will be stricter now, I promise you.'

'That makes me very happy.'

'Guid. Guid. Now, Superintendent, he's been there a few times. I have a note of the dates; only for a few days at a time, and not on holiday, it seems. At least he didna act like a man on holiday.'

'How *did* he act?'

'Like a businessman, they say. And from something the reception lassie heard him say one day, it seems he might be connected with the Nordrill Mining Company.'

'Who the hell are they?'

'Well, if you lived up here, you wouldna need to ask.'

'Sergeant, if you lived down here, you'd bloody well feel the need to answer! Get a move on.'

'Aye. They're one of these companies that are going around everywhere these days, it seems, sinking test shafts to see what's worth ploughing up the earth for. You may have read about them in Wales and the Peak District in England? Well, we have the same trouble.'

'And Atkinson's probably working for them?'

158

'So it seems.'

'Well done, Lauder,' said Dalziel. 'Just give me those dates and you can get back to the peat fire.'

The phone rang once more before Dalziel could leave. He listened for a long while without offering to interrupt.

'Right,' he said finally. 'Yes, I'll tell him. Good night.'

But not tonight, he thought, glancing at his watch. He'll be out with that girl. Let them enjoy themselves tonight if they could.

Besides, he had no idea where they were.

Chapter 7

Pascoe was breakfasting on the run when the morning paper arrived. Ellie who had farther to go but was a much later starter wandered in from the kitchen from time to time, placing cups of coffee and slices of toast at strategic points along his route.

'Why don't you set your alarm earlier?' she asked.

'When I'm sleeping by myself, it's early enough.'

'It's my fault, is it?'

He didn't answer, but went out into the small, dark hallway of his flat and picked up his mail and the newspaper.

'Catch,' he said, throwing it at Ellie who settled down on the rug in front of the gas-fire to drink her own coffee and read the headlines.

He was in the bathroom when she called his name. He came instantly, recognizing a note in her voice which told him something serious had happened.

'They've found him,' she said.

'What? Let me see.'

He took the paper and read the report. It told of the discovery of the car, mentioned that a note had been found in it, and gave the gist of an obviously non-committal interview with Backhouse. He refused to comment on the suggestion that his murder investigation was now completed, and when asked about the clay-pit merely said that a thorough search would take place. The report ended with a reference to the other lives lost in the pool.

'You said they'd found him,' said Pascoe accusingly.

'It's as good as,' said Ellie, white-faced.

'No such thing. Can you see Colin killing himself?'

160

'It would depend on what he had done.'

Pascoe held his hand to his forehead and closed his eyes tightly. Night. Wind in the trees. Moonlight through the driven clouds touching the ruffled water far below. A step forward. It was all too Gothic.

And then, not to struggle! Colin had been a fine swimmer. It could *not* be true!

But the rest was true. He had seen that himself; Carlo and Tim lying dead, and above all, Rose bleeding her life away at the foot of the sundial. If that was true, then anything could be.

'Come on,' he said suddenly. 'Let's move. I'll find out what's really going on from Dalziel.'

'I don't know if I can,' said Ellie dully. 'I'll stay here, Peter. You go.'

'No,' he said. 'You're not coming with me, love. You're going into college like a good little lecturer. That's what you're overpaid for. So let's get a move on, shall we?'

It was important to be busy. Action impeded reflection. Action would keep them for a while at least from visualizing the policeman, awkward in his stiff blue raincoat, probing the pool depths with a boat-hook as the leaky, creaking cockleshell wove a careful searcher's pattern across the dark water. Back and forth, back and forth, till the hook snagged . . . thank God there was lots of work to do.

It was not quite as Pascoe visualized it. The boat *was* there, picking up the search where darkness had halted it the previous evening. But the warm weather of the previous weekend had returned and the quarry pool reflected blue sky and morning sunlight. It would have been idyllic, had it not been for the evil smell stirred up by the probings below. Still, it would be shirt-sleeve order before the day was out, thought Backhouse. Of all the seasons of the year, he loved an Indian summer best. It

161

was a comforting allegory of middle age; a golden time of warmth and maturity, with just enough of the elegiacs to be piquant without being depressing.

It would be pleasant to slip away for a few days and enjoy the company of Proust in the small walled Dorsetshire orchard which lay behind his brother's farm like an earnest of Eden. It would be very pleasant. The price was simple. A water-puffed, rotting corpse, dragged reluctantly to the sun-polished surface of the waters he looked down on. He had seen it before. No other form of death seemed to write such despair on a man's face. It was a matter of time, he supposed. Other deaths had to be satisfied with what they could set in a man's features in the actual moment of dying. Only water kept on working, smoothing, shaping, after life had fled.

A few days in the orchard would be dearly bought at that price.

'Hello, Superintendent!'

It was French, the coroner, sensibly clad in gum-boots which would probably spoil the crease of his well-cut country solicitor's suit.

'Anything yet?'

'No, sir.'

'It's a nasty place, this,' said French. 'I've been in charge of too many inquests connected with this water already.'

'We don't know for certain yet there'll be another.'

'No. Of course not. Still, it looks odds on. The first one was my first inquest ever. Poor Pelman's wife – you must recall it?'

'Only from the papers, sir.'

'And then there was that boy. It was after that they put this wire round the place. Totally inadequate.'

'Especially if someone cuts a hole through it with wirecutters,' said Backhouse grimly.

162

'Really? How odd. You need to be a pretty determined sort of suicide to go to those lengths.'

'You would be. But this was done before last week-end. We have an expert witness. Master Eric Bell with whom I made a deal. He told me everything he knew, in return for which I only told his parents what they needed to know.'

French laughed.

'I see. But why should anyone . . .?'

'I have an idea, sir. We'd better leave it at that for the moment.'

By mutual accord, they turned from the quarry and walked towards the tangle of bushes in which the Mini had been found.

'The ground's very churned up,' observed French.

'Yes,' said Backhouse. 'Was there something special you wanted to discuss with me, Mr French?'

The coroner looked at him assessingly.

'What do you think you're going to find in the pool, Superintendent? Be frank.'

'I can just tell you what the evidence so far suggests. It suggests that we should find the body of Colin Hopkins.'

'Part of this evidence being a note left in the car, I believe?'

'That's right, sir. A note which will, of course, be put into your hands as soon as a body is found and an inquest required.'

'And till then . . .?'

'Till then it's just police evidence. Like anything else we find in the car.'

French sighed deeply.

'From that I take it that I may not see it?'

It is foolish to fall out with your coroner, thought Backhouse. But for some reason he felt like digging his heels in. He had never taken kindly to any feeling of pressure.

'I didn't say that, sir,' he said cautiously. 'The note is at present undergoing examination in our labs. It is, I hasten to add, an extremely incoherent note, not one that I would care to repeat from memory. Of course, we shall also be getting an expert psychiatric assessment of the writer's state of mind.'

French nodded as though satisfied.

'There is, as you must know, a great deal of unease in the village,' he said. 'Everyone is very keen for this unfortunate business to be laid to rest. This unease is likely to continue until there's been an arrest, or something else.'

He made an uncertain gesture back towards the quarry.

'I think, not to put too fine a point on it, that the sooner someone can say officially what everyone seems to be saying privately, the better it will be.'

'It's just my duty to investigate crime, sir, and publish to my superiors the results of my investigations,' said Backhouse coldly.

'I know that, Superintendent. My duty is not dissimiliar. Only my duty is to publish to *everybody* the results of my investigation. I hope you find what you're looking for here. You may recall it took over three weeks to find the body of Robert Hand. It's a great deal of time.'

'Hand?'

'Mrs Pelman's lover.'

'Yes, I do recall that. As I said, I read the reports. I also recall a police frogman almost lost his life in the search. It's a nasty piece of water this, sir. It's filthy black and there are all kinds of hollows and tunnels into the sides of the pit. I shall do everything I can to ensure a thorough search, but if it takes three weeks, it takes three weeks. It may even take longer. But I will not risk lives. Nor will I anticipate results.'

'Of course not, Superintendent,' said French, suddenly

smiling. 'It would be wrong of you to do that. Good day to you.'

'Good day,' answered Backhouse. He felt unhappy for some reason. The sun-filled orchard suddenly seemed like a completely substanceless dream.

Dalziel had arrived in his office that morning to find a most unwelcome note inviting him to call on Dr Grainger at midday if it were convenient. He called Grainger's surgery straightaway but no further than a sweet-tongued receptionist who seemed to his sensitive ear to become suspiciously sympathetic when she learned his name. But Grainger was very busy, she insisted, and a couple of hours wasn't *too* long to wait, was it? Again Dalziel felt he caught a suggestion that he might well be wishing at noon that the waiting had been even longer.

Like Pascoe, he seized upon the anodyne of work and began busily examining the results of various inquiries his minions had undertaken.

The Nordrill Mining Company, he was intrigued to discover, did not employ (and, to the best of their knowledge, never employed) a John Atkinson. He thought about this a while, then reached for his phone and dialled a local number.

'Superintendent Dalziel here,' he said to the girl who answered. 'I'd like a word with Mr Noolan please.'

There was a brief pause.

'Hello Andy,' said a lively Yorkshire voice after a few moments. 'Are we going to be robbed?'

'No. But you might have been. Have you checked your vaults yet?'

'What!' said Noolan in alarm.

'Joke, Willie,' said Dalziel. 'Just checking to see if you're wide awake like a good little bank-manager should be.'

'Some joke! I nearly wet my pants. What is it you want, Andy? I have work to do.'

These two had known each other for a long time and had built up a mutually advantageous system of favour-exchanging over the years. It was based on a form of oblique questioning which allowed both to avoid too much damage to their professional consciences.

'If I was wanting to buy a house, who would you advise to use as an agent?'

'That would depend on what you had in mind.'

'Something pretty high-class, I think. You know me. Nowt squalid. What do you reckon to Lewis and Cowley?'

There was a long pause.

'I was sorry to hear what happened to Lewis,' said Noolan finally.

'Were you?'

'Yes. Nice family. They'll be hard pressed now.'

'There must be a good lot coming to them, surely,' said Dalziel, infusing surprise into his voice.

'They could be in trouble if they're relying on money from the firm,' said Noolan.

'Really? But there must be other things. That's a nice house. And there's their cottage in Scotland. Oh, she'll be all right, never fear, Willie. A businessman like Lewis looks after his dependants.'

'You may be right, Andy. Perhaps his assets are looked after somewhere else.'

'I see. Well, perhaps I'll stick in my own place for a bit. Cheers, Willie. See you at the club some night.'

So. As far as Willie Noolan knew (and on matters financial there was little that happened locally without Willie getting a sniff of it) Lewis and Cowley were in a bad way, a business crisis which overspilled into Lewis's private life. It would be easy to check Noolan's hints, but hardly necessary, he felt. The house must be heavily

166

mortgaged, the cottage too, and from the sound of it, there might not be a lot of insurance cover there.

All in all, one ought to feel very sorry about Matthew Lewis. But there was something in all this which bothered him. Perhaps it was time James Cowley was confronted with the full majesty of a detective-superintendent instead of the lightweight threat of a sergeant.

Which reminded him of Pascoe whom he had not yet seen. He felt slightly guilty. The lad would probably have read about it in the newspapers now. Still, that was what life was all about. You opened a paper and read that someone you knew had died. Or was dying. Or was going to be killed.

And one day the name you read was your own.

There was a knock at the door and it was no surprise when Pascoe walked in.

'You've seen the papers, Sergeant?'

'Sir.'

'I'm sorry. If I'd known where you were last night, I'd have told you. But there's still no body been found.'

'No, sir.'

'Tell me, Sergeant, this friend of yours, would he write a suicide note in poetry?'

'What?'

'Poetry.'

'The note was in poetry?' Pascoe thought hard. 'I doubt it . . . well, no one would . . . but he might *quote* somebody else's. He was – is – a great lover of the apt quotation. You don't happen to know what the note said?'

'No, lad. Such things are not revealed lightly, even among policemen. Anyway, put it out of your mind. There's other work to be done. This Lewis business.'

Quickly he filled Pascoe in on the new information they had.

'Nothing gels,' he said in conclusion. 'It's all scrappy. I think you'll have to go and talk with Sturgeon if you can.'

'To Doncaster?'

'If it's inconvenient,' said Dalziel wearily, 'we could ask him to meet you half-way. He is after all merely a sixty-eight-year-old man, half dead after a car crash. He is also the only person who can confirm or deny what seems to be a nutty idea on the face of it – i.e. that he killed Lewis. If he *did*, I'd like his word on it before he snuffs it. So hurry.'

'Yes, sir,' said Pascoe without enthusiasm.

'How's his wife?' asked Dalziel.

'Still in hospital, but getting better. She was worried about the cats.'

'Hospitals,' said Dalziel gloomily. 'It's been a good week for the doctors. Off you go then, Sergeant. We might as well keep up the illusion of motion, though it's all running on the bloody spot. By the way, while you're at it, find out anything you can on the circumstances of Sturgeon's crash, will you? I'm beginning to have a feeling about this.'

'Me too, sir. But I'm not sure what.'

'Suicide after murder. It's not uncommon.'

'No, it's not,' said Pascoe flatly.

'Oh, shit!' said Dalziel. I'm sorry. I keep forgetting . . . look, just how concerned are you about this other business, Sergeant? How delicately do you want people to tread?'

'It bothers me,' admitted Pascoe. 'It's getting better but it's always there. And sometimes I feel this anger stirring inside. Such an anger that I could . . .'

He found he had clenched his fists and forced himself to relax. Why am I telling Dalziel this? he wondered. A fat old copper who thinks tears in a man are proofs incontrovertible of homosexual tendencies.

'Hold it in, lad,' advised Dalziel. 'One of these days

168

it'll mebbe come in handy. By the way, I forgot. We never asked Lauder if he knew anything about Lewis. Give him a ring before you set off for sunny Doncaster.'

He said I *forgot,* noted Pascoe. Coming from Dalziel this was a kind of sympathy.

'You've been worried, have you, Andy?' asked Dr Grainger. 'That's good. I hoped you might be.'

'Hoped?'

'That's it. I bet your fertile imagination's run through every disease known to man and invented a few more besides. Well, you'll be pleased to know you've got none of them.'

'None? You mean there's nothing wrong with me?' growled Dalziel, beginning to bristle with anger.

'Don't sound so disappointed. Anyway, you're far from perfect, I assure you. That's why a bit of good honest fear might be a help. Let me list your faults. You smoke too much, you drink too much and you eat too much. In addition you try to interrupt your doctor. You wanted bad news. I'll give it to you. You follow my advice or within a twelvemonth, two years at the most, I reckon you'll be laid low, perhaps permanently, by one or more of half a dozen complaints.'

'Such as?' said Dalziel almost humbly.

'You name it. High blood pressure, bronchitis, cirrhosis, thrombosis.'

'God Almighty!' said Dalziel disbelievingly. 'I can't have them all!'

'Believe me,' said Grainger, 'we all have them all. Only some people have them more than others. I've made out a diet sheet for you. You'll need to drop at least a stone, to start with. It'll be difficult for you, especially without the comfort of tobacco and alcohol, so I'm giving you a prescription for a mild tranquillizer, just

169

so you don't become too unbearable to yourself and others. OK?'

'OK,' said Dalziel helplessly. 'You're a bloody sadist though.'

'Do as I say and you may yet live to dance lightly on my grave.'

'One thing before I go,' said Dalziel, looking with distaste and disbelief at the diet sheet he held. 'You're on the committee at the Liberal Club aren't you?'

'That's right. You're not going to join after all this time?'

'I'm not that sick,' grunted Dalziel scornfully. 'No, it's just that a couple of your members have come my way lately.'

'Matt Lewis and Edgar Sturgeon, you mean? Tragic, tragic. Everyone at the club's desolated.'

'Were they very friendly? With each other, I mean.'

'Not particularly. Though I've seen them together once or twice since Edgar retired.'

'I see. Any word on either of them round the snooker table?'

'Pardon?'

'Come on!' said Dalziel. 'I know clubs. Any little titbits of gossip, scandal, you know?'

'I'm your doctor, Andy, not one of your snouts!' said Grainger indignantly.

'All right. No harm in asking, I've got some right surely after *this!*'

He waved the diet sheet violently in the air.

'You think so? All right then. I shall deny having said it but, in confidence, the word was that Lewis was a very sharp man on a business deal.'

'You mean a crook?'

'I mean he worked on a large profit margin in everything he did.'

'Oh aye. Suppose I told you he was financially in Queer Street when he died?'

Grainger nodded, unsurprised.

'Why not? The trouble with being a crook in a place like this is, it gets known. That little firm has always gone in for the "class" stuff – none of your suburban semis. So the people interested in the kind of property market Lewis and Cowley catered for are the same people who'd have heard the rumours. Businessmen, the aristocracy of brass. So a spiral starts. Less business for the firm, and then still less business because everybody knows they're doing less business! Add to this the rate at which Lewis could spend money.'

'What on?'

'Dear me, Andy, what do your underlings do nowadays? He's a lover of the good life, or was. Wine, women and song. So they tell me, I hasten to add. I have never been involved in any of his excesses.'

'Don't sound so regretful,' said Dalziel, rising and making for the door. 'And Sturgeon?'

'Pleasant chap. Self-made man, rose from having nothing to owning a nice little timber business. His wife talked him into selling up and retiring I believe; *he* didn't want to sit back and do nothing, you know what these blasted Yorkshiremen are like!'

'None better. Thanks. I must be off. You'll send me a bill?'

'Too bloody true,' said Grainger, picking up the diet sheet which Dalziel had replaced on the desk. 'And pay it quick if you're leaving this behind you. I don't want all the trouble of making claims against your estate.'

'Oh, give it here!' said Dalziel, taking the paper and thrusting it carelessly into his jacket pocket. 'Don't do too many illegal operations. Cheers.'

He left noisily. Grainger shook his head, smiling. But there was a shadow of worry in his eyes.

Chapter 8

Pascoe seemed to have spent the entire morning on the telephone, preserving a steady balance between official and unofficial business. First call was to Sergeant Lauder of Lochart who recognized his voice instantly.

'It's nice to hear from you again, Sergeant Pascoe,' he said. 'The day isna' complete without it.'

'Should auld acquaintance and all that,' said Pascoe. 'This time it's a man called Lewis, Matthew Lewis. He had a cottage somewhere near Lochart, I believe.'

'Now why was I just pondering that?' inquired Pascoe.

'Because I am by the way of being a distruster of coincidence, Sergeant, and when I have to tell a woman called Mrs Lewis who has a week-end cottage in Lochart that her husband had been murdered, and when my colleagues in Yorkshire start ringing me up twice or thrice a day, why then I suspect a connection.'

'I hope this means you've anticipated my inquiries.'

'Perhaps so. The man Lewis has been coming here for nearly three years now. Week-ends and longer in the summer. He keeps himself to himself as far as the locals are concerned. He's usually with his wife and family.'

'Usually?' asked Pascoe, alert.

'Aye. But there have been others. Men and women. Such things are noticed. One other woman in particular.'

Dirty old Lewis, thought Pascoe.

'Anything else?'

'Nothing much. Some people in the village are looking after their dog. Mrs Lewis just wanted to get home as quickly as possible that night, you'll understand. Perhaps you might inquire about returning the beastie.'

172

'I will. Many thanks, Sergeant.'

'Just one more thing. Since you were so interested in this man, Atkinson, who stayed at the hotel, I went back through the hotel register just to see if anything else struck me. I made a note of one or two names, people with addresses from your part of the world who'd stayed there this summer. Would you be interested?'

'I certainly would.'

The list was not very long. Only one name was notable and Pascoe was less than surprised. Mr and Mrs E. Sturgeon. He checked the dates. They had been there for three nights early in the summer; clearly the holiday during which their house had been burgled.

'Thanks, Sergeant,' he said. 'I've no doubt we'll be in touch again.'

Doncaster Royal Infirmary was next on his list. Sturgeon's condition was unchanged. It was impossible to say whether or not a visit would be worthwhile. The tone used here was clearly disapproving. But they had never heard Dalziel's disapproval, thought Pascoe as he replaced the receiver. He would have to go.

Finally he contacted the garage to determine the results of the examination of Sturgeon's car.

He thought of this some time later as he drove by the scene of the crash. Not that there was anything to see. Sturgeon's car had, of course, been lifted away, and at Pascoe's speed, a broken hedge and ploughed-up grass were hard to spot.

The car was being closely examined, and according to the reports which he had got via the telephone, there seemed to be little reason for the crash. Tyres were all OK and the steering was absolutely sound. No evidence had yet been discovered of mechanical failure. The full report might show otherwise, but Pascoe's uneasy feeling was getting worse.

The doctor he spoke to confirmed it. So far as they

could tell there had been no physical explanation of the crash in Sturgeon himself. All damage had clearly stemmed from the accident, not contributed to it.

'What are his chances?' asked Pascoe.

'Pretty slim, I'd say,' answered the doctor. 'He was badly knocked about, lost a lot of blood. But it's not just that. He dosen't seem to have the least interest in staying alive.'

'How can you say that?' protested Pascoe. 'He's only been here twenty-four hours. You can't expect much joy and laughter after what he's been through.'

'Listen,' said the doctor, 'I won't arrest any motorists if you don't make diagnoses. All right? And I'll tell you this. If it wasn't for the fact that I believe he might well be dead before morning, you wouldn't be going to see him now.'

What there was to see of Sturgeon's face confirmed the doctor's words. It was deadly pale and pinched-looking, as though the blood had been squeezed out of it by force. His eyes miraculously had escaped the onslaught of shivered glass which had gashed his scalp and brow as he pitched forward into the windscreen. But the flicker of recognition as they stared up at Pascoe was a mere movement on the surface of despair.

It was no time for social exordia.

'Mr Sturgeon, I rang Lochart,' said Pascoe deliberately. 'The constable there says there's no one called Archie Selkirk in the district.'

There was no response.

'He told me you'd phoned as well. What did you want with this man, Selkirk?'

Sturgeon closed his eyes, but he was still listening.

'What about John Atkinson then?' asked Pascoe. 'What's your connection with him? Do you know James Cowley? Did you know Matthew Lewis?'

The eyelids perceptibly pressed down more tightly on

174

the eyes. This was getting them nowhere. A passing nurse pushed the door open, peered assessingly at Pascoe, and went on her way.

'Listen, Edgar,' urged Pascoe leaning closer, 'this is doing you no good. I want to help. You *wanted* me to help. Just tell me what it's all about and I'll try to sort things out. Is it something to do with the robbery? Your stamps?'

Still nothing. It was difficult to know where to go from here. The man was in no state to withstand the kind of shock being questioned about a murder could give him. Pascoe could hardly believe that a man like Sturgeon could have had the will or the strength to kill Lewis, but his innocence would possibly just increase the shock.

'All right, Edgar. I'm going now,' he said to the closed eyes. 'I'll come again.'

He rose to leave. The eyes opened.

'Mavis?' whispered Sturgeon.

'Mavis? Yes, I've been to see her.'

'To see?' Sturgeon was puzzled. Of course, he doesn't know she's in hospital as well, thought Pascoe. He's wondering why it's me standing here, not her.

'I'll tell her,' he said reassuringly, eager to get out now.

'Let her come. I want to explain.'

The words were almost inaudible. The door opened and the doctor and nurse appeared. Pascoe ignored them.

'Explain what, Edgar?'

'I can see you've cheered him up,' said the doctor. 'What's he said?'

'He was asking for his wife.'

'His wife? For God's sake man, you didn't tell him she was in hospital too, did you?'

'Hospital? Mavis in hospital?'

There was nothing inaudible about Sturgeon now.

'No, but you did,' Pascoe answered the doctor. 'Listen,

175

Edgar, it's all right, she'll be all right. She was just upset when she heard about your accident, that's all. You get better, she'll get better, it's as simple as that.'

Sturgeon stared up at him, his eyes alive with feeling now.

'Damn them,' he said. 'Damn them to buggery! Damn them!'

'Who, Edgar? Who?' said Pascoe, feeling it should be 'whom?' Sturgeon ignored him. He took two or three deep breaths.

'How am I, Doctor?' he asked feebly. 'Will I mend?'

'Certainly, old man. With care you could be your old self in a couple of months.' He sounded very convincing.

'Right,' said Sturgeon. 'I want a word with Sergeant Pascoe now.'

The doctor looked down at him dubiously for a moment, but whatever he saw in the old man's face seemed to satisfy him.

'Five minutes,' he said. 'That's all.'

Sturgeon was talking before the doctor and nurse had left the room. His voice was low and shaky, but he spoke fast, like a man in a great hurry. Pascoe asked no questions, did not interrupt at all. After ten minutes the nurse returned and angrily chased him.

He met the doctor outside.

'Any use?' the man asked cheerfully.

'I think so. What about him?'

He looked backwards to the now completely still figure in the bed.

'Well, I'd say you've either killed or cured him, wouldn't you? Time will tell. We'll let you know.'

It was with relief that Pascoe had stepped out into the dingy sunshine of a Doncaster day and made his way to a phone box. He could have begged the use of one in the infirmary, but it had seemed important to get out into the

176

open as quickly as possible. Even spacious, modern, well-equipped hospitals could deafen the mind with imagined screamings of pain and despair.

Dalziel listened with interest to what he told him. He sounded unsurprised.

'I thought it must be something like that,' he said. 'Silly bugger. You wonder how they make a living, don't you?'

'He'll be lucky if he makes much more of one,' said Pascoe.

'What? Oh aye. Do you think he killed Lewis?'

'No.'

'You're very certain. You can't expect a deathbed confession if the sod's decided not to die after all. Here. Have you thought on? That break-in. No, not at Lewis's, at Sturgeon's own place. Could he have done it himself to get the insurance money, tide him over a bit?'

'Hardly, sir,' said Pascoe. 'He was in Lochart that week, remember? He hadn't signed up yet, and even when he did, it took a long time for disenchantment to set in.'

Sturgeon's story had been so incredible it had to be true. Bored with inactivity after a few months' retirement, he had been rash enough to reveal his malaise in the company of Matthew Lewis. Lewis (as Pascoe reconstructed) had taken care to bump into Sturgeon fairly frequently at the Liberal Club in the following weeks and had steered conversation round to his own adventures on the stock market, expressing a special interest in Nordrill Mining (whose shares, Pascoe later ascertained, were moving steadily upwards at this time). Sturgeon had been fairly interested by this, but he became really interested when Lewis started dropping hints that he was going to cash in on Nordrill in more ways than one. He probably pretended to drink too much one night and revealed that he had inside information of a potentially rich mineral strike at Nordrill's test bore not far from his holiday cottage at Lochart. After that things had moved with tragic inevitability, with Sturgeon, like the hard-headed, clear-sighted Yorkshire businessman he imagined he was, measuring every step he took with the utmost care and Lewis with even greater care making sure that there was always a small piece of firm ground under Sturgeon's foot.

First Atkinson was introduced as Nordrill's site engineer. He had even taken them round the drilling site one Sunday afternoon, the watchman doubtless having been persuaded to stick in his hut with a couple of fivers for company. Naturally Atkinson confirmed the strike.

Next Archie Selkirk of Strath Farm had appeared on the scene, the alleged owner of a large tract of what was euphemistically called hill-farming land under which most of the mineral ore would probably lie. He was willing to let others take the risk of negotiating with Nordrill, if it ever came to that, and was selling the land at a mere half of its potential price. Lewis bought as much as he could afford. Sturgeon acted as a witness of the deal. By now he was firmly hooked. An agreement was drawn up for another parcel of land. Atkinson suddenly let slip that the news was going to break in the national Press the following week and Nordrill's own land-agents would be getting to work the very next day. Sturgeon went the whole hog, cashed in on all his resources including using his house as security for a loan, and bought every acre Selkirk had to offer. It cost him over forty thousand pounds.

'He hasn't a penny left in the world,' Pascoe had concluded. 'It took a long time for him to get suspicious but when he read in Monday's paper that questions were being asked about Nordrill's intentions in Scotland, he got worried. He tried to contact Lewis at his office, but he wasn't there of course on Monday morning. Then

178

when I got in touch with him about the stamps, he took the opportunity to ask me to check on Archie Selkirk. I was too busy to do anything. Perhaps if I'd pressed him more . . .'

'Stop being a bloody martyr and get on with it,' interjected Dalziel.

'So he rang Lochart police-station for himself on Tuesday. Lauder told him emphatically no such person existed. Next thing, he looks in the paper and sees Lewis is dead. And on Wednesday morning, Nordrill announce they're stopping work in Scotland. He tried to ring me, God knows why. I wish that . . . anyway, by Wednesday lunch-time he'd got it into his head that the important thing was to see his wife well cared for financially. With Lewis dead, he could see little hope of regaining his money. But he was well insured, so off he set down the A1, bent on killing himself and making it look accidental. Fortunately he was determined no one else would be affected, so instead of making sure of it going across the central reservation and getting a seventy plus seventy crash, he went over the edge. When he realized the news of his accident had put Mavis in hospital, he saw what a bloody fool he'd been. And he talked.'

'Christ. And we laugh at stories of Americans buying the Eiffel Tower!' Dalziel had commented. 'What about Cowley? Did Sturgeon mention him?'

'No. Knows nothing about him as far as I could make out.'

'But you saw him with Atkinson? We'd better have a word. I was going to see him anyway. Let's get him to ourselves. Five-thirty, that's probably when they close. That give you enough time? Right. I'll see you there.'

He joined Dalziel in his car by the kerbside just on five-thirty.

'What if he's not in, sir?' he asked, looking across the street at Lewis and Cowley's offices.

179

'He'll be in all right,' said Dalziel cheerily. 'I rang him up and made an appointment.'

'Oh,' said Pascoe. Then, realizing he had let his surprise show, he added, 'I thought you'd be wanting to catch him off guard, that's all.'

'What? Don't be soft, lad. He doesn't know *we're* coming. He's expecting a rich touch in search of a house! Come on.'

The signal was the appearance at the door of the two secretaries, Marjory Clayton and Jane Collingwood.

The latter recognized Pascoe as he and Dalziel strode purposefully across the street and he gave her a little wave.

'Mr Cowley!' bellowed Dalziel in the outer office.

The door marked Cowley opened and the man stood there, his customer-reception smile slackening into puzzlement as he caught sight of Pascoe.

'Mr Cowley? I'm Detective-Superintendent Dalziel. We haven't met, though I believe you know my sergeant here. May we have a few moment of your precious time?'

Dalziel advanced powerfully so that Cowley had to step aside or be crushed. Pascoe meekly followed his leader into the inner office. It was expensively furnished in a rather unintegrated way. An oval-shaped Indian carpet caught at the feet. On the leather inlaid desk an onyx cigarette-box stood open, obviously newly filled. Dalziel picked it up and looked at it admiringly.

'Nice,' he said. 'Is it convenient to talk with you now, sir?'

'I *am* expecting a client,' began Cowley, glancing at the ormolu clock resting on a shelf above what looked like the room's original fireplace, carved out of York stone before it started getting pretty. Something had been worrying Pascoe and now he recalled that on his previous visit just over twenty-four hours earlier, Cowley's room had been the other one. He had wasted no time. And this room clearly bore the mark of the kind of man Lewis had been if Dalziel's sources were good. He remembered also the kind of thing stolen from Lewis's house. It all fitted a picture of a man who enjoyed the good things of life with a fine indiscrimination.

'Just a couple of minutes, please,' said Dalziel, adding magnanimously, 'we shall leave, of course, as soon as your client arrives.'

He put down the cigarette-box and seated himself in the most comfortable-looking chair. Cowley, butler-like, picked up the box and took it to Dalziel.

'Cigarette, Superintendent?'

'Thank you, no. It's a habit I've broken.'

Since *when?* wondered Pascoe. This morning at the earliest! Some people break habits quicker than others.

'Now, Mr Cowley, the thing is this. We're anxious to get in touch with an acquaintance of Mr Lewis's, a Mr John Atkinson. Do you know him by any chance?'

'Well, yes. I think so. If it's the same one. Hang on a moment, will you?'

He rose, opened a rather over-ornate walnut cabinet and took from it a folder.

'Here we are. Atkinson, John. This was one of perhaps half a dozen clients Matt took a very personal interest in. Looking at the file, I remember why now. He met Mr Atkinson up at Lochart, that's where he had his cottage, you know. That's one of the addresses we had for him, the Lochart Hotel.'

'And the other?' asked Dalziel.

'Another hotel. The Shelley in Bayswater. That's in London.'

'Thank you,' said Dalziel. 'What was Mr Atkinson's interest down here?'

'He was nearing retiring age, I believe. Had known the area a long time ago and talking with Matt had revived old memories. So he was looking round in a rather desultory fashion. You know, popping in occasionally and breaking his journey between London and Scotland.'

'When did you last see him, sir?' asked Dalziel.

'Only yesterday morning. In fact, I think he was here when your sergeant came. If only you'd thought to mention him then, Sergeant.'

Dalziel looked reprovingly at Pascoe and shook his head.

'Can't be helped. Why was he here, sir?'

'Why, he'd read about Matt's death, of course, and come down specially to find out what had happened. He called on Mrs Lewis, I believe. He was most upset. The odd thing was he'd turned up by the chance on Monday afternoon and seen Matt then when he came back from Scotland.'

'By chance you say?' said Dalziel, exchanging glances with Pascoe.

'Oh yes. He just drifted in. He didn't realize the office is normally closed that afternoon. So he chatted for a while, saw that we were busy, and went on his way. He was very struck by the coincidence.'

'Yes, yes, he would be. Yesterday you said he came *down*, didn't you. From Scotland, you mean?'

'I've no idea,' said Cowley. 'Possibly.'

He took a cigarette and lit it from a table lighter which matched the box.

'Which would mean he was on his way *up* from London on Monday.'

'I suppose so.'

'But he wasn't in Lochart on Monday or Tuesday, Mr Cowley,' said Dalziel mildly. 'We checked.'

'Perhaps it was the other way round.'

'You mean he came *down* from Lochart on Monday? And called in here, knowing his friend Mr Lewis was still in Scotland?'

182

'I don't think they lived in each other's pockets, Superintendent.'

'No. Of course not. Where did he stay overnight when he was house-hunting.'

'Really, I've no idea. This was Matt's client, as I've told you. I only met the man two or three times. And then just for a couple of minutes. Is that all you wanted to ask me, Superintendent!'

He stood up, looking very irritated, stubbed out his cigarette and glanced at his watch. Dalziel ignored the hint.

'Have you ever been to Lochart yourself, Mr Cowley?'

'No. Never.' There might have been a hesitation, thought Pascoe. An idea was forming in his mind.

'Do you know a Mr Edgar Sturgeon?' he interjected. Dalziel looked sharply at him, then settled back in his chair as if to enjoy the act.

'No. I don't think so,' said Cowley.

'Stocky. Gray-haired. Mid-sixties. Retired,' rattled off Pascoe.

'Sorry, he doesn't ring a bell.'

It was probably a daft idea, thought Pascoe, but he might as well try. He took out his notebook.

'I wonder if you can recall where you were on this week-end, sir,' he said. He read out the date of the meeting between Archie Selkirk and Sturgeon.

Cowley whistled.

'God knows. That's a while ago, isn't it?'

'I realize that, sir. Do try. A diary, perhaps?' suggested Pascoe.

'I don't keep one. Only my office diary and that doesn't run to week-ends,' said Cowley, flicking through the pages of his leatherbound desk diary. 'Hang on though. You're in luck.'

'Yes?'

'Well, most of that week-end I was here. Working on

183

accounts, checking our mailing list and property details, that kind of thing. It's a half-yearly job. We take turns at it. This was mine. Poor Matthew, I remember, was in Scotland.'

He turned the book round so that they could see the entry.

'So you were alone, Mr Cowley?'

'Yes.'

'You live by yourself as well, don't you?'

'You seem to know a lot about me,' said Cowley aggressively.

'We took closely at everyone connected with a murder victim,' said Dalziel placatingly. 'Sergeant, what's your point? We mustn't keep Mr Cowley from his customer.'

Cheeky sod! thought Pascoe.

'No point really, sir. I was just interested in Mr Cowley's whereabouts that week-end. I'm sure someone saw him . . .'

'Saw me? Of course someone saw me!' Cowley looked at Pascoe as if he were some rare and rather unpleasant animal. 'For a start I don't do the job by myself, you know. Miss Clayton and Miss Collingwood were here too doing their bit. Ask 'em! Superintendent, I don't understand your underling. If he'd wanted to know about this week-end or Monday afternoon, that would figure. But all that time ago . . .!'

'Don't worry, sir. We're checking that too,' said Dalziel, rising. 'No sign of your client yet? Sergeant, have a look.'

Solemnly, Pascoe peered into the outer office.

'No, sir. Empty.'

'Dear me. I hope we haven't chased him away. Well, thank you for your time, Mr Cowley. Sorry to have troubled you. If Mr Atkinson should get in touch again, please let us know. Good evening.'

Outside Dalziel looked assessingly at the sun's declension.

'You can buy me a drink,' he said finally.

'The Black Eagle, sir?'

'No. Somewhere where telephones don't ring. Round the corner here'll do.'

At this time of evening they were the only customers in the ugly little pub Dalziel had discovered. Instead of his usual scotch he ordered a gin and a sugar-free tonic.

Pascoe expressed surprise.

'I'm cutting down,' said Dalziel, adding two drops of the tonic to his gin and drinking the mixture with a shudder.

'Ah,' said Pascoe.

'Your bright idea that Cowley and Selkirk might be one and the same sank like turtle-shit, didn't it?' said Dalziel gleefully.

'It was a thought,' said Pascoe. 'I'll check with the girls all the same. If it wasn't that, then what part could he have played? I suppose he could be in the clear?'

'Who knows? I doubt it, but I could be biased. He's not a kind of man I care for.'

It was like the Pope admitting some uncertainty about the position of the Mormons.

'What's the next move, sir?'

'We'll try the Shelley, but I doubt if we'll have much luck. Have a word with Mrs Lewis, see what she can tell us about Atkinson. After that, God knows.'

He shrugged fatalistically and finished his drink. He looked tired.

'Is it possible Lewis got taken as well? That he wasn't in the con after all?'

'No. Cowley I'll admit some doubt about. Lewis, no. We'd better get some expert help from the fraud lads on this. That forty thou's got to be somewhere. Do you want another?'

185

'No, thanks. I talked with Lauder about the Lewises. He reckoned Lewis sometimes took a bit of spare up there.'

'It figures. A man needs his hobbies. Anything else?'

'No. Except he wants to know what to do with the Lewises' dog.'

'Dog?' Dalziel looked interested. 'Dog? That reminds me, I had a notion earlier. But no. It doesn't help much, does it?'

'What doesn't?' asked Pascoe patiently.

'These break-ins. There seem to be a lot of pets around. Sturgeon's cats. Cottingley's dog. You keep on coming back with more hairs on you than a gorilla's arse. If there was a tip-off coming from a kennels, it'd explain how our friend knew whose house is empty when. But if the Lewises' dog went with them, it doesn't work.'

'Unless, as you suggested before, the Lewis job wasn't in the series,' said Pascoe.

'But you don't reckon Sturgeon?'

'No. But that still leaves Atkinson. And perhaps Cowley. And forty thousand pounds.'

'True, Sergeant. Check the other houses that got done for pets, then. See if there is a connection.'

'Now, sir?'

'You said you didn't want another drink, so you can't have anything else to do.'

The old Dalziel logic. Pascoe drank the last of his beer. He must be reaching maturity, he hardly felt even slightly irritated.

'I think I can spare you half an hour of my time, sir,' he said lightly. The reaction surprised him.

'You can spare me as much of your bloody time as I require,' said Dalziel with some force. 'We don't work nine to five and we can't afford private lives. Haven't you learned that much yet?'

'I've learned that if you're one thing all your life you

186

become less than that one thing,' answered Pascoe, feeling his recent sense of mature invulnerability evaporating. 'You can be too dedicated.'

'Can you? What the hell do you know, Sergeant? Do you want to spend you life in the company of people who think of us as "pigs"?'

'You're talking about Ellie Soper?'

'I didn't mention her,' grunted Dalziel.

'Now listen,' said Pascoe with quiet vehemence. 'I've had the gist of what you said to her on the phone the other day. You'd better understand, sir, I make my own decisions. I need no keeper, no protection. You're my superior officer, but what I do with my life's my own business. And who I do it with.'

Dalziel didn't speak but went to the bar and bought another round. Pascoe's was a large scotch, his own another gin and tonic.

'What's this for?' asked Pascoe, looking suspiciously at his glass.

'Drink it down. Your promotion's through. It'll be published next week.'

'What?'

'Yes. Congratulations.'

Pascoe drank, his mind full of fragmented thoughts.

'You'll probably be off somewhere else.'

'Will I?'

'It's usual.'

Pascoe smiled almost apologetically.

'You'll have to find youself another boy,' he said.

'This time I might try for a man,' answered Dalziel.

But there was no force, no passion behind the exchange. Instead it hung on the air like the dully resigned, totally inadequate farewells of friends who part, uncertain whether they will ever meet again.

The next morning Pascoe heard that the Thornton Lacey inquest was to be reopened and would take place on the following Tuesday.

187

PART THREE

Chapter 1

What sudden horrors rise! a naked lover bound and bleeding
  speed the soft intercourse from still on that breast enam-
oured let me he best can paint 'em who shall give all thou
canst and let me dream the rest her gloomy presence a
browner horror all is calm in this eternal sleep here for
ever death, only death, can break here, even then, shall my
cold dust remain I view my crime but kindle at I come, I
come! thither where sinners may have rest I go in sacred
vestments mayst thou stand teach me at once and learn of me
to die condemned.

The piece of paper was crumpled and grubby from
much handling and examination. A jagged upper edge
showed it had been torn off a larger sheet. But the
handwriting was indisputably Colin's as far as Pascoe
could assess, and the experts had agreed.

'What did they find?' he asked, just for the sake of
speaking rationally through the confusion of thoughts
stirred up by what he had read.

'Fingerprints – Hopkin's – they checked them against
sets in the cottage known to be his by elimination. Also
the young lad's who found the car. No others. Written
recently. Ink and paper of a kind discovered in the
cottage. What do you make of it?'

'It's confusing sir,' answered Pascoe, returning the
plastic encapsulated paper to Backhouse.

'It's certainly that. Our pet psychiatrist took several
hours to come to the same conclusion. Or rather that
whoever wrote it was in a state of confusion. Which

would fit the suspected circumstances. He also talked a lot about quotation. The use of other people's words in a situation where a man's own mind refused to confront directly what had happened.'

'You think he's in the quarry pool then?'

Backhouse looked thoughtful. He also looked very tired and drawn. Pascoe thought of Dalziel. Was this kind of strain the price of promotion?

'It seems possible. We found a shoe.'

'Colin's?' asked Pascoe.

'It's being checked as best we can. But it's not that. If you were going to write a suicide note and *not* commit suicide, what kind of note would you write?'

Pascoe thought for a moment, then nodded.

'I take your point, sir.'

'That's right. Something traditional, clear, unambiguous. *I have done wrong and I cannot go on living.* That's what you'd write. Unless you were very clever, of course.'

Pascoe stared out of the window of Constable Crowther's office. The sun was continuing to pour its late blessings on Thornton Lacey's mellow stone.

'Colin was clever,' he said.

'Yes. I gathered so much,' said Backhouse. 'This clever?'

He waved a sheet of paper in the air.

'Not in those circumstances. I can't see it.'

'You know, Sergeant, you're beginning to talk as if you're ready to think Hopkins might after all have done the killings,' said Backhouse with a note of compassion in his voice.

'I suppose I am,' replied Pascoe, making the admission for the first time even to himself. 'That's the trouble with our job, isn't it sir? After a while you begin to believe anybody could do anything.'

'Given the right pressure in the right places,' agreed Backhouse.

'Though if you don't mind me saying so, sir, you seem to have moved a little bit the other way.'

'Away from a firm conviction of Hopkins's guilt, you mean? No. It was a theory. It still is. Information accrues and the theory might have to shift or take a different shape, but it remains. Tell me, Sergeant, given a choice between drowning and blowing you head off with a shotgun, how would you dispatch yourself?'

'I wouldn't fancy either much,' said Pascoe. 'The gun, I suppose, but it's not like using a revolver, is it? I mean, a single bullet's one thing, but a headful of shot . . .!'

'A point,' mused Backhouse. 'Well, I should like to find the gun all the same. Would you jump over a quarry edge with a shotgun in your hands?'

'No. But if I was a local peasant and came across a car with a shotgun lying around on the back seat, I might very well lift it.'

'My men are out talking to all likely candidates,' said Backhouse in a tone of mild reproof. 'Well, I must be off. I shall see you at the inquest tomorrow, Sergeant.'

'Why is the inquest being reopened now?' asked Pascoe.

'It's well within the coroner's powers at present,' said Backhouse. 'Though, as you are clearly aware, it is unusual in a case like this. I am not privy to the working of Mr French's mind, but I surmise that some kind of local pressure is bearing on him. People want to sleep untroubled in their beds. A verdict of murder against Hopkins would do this nicely.'

'But it's almost unheard of nowadays!' protested Pascoe.

'You may hear it tomorrow,' warned Backhouse as he left. 'Behave youself, Sergeant.'

Whether he meant during the proceedings or during the intervening period, Pascoe didn't know. It was not altogether unflattering, he discovered, to be regarded as potentially dangerous. Like the Western gunman enjoying the noise-hiatus as he entered a bar.

The thought made him glance at his watch. Far too early for a drink, alas. He stared glumly out of the window once more. He could not imagine what had prompted him to sacrifice a precious rest day in travelling down here. The adjourned inquest was not due to restart until ten o'clock the following morning. Ellie had absolutely refused to come near the place till then. She was probably wise. One thing he wanted to do was take another look at the cottage. Backhouse had not raised any objection and no one else was likely to. Crowther was looking after the key in case anyone with a legitimate claim to it turned up. It now rested in Pascoe's pocket but he felt reluctant to set off to use it.

Mrs Crowther poked her head through the door.

'Cup of tea, Sergeant?' she asked. 'And a piece of my shortcake?'

It was a tempting offer but, like a bare bosom shaken alluringly at a devout puritan, its effect was opposite to that intended.

'No, thanks,' said Pascoe. 'I must be off.'

'Please yourself,' grunted Mrs Crowther. 'We'll see you for supper?'

'Yes, please.'

Pascoe was staying with the Crowthers. The only alternative had been to thrust himself upon the Culpeppers once more, and his memory of his last stay there did not encourage this. Of course, he could have stopped at a hotel, but this would have meant being some distance from the village and this did not suit his albeit unformulated purpose in coming down that day.

He left his car by the kerb and set off on foot, enjoying the late afternoon sunshine. Soon he reached the edge of the village and the houses began to thin out. A small scattering of 'executive residences' had erupted on the right of the road. He thought he saw Sandra Bell by the garage of one of them but she made no sign of recognition. Then came a small block of old cottages, untouched though probably not undesired by the renovators. Culpepper's modern stately home lay somewhere along the ridge to the left. It would probably be visible from the road when autumn finally got among the trees and started shaking the branches bare, but the foliage still had all the fullness of summer, edged now with gold but not yet weighed down by it. On the right now he passed the narrow ill-kept track which must lead up to Pelman's house; Pelman's woods looked denser, more sombre, perhaps because the sun was throwing the shadows of these trees across his path as he walked.

Pelman. There was an interesting figure. He would not have thought him a man to take lightly his wife's affairs with a farmhand. Tenant farmer, he mentally corrected himself, recalling what he had learned from Crowther. It would not do to over-Lady-Chatterley-ize the situation. Yet they had both ended up in the quarry pool, which out-Lawrenced Lawrence.

A Land-Rover approached him, slowed down and pulled into the side.

'Pascoe, isn't it?' said the driver, leaning out and peering into the side.

It was Pelman. Pascoe felt as though he had conjured him up.

'Hello,' he said.

'Down for the inquest? I don't understand the workings of the Law, though I suppose it makes sense to you.'

Pelman was in his shirt-sleeves. He looked as if he'd done a hard day's work.

'Can I give you a lift anywhere or are you just taking the air?' he went on.

'I'm on my way to Brookside,' answered Pascoe. 'Thanks for the offer, but it's only round the bend.'

A Citroën GS sped by them towards the village. It slowed momentarily as if the driver thought of stopping, then picked up speed again. Davenant, thought Pascoe. He had told Backhouse his thoughts about the man, but received nothing in exchange. Except courteous thanks.

'What are you doing tonight?' asked Pelman. 'Come round for a drink if you can. There'll be one or two others there, most of 'em you've met. We're having an Amenities Committee meeting – can't use the village hall, of course. But we should be done by eight-thirty.'

'Thanks,' said Pascoe. 'I'll try to make it.'

A very interesting man, thought Pascoe as he watched the Land-Rover disappear. He couldn't really see him as a good committee man. He was an individualist, not to be ignored. Pascoe hadn't made up his mind about him yet, but the man's instinctive defence of Colin still shone out like a golden deed in the angel's book.

A few minutes later without seeing another soul he reached Brookside.

Precisely why he wanted to look at the cottage, he found it hard to explain. It was not with any serious hope of finding clues that Backhouse had missed that he had come, but certainly part of his motive was a desire to try and view the place with a policeman's eye, impossible on his last visit there. In addition there was a feeling of responsibility. Someone ought to take a look through Rose and Colin's things, not officially but with a view to disposing of them. Doubtless someone would be appointed to do this eventually, but up till now nothing had happened. Nothing could happen, of course, in law. Rose was dead. All that was hers became Colin's. Colin was still alive legally. Therefore no one could act.

Except perhaps a friend who happened to be a policeman who happened to be admitting openly to himself now his firm conviction that Colin was dead.

An attempt had been made to tidy up after the explosion and, kitchen apart, the place looked almost normal. Someone had closed the curtains, whether as an act of decency or of defence it was impossible to say. He fumbled around till he found the light switch. The electricity was off. Naturally. Gas and water, too, after the bang. It was like the work of a careful family going on holiday. He turned to the rear window and began to open the curtains, pausing as the sundial came into view. *Horas non numero nisi serenas.* A nice thought, if you were a sundial.

Behind him a telephone rang.

He span round. It was on the floor. He recalled that it had been there when he and Ellie arrived nine days earlier. It only let out a single ring, then became silent again. After a moment, standing looking down at it, Pascoe began to wonder if he had perhaps imagined the noise.

He squatted over it, hand on the receiver willing it to ring once more. It suddenly seemed very important. He began to count seconds. One thousand, two thousand, three thousand . . . He had reached ten when it rang again.

At the same time something descended heavily on the back of his head; the bell sound entered his mind and turned it into a belfry which sent wild peals buffeting about the inside of his skull seeking a way out. Finally they found it and fled, leaving only darkness.

* * *

194

When he opened his eyes it was like waking into a drunkard's paradise. He was surrounded by publicans.

Sam Dixon was bathing his head while Major/Sergeant Palfrey hovered uselessly around.

'Brandy,' said Pascoe in happy anticipation.

'Hush,' said Dixon. 'There is none.'

'Two publicans and not a brandy between you? You ought to lose your licences.'

'I'm pleased to hear you so chipper, Mr Pascoe,' said Dixon with a relieved smile. Even Palfrey looked happy to see him sitting up.

He glanced at his watch. Ten past five. He must have been out for nearly ten minutes.

'What happened?' asked Palfrey in his over-clipped military accent.

'God knows. I had just come into the cottage when the phone rang. I bent to pick it up and crash! everything fell on me.'

'You've been coshed,' said Dixon, with the expertise of one who had managed a pub at the rough end of Liverpool. 'We probably disturbed whoever did it or he might have given you a couple more for luck.'

'Thanks,' said Pascoe, wincing as Dixon continued his mopping-up operation. 'How did you get here?'

'I was driving by,' said Palfrey. 'Saw the cottage door was open as I passed. It seemed odd in view of . . . well, you know. So I stopped and then came in to investigate.'

'And I did the same a couple of minutes later when I saw the major's car,' said Dixon. 'Now we'd better let Dr Hardisty have a look at you. The skin's broken but I can't say what else might be wrong.'

'No, I'm fine,' said Pascoe, standing up and staggering against Palfrey. The man might not have had any brandy about his person, but from his breath he certainly had a great deal within.

'Come on,' said Palfrey with something approaching kindness. 'Best get you patched up.'

'OK,' Pascoe answered, admitting the sense of it. 'But we'd better let Crowther know.'

'I'll give him a ring while you're getting in the car,' said Dixon.

Helped by the major, Pascoe walked with increasing steadiness to the car. It was pleasant to be out in the fresh air again after the warm, unaired atmosphere of the sealed cottage.

He suffered a bit of a relapse in the car, perhaps because of the movement. His mind wouldn't fix on what had just taken place, but wandered back over the whole of the past week. Sturgeon appeared before him. He had seen him again at the week-end, this time taking with him Mavis Sturgeon, now recovered sufficiently to travel. He had hated to impose his presence on their reunion, but the doctor had only permitted a limited time for the visit in view of Sturgeon's still critical condition. And they needed anything Sturgeon could tell them. Atkinson had proved untraceable, as had the man known as Archie Selkirk. There was no tie-up with Cowley and no sign of forty thousand pounds.

'I couldn't see you poor, love,' explained Sturgeon. 'Do you remember those first days? Making a meal off a couple of stale crusts and a potato? Them were hard times. I couldn't see you face them again.'

'Things've changed,' protested his wife. 'It wouldn't happen now. Besides we managed. As long as I've got you, Edgar, I could manage.'

'Aye, aye. But it seemed best. I've been a fool, Mavis. All that money, all we had, gone. And the bungalow. It seemed best . . .'

His voice tailed away and he and his wife had wept comfort to each other.

196

The picture broke up was replaced by thoughts of Ellie. She was somewhere being threatened, but he didn't know who by. Unless it was Anton Davenant, but why should he . . .

Again the picture collapsed and when it reformed it was in the likeness of Dr Hardisty with Backhouse standing in the background.

'You'll do,' pronounced the doctor. 'There may be some mild concussion, but you're not cracked open. These fellows should stop the headache from taking you apart.'

He handed over a bottle of tablets. From his demeanour Pascoe gathered that he must have been giving an appearance of rationality while he was being examined. It was not a comforting thing to be aware of the body's capacity to carry on in a straight line while the mind was circling quite other spheres of time and space.

'Thornton Lacey has not been a happy place for you, Sergeant,' said Backhouse.

'No, sir.'

'We'll get you back to Crowther's now. You need some rest.'

'What about the man who attacked me, sir?'

'The police are being as efficient as you could wish, Sergeant,' said Backhouse smiling. 'It was probably just some local tearaway who knew the place was empty.'

'Probably,' agreed Pascoe. But a telephone bell kept ringing in his mind as he went out to the waiting car.

Chapter 2

Dalziel didn't know whether to be happy or ashamed at the growing frequency of his bouts of lust. In his league of gross appetites, sex had always come a very poor third to whisky and food. Perhaps it was his recently initiated diet which had unbalanced things, but lust had suddenly rocketed to the top, taking him quite by surprise. Also surprising was the cause of it, Ellie Soper in a simple cotton dress which let the sunlight filter through.

He stood up as she approached his table. It was pleasant out here in the little garden of the Jockey with this extra bonus of summer making the Martini sunshades rather less ludicrous than usual.

'Like what you see?' she asked as she sat down. He realized he had been staring.

'It'll be cold in an hour,' he said.

'What will be?'

It didn't do to start lusting after subordinates' womenfolk, he thought. Especially when they were sharp-tongued and ill-disposed.

'What'll you drink?' he asked, sitting down abruptly. 'Sam!'

'Yes, Mr Dalziel?' said the barman, appearing with great smartness.

'Gin and tonic,' said Ellie. 'It must be nice to be known.'

'Not always. It's nice here though.' He nodded approvingly at the village of Birkham.

'It's convenient,' said Ellie. 'It's half-way. I like to meet people half-way.'

What am I doing here? wondered Dalziel.

'Now, what are we doing here?' asked Ellie.

'Christ knows,' grunted Dalziel. 'I'm giving an explanation. You might like to think it's an apology.'

'As long as it's just that. I get suspicious when middle-aged men start ringing me up as soon as my boy-friend's gone away for the night.'

'Don't flatter yourself,' said Dalziel. He scratched his armpit. If they thought he was bloody repulsive, he might as well look bloody repulsive.

'It's the inquest tomorrow then.'

'Yes.'

'You know why they've reopened it? Normally nothing'd happen. The police would get a man, he'd be tried, found guilty. The registrar of deaths would put it in his book. Murder, manslaughter, whatever. This lot's different. They'll bring in a verdict of murder and name Colin Hopkins.'

'But why?'

'No one down there thinks the body's ever going to come up. At least it might not. It's hard to do things in law without a body. But they've got three others for the coroner to work on.'

Ellie's drink arrived. The barman looked in mock amazement at Dalziel's still untouched glass.

'On the wagon, Mr Dalziel?'

'I'm being dragged behind, Sam.'

'Well, don't forget, there's a big one in the bottle for you.'

Dalziel waited till he had left their table.

'There was a note, you know. It'll be read. Conclusions drawn. Hopkins named. Everyone sleeps happy in their neighbour's bed.'

'But what if Colin's still alive?' protested Ellie.

'What's the odds? A fake suicide note's as good an admission as a real one.'

'I see,' said Ellie hopelessly. 'Peter thought much the same.'

'He would,' said Dalziel approvingly. 'You know his promotion's through? It'll be official tomorrow.'

'I heard. You're not building up to another warning, are you?'

Dalziel laughed.

'Not really. No. We had a few words about that. I must be getting soft. I can take anything from these lads now. Anything.'

'So I've heard,' said Ellie drily.

'But it made me think. I shouldn't have talked to you on the phone the way I did.'

'No. You bloody well shouldn't.'

'No,' agreed Dalziel.

'So you're sorry?'

'No point in being sorry. It's past now.'

'Jesus! So?'

'So what?'

'So what are we doing here?'

Abstractedly, Dalziel downed his drink in one swallow then stared at the glass defiantly.

'Listen, I'm good. Of my kind of policeman, I'm probably one of the best Pascoe will ever know. Mind you, I've peed behind too many doors to get much farther. Pascoe, I reckon, of his kind, which looks like being the new kind, can potentially be very good too. Excellent. If I live that long and he keeps going, I could be sirring him before we're finished. So my interest in him is self-interest in a way.'

'You couldn't perhaps like him just a bit as well?' inquired Ellie. She had softened a little but was still very suspicious of this fat bastard.

'He amuses me sometimes,' said Dalziel. 'There's not many as do that.'

'I think I may marry him,' said Ellie thoughtfully.

'Good,' said Dalziel. 'Good. That would be best. I'm glad to hear you say that. Good.'

'Good?' repeated Ellie. 'Why, you fat bastard, that's what you want, isn't it? If you can't get us apart, you might as well get us respectable!'

'I told you I belonged to the old school. There's nowt wrong with a woman that can't be cured by colour telly, wall-to-wall carpeting and a couple of rounds up the spout,' he said with exaggerated coarseness.

Ellie thought of kicking him in the crotch. Then she started laughing. She laughed so much that people turned and stared and the dogs in the nearby kennels started barking wildly as though in reply.

'Let's have another drink,' Dalziel said when she had recovered.

'All right. Just one. Peter's going to phone me at eight. We can breathe heavily down the phone before we're married, can't we?'

She started laughing again. This time Dalziel laughed too.

Pascoe slept for an hour and woke up feeling rotten. He got out of bed to take another pill, felt slightly better and decided to ring Ellie. The phone rang a dozen times. No one answered. He glanced at his watch. Seven o'clock. She'd be having dinner. He went back to bed.

Ellie was enjoying herself. Her previous encounters with Dalziel had always been in polarizing situations. This evening they were keeping steadily on neutral ground and she was finding it a pleasant experience. Like football in no-man's-land during a Great War Christmas.

201

He was talking about Sturgeon.

'There's only one crime and that's being poor,' he asserted.

'Shaw,' said Ellie, through her fourth large gin. Dalziel took it as an expression of drunken agreement.

'You can grade men according to the way they react to being without money,' he continued.

'You're not going to tell me that the more you've had, the worse it is?' asked Ellie suspiciously. 'More sympathy for the rich, that kind of bullshit?'

'Not at all. Some people can take it. Some are so fond of luxury and position they'll do anything to conceal it. Others have been there before and are absolutely resolved they'll never be there again.'

'Scarlett,' said Ellie. Even making allowances for gin, the chatter of people and the howling of dogs, Dalziel couldn't make sense of this.

'O'Hara,' said Ellie. 'End of *Gone With The Wind* part one before the intermission.'

'Yes,' said Dalziel. 'Great movie. Sturgeon was like this. Not for himself, mind you. For his wife. He decided she would be better off with the insurance money. She didn't think so.'

'Get his money back.'

'What?'

She leaned towards him, exquisite in the darkling air.

'Get his bloody money back. That's what you're paid for, isn't it?'

'I wish it was as easy as that.'

The Fraud Squad's preliminary report had arrived that afternoon. Quite simply, they could find no case to answer, and as Dalziel could find no one to answer this non-existant case, things were at a stand-still.

It appeared that land had been bought, legitimately bought, from the fringes of the Earl of Callander's huge estate near Lochart. It was land fit for little except grazing sheep and by the terms of the sale not usable for anything else either. A fair price had been given. The land agent who negotiated the sale was acting for a Mr Archibald Selkirk about whom he knew nothing except that he had placed at his disposal an amount of money sufficient to cover the land price and expenses.

On the land was a small dilapidated croft. In the record of the sale Archibald Selkirk had inserted after the single mention of the croft the words *hereinafter known as Strath Farm*.

So the land Edgar Sturgeon had purchased for something like thirty times its original value had legally been the property of Archie Selkirk of Strath Farm.

Where Archie Selkirk was now, or the money for that matter, was impossible to determine. No papers Sturgeon possessed were anything other than strictly legal. The only evidence of fraud was the extortionate price paid by Sturgeon for the land. And, of course, Sturgeon's story.

'So the poor sod's had it!' exclaimed Ellie indignantly.

'Not altogether. If we can trace the man Atkinson, or Selkirk, we'll have something to work on. But our best bet's dead, of course. Lewis.'

'He was definitely in it?'

'Oh yes. None of the land *he's* supposed to have bought from Selkirk is registered to him. Poor Sturgeon got the lot. It's a good thing in a way.'

'Why?'

'Well, it's his only asset!' said Dalziel with a grin.

Ellie stood up clutching her handbag to her stomach.

'I was right about you,' she said clearly. 'You're a heartless old bastard.'

'Are you going?' asked Dalziel.

'Only to the loo. I'll have another gin when I get back.'

The Jockey's conveniences were misnamed. The gents

consisted of a small brick outhouse, a fearful journey on a rainy night. The ladies was inside at least, but at the end of a long, gloomy corridor at some remove from the drinking areas. In rural Yorkshire the age when women didn't drink and men used the wall outside was never far away.

Ellie was half-way down the corridor when she heard a noise behind her. She began to turn her head, but had only moved it through forty-five degrees when something cold and slimily smooth was thrust down over it. At the same time a knee was rammed jarringly against the base of her spine.

She drew her breath to scream and sucked in a mouthful of the cold and smooth material. She felt her handbag being removed for her unresisting fingers. For a moment the attacker's hand moved to her breast but the movement was acquisitive not exploratory and she felt her pendant being torn from her neck at the same time as she was pushed roughly sideways. Her shins struck something hard and metallic and she fell to the ground. A door clicked shut. Then everything was quiet except for her own spasmodic breathing.

It took her several minutes to realize that she was lying among the buckets in a cleaning store-cupboard, that over her head had been a plastic carrier-bag and, most mercifully, she was alone.

The door turned out to be without a handle on the inside and it took another five minutes to attract attention.

'You've been a long time,' said Dalziel.

'A funny thing happened to me on the way to the loo,' she began.

Pascoe had been sleeping well the second time round. Mrs Crowther's knock woke him from a rather soothing dream in which he was pursuing Pelman slowly round the Kruger National Park.

'I wouldn't have woken you,' said Mrs Crowther, 'only it's your young lady, Miss Soper, and if she don't speak to you she's going to think you're dead.'

It took several minutes to convince Ellie that he was in fact far from death's door, but finally she rather grudgingly accepted the fact.

'It's been a hell of a night so far then,' she said. 'I've been attacked too.'

'*What!*'

'Yes. A violent assault on my way to the loo in the Jockey. I'm probably dreadfully bruised. And then I was robbed.'

She told the story lightly, but Pascoe was extremely worried.

'Look, love, if they got your keys, you shouldn't stay there alone.'

'Oh, I'm not alone. I'm well protected.'

'Who by?' asked Pascoe with sudden suspicion.

'That very perfect gentle knight – who else? Superintendent Dalziel. He's hovering. I think he'd like a word.'

'Evening, Sergeant. Been in the wars again? Mr Backhouse'll be getting ideas we can't handle ourselves up here.'

'What's the form on this business, sir?' demanded Pascoe impatiently.

'God knows. Accident? Someone saw his chance in the pub, made a grab, then probably drove off home. No one noticed a thing of course!'

'What's been taken?'

'Precious little. A few quid. Toilet stuff. Her pendant. Nothing very valuable, Miss Soper assures me. It seems her men friends don't run to diamond bracelets and strings of pearls.' He laughed throatily. 'It hardly seems worth the effort, does it?'

'That's what worries me, sir.'

'Not to worry, Sergeant. Happens all the time, as we policemen know, eh?'

Dalziel was being diplomatic, Pascoe realized. His light-hearted tone was for Ellie's benefit. But all possible implications of the crime would be considered. Dalziel talked for some time longer, whether to reinforce his carefree role or whether because he believed in cramming every rift with ore it was hard to tell. He passed on the latest reports on the Sturgeon case.

Pascoe's reaction was the same as Ellie's.

'Poor sod!'

'Well, he does own the land. He'll probably be able to flog that for enough to stave off the mortgage sharks from his bungalow for a while. Then I suppose he'll either live off social security or go back to work. He sounds like one of the independent ones to me. No bloody charity and all that.'

'It's a hell of an age to be broke,' said Pascoe.

'Any age is. Lewis must've felt the same. The business was right up shit-creek. Cowley's claiming that things are far worse than he imagined. Says that his partner must have been milking money steadily out of the business account without him knowing.'

'Yes. I was there this morning.' reminded Pascoe.

'So you were. It seems longer. You didn't see that report we got in from that comic Scotsman, though. Jesus! the detail! Nothing new. A bit of a description of Lewis's girl-friend, obviously seen through lust-coloured spectacles. Very exotic she sounds, lots of make-up, revealing clothes, big knockers, just the job for these cold Highland nights.'

'Is Ellie still there, sir?' asked Pascoe reprovingly.

'Yes. She seems to find our constabulary business very amusing. You sure you're OK? Don't hang about after you've given your evidence, will you? We need you here. 'Bye, Sergeant.'

'Hello, love,' said Ellie. 'You take care, will you?'

'Is Dalziel still there?'

'No. He's diplomatically gone for a pee.'

'What the hell were you doing with him tonight? He's not been sticking his nose in again, has he?'

'Calm down, love,' laughed Ellie. 'No. *Au contraire,* as they say. He wants us to get married.'

'He wants what?'

'Us to marry. You and me, that is, not me and him!'

'Well thank God for that.'

'I told him I'd think about it.'

'Why not?' said Pascoe. He glanced at his watch. Just after eight. It seemed early still. He shook it to make sure it was still going.

'Are you still there?' said Ellie.

'Yes. Just checking the time.'

'Oh.' She sounded faintly disappointed. 'I won't keep you from your sick-bed, love. See you tomorrow.'

'Yes. Sure. Take care now.'

He felt much better, he realized. Only the slightest headache.

He replaced the receiver and looked at his watch again. He really did feel better.

Chapter 3

'Order! Order!' commanded Angus Pelman. 'We really must give John a hearing.'

'We give him a hearing every time,' said the Reverend Matthias. 'I propose an amendment whereby John give us a rest.'

'That's not very Christian of you, Vicar,' said John Bell. 'I wouldn't put that in the minutes, Marianne. We don't want the vicar, defrocked.'

'Order,' said Pelman. He sounded less than his usual forceful self, thought Marianne, glancing at her watch. This meeting seemed to be going on for ever. As usual the main delaying factor was John Bell's anti-pollution campaign.

'Sorry, Mr Chairman,' he said. 'As you know, I've been worried for some time about the stream that runs through the village. Its course is familiar to you. It runs down from Cobbett's farm, through Angus's woods, and then follows the line of the road to the village, passing behind the small development which contains my house. We are all on main drainage, but next to this development, just fifty yards up stream, are three older cottages which aren't. Now I have a contact in the Water Board and, with his help, I've been testing the water over the past week.'

He passed out some photostatted sheets.

'Look at this. Firm evidence of pollution.'

He smiled triumphantly. The others stared at the sheets.

'I'm sorry, John,' said Pelman, 'but this doesn't mean a damn thing to me.'

'Let me explain . . .'

'No. Don't bother. I'll get someone who understands to have a look at them.'

'But the evidence is there! Or if you don't believe in science, go and sniff at that water. Since it got warm again and the brook level dropped, it's begun to stink. There must be some deficiency in the sewage systems of those three cottages.' He pounded the table in emphasis.

'Why the cottages, John?' asked Matthias. 'The stream goes back all the way to Cobbett's farm.'

'Yes. But there's only Brookside on the other side of the track up to Angus's house. And anyway, I sampled the water in the woods as well for comparison.'

'You did what?' said Pelman coldly. 'You must have been trespassing, you realize that? I don't put up those signs for nothing.'

'For God's sake!' cried Bell. 'You can't stop people going into your bloody woods, you know. The days of the lord of the bloody manor are long past, Angus, and it's time you realized it.'

A confusion of voices arose, apparently far in excess of what might reasonably be produced by the six-member Amenities Committee.

Pascoe and Hartley Culpepper, drinking scotch in the adjoining room, had till this moment not openly admitted they were listening to the discussion through the not quite closed door. But now they smiled at each other and Culpepper said, 'It's comforting to know that Westminster is not the only place where democratic debate degenerates into riotous assembly.'

'I've never been,' said Pascoe. 'To Parliament, I mean. Do you spend much time in the corridors of power?'

'Sorry?'

'In your job, I mean. I see you're pulling out of Scotland, but Nordrill must need a pretty strong lobby even to get a toe-hold on the National Parks.'

'Yes. Yes, we do. Another drink, or won't your head take it?'

'I'll manage one more, I think.'

'Here you are,' said Culpepper, handing over a well-filled tumbler. 'Nice place Pelman has got, hasn't he? He's not a collector, of course. He's far too busy planting and ploughing and breeding and killing. But if your family stop long enough in one place, you're bound to collect one or two nice things.'

'I suppose so. Have you added to your porcelain lately?'

'Not a great deal, no. I was at Sotheby's last Wednesday for the Cantley collection sale. One or two very nice pieces, but a bit beyond my price, I'm afraid. Still, it was pleasant just to look. You can't have everything.'

'I thought it was the collector's creed that you can? The kind of collectors I deal with certainly believe it!'

'Perhaps I should emulate their methods,' said Culpepper.

It suddenly struck Pascoe that though Culpepper's collecting enthusiasm might stop a long way short of theft, he had just admitted that while Rose Hopkins was being buried, he had been wandering around Sotheby's feeding his passion.

Perhaps an hour snatched out of a hard day's work, he thought, trying to be charitable.

The door of the meeting-room opened and the committee members started coming through. They all sounded amiable enough now, observed Pascoe. Sam Dixon gave him a cheerful nod.

'Sorry to keep you waiting,' said Pelman. 'But duty

must be done. Alan, I don't think you've met Sergeant Pascoe. Alan Matthias, our padre.'

'Glad to meet you, Mr Pascoe. I was deeply distressed to hear of your murdered friends.'

Well, he's direct anyway, thought Pascoe. Marianne Culpepper joined them. She looked in surprise at her husband.

'Hartley, I didn't realize you were coming back from town tonight.'

'I did say I wanted to be here for the inquest tomorrow.'

'Did you? I don't recall.'

'Don't let me upset any plans you may have, my dear,' said Culpepper. 'Mother will look after me, I'm sure.'

'I'm sure she will. She looks after me very well while you're away.'

'How do you like it here?' said Pascoe to Matthias in order to fill the slight pause which followed this barely concealed gibe. 'Different from the valleys.'

'I don't know,' answered the vicar. 'There are dark tunnels beneath the surface wherever you go.'

'Alan is an allegorical moralist,' said Pelman. 'It's the Welsh disease. Hartley, you're very welcome of course, but was there something special?'

'Nothing important. I just felt like a stroll to get the London dust out of my lungs.'

'It must be tough at the top!' interjected John Bell. 'I must be off, Angus. Thanks for the drink. You'll look at that report I prepared, won't you?'

'I'll take it to bed with me,' promised Pelman. 'It may do what Hardisty's pills can't manage. Get me to sleep!'

A good area for insomniacs, thought Pascoe. He himself felt there would be little difficulty in getting to sleep. A cloud no bigger than a thumb-nail seemed to be floating in his mind. Another drink, and great billows of cumulus would obscure things completely. And if he hung around

211

too long, they might be torn apart by jags of lightning and made terrible by the noise of thunder.

'Would you excuse me too?' he said to Pelman.

'But the night's young. You've only just arrived.'

'Hush, Angus,' reproved Marianne. 'Mr Pascoe's had a nasty bang on the head today. It must have been a great shock for you. I hope they catch whoever did it.'

'So do I,' said Pascoe. 'Yes, I think I've overestimated my powers of recovery. Do forgive me. Good night. Good night.'

He left quickly, feeling very faint. It passed off in the evening air and he drove down the long track to the road following the tail-lights of Bell's car. Culpepper had at least turned the immediate approach to his house into a proper drive, but Pelman as a working land-owner obviously accepted bumps, ruts and puddles as part of the facts of existence. He drove carefully to preserve his car-springs, but the lining of his head proved much more sensitive to the lurchings of the vehicle and he had to stop before he reached the road.

Pelman's woods stretched darkly to his right, and to the left about fifty yards away he could see the lights of the group of cottages whose owners were so suspect in John Bell's eyes. Faintly among all the other night sounds he could hear the murmur of water. It must be the contentious stream. Presumably a culvert of some kind carried it beneath the ridge of land bearing the lane to Pelman's house.

He opened the car door and stepped out for a breath of fresh air. It was a disappointment, smelling none too fresh. But he did not feel like resuming his journey straightaway. He leaned back against the car-bonnet and let images crowd uncensored into his mind.

Places – Thornton Lacey, Birkham, Lochart. The dead – Rose, Timmy and Carlo, Matthew Lewis, Sturgeon almost. The missing – Colin, Archie Selkirk, Atkinson. The betrayed – Mrs Lewis, Culpepper. The enigmatic – Davenant, Etherege.

Etherege. Why did he think of Etherege? Because of Birkham. Too much was happening around Birkham. Too much? An antique shop which had sold a few quids' worth of stolen stamps. That wasn't much. What else? The Jockey, of course. Ellie had been attacked. Connection? Ellie was known to be connected with one fairly minor policeman, himself. Then she turns up with the big fish, Dalziel. Touching pitch and being defiled.

The image amused. He climbed back into his car, his mind working too hard now to be affected by Pelman's lane, and drove rapidly to Crowther's telephone.

'Why aren't you in bed?' demanded Ellie.

'I've just got up for a moment,' lied Pascoe. 'Listen, love. Dalziel said that one of the things you lost tonight was a pendant. Would that be the one I bought in Birkham?'

'Yes, I'm afraid it was,' said Ellie. 'Why do you ask?'

'I'm not sure,' said Pascoe.

'There's something rattling round your nasty suspicious mind,' said Ellie. 'Hang on. There's something I can tell you about it which might or might not help. That bit of rock certainly wasn't a local pebble like the chubby fellow in the shop said. One of the geologists at college was admiring it. I think he fancies me. Anyway he said it was some kind of bloodstone probably originating from South America. Which makes the local craftsman angle a bit fishy! They probably came in a job lot from Buenos Aires!'

'You are beautiful,' said Pascoe. 'Beautiful! I love you!'

* * *

'You must have been hit harder than you think,' said Dalziel. 'Let's get this straight. You reckon that Mrs Cottingley's collection of bits of stone has been passed to Etherege who polishes 'em, sticks 'em in a bracelet or whatever, and flogs them in his shop?'

'Why not? It'd make a perfect outlet for unidentifiable stuff. Or nearly unidentifiable.'

'Unidentifiable,' grunted Dalziel. 'You can't identify a lump of rock.'

'You can say wherever else it was picked up, it wasn't Yorkshire!'

'You might be able to, if you had it! And this is why you think your lass was attacked? For the pendant?'

'It's possible.'

'You've been watching too much telly,' said Dalziel. In the background, Pascoe could hear Dalziel's own television set blaring away, but diplomatically he said nothing.

'Well,' resumed Dalziel. 'If you're thinking it was Etherege as robbed your girl, you'd better think again.'

'I never said . . .'

'Because I called at his shop when I was on my way to meet Miss Soper. I had those stamps. Sturgeon wasn't able to say yea or nay about them, so I thought as I was passing I'd have a look in. Anyway, he wasn't there, but an old bird who looks after his house for him told me he was at a sale in Durham somewhere, not expected back till late.'

'It was just an idea,' said Pascoe dispiritedly. All their bright ideas seemed to be leading nowhere in this case. Dalziel's suggestion about a kennels being the source of information about empty houses had proved fruitless too. It was in fact true that all the people robbed had owned animals, but a variety of kennels were used and in at

214

least one case, Lewis's, the dog had been away on holiday with the family.

'Get some sleep,' advised Dalziel. 'I'll see you tomorrow.'

He replaced the receiver and stood in thought for a moment. The television raged in the neighbouring room, but the house still sounded empty. His stomach rumbled, reminding him of the inroads Grainger's diet was making on his flesh.

Pascoe's a good lad, he thought. He has his daft moments, but who doesn't? Most of what he said was worth thinking about. He looked at his watch. It was only quarter to ten. Worth a call.

Chapter 4

Thornton Lacey was lovely in the morning sunlight, and surprisingly quiet. Ellie glanced at her watch as she drove down the High Street. She was too late for the nine o'clock captains of industry. She realized she had been externalizing her own feelings of tension at the imminent inquest and had somehow expected the place to be as nervously taut as a Western Frontier town before the big shoot-out.

Pascoe met her outside Crowther's house and greeted her with a satisfyingly passionate kiss – satisfying not because she felt much like bed at the moment but as a reassurance of his physical well-being. For all that, he looked pale, and she examined the dressing on the back of his head as though it could tell her something about the nature of the wound beneath.

'I'm all right,' said Pascoe, who had in fact slept well until about six o'clock, when he had woken with his mind chaotic with thoughts which he had only begun to put into some kind of order. He had long since acquired the habit (most suggestively amusing to Ellie) of setting out his notebook and pencil on his bedside table every night so that intuitions of the night should not be sacrificed to indolence. It rested in his pocket now.

He led Ellie into the house.

'How about you?' he asked. 'That was an odd business.'

'Too true, I'm fine. Fat Dalziel had pumped so much gin into me that I slept like a log. He's quite a kind old sod, really. He rang me up again later to check that I was OK.

216

'Did he now? About quarter to ten?'

'That's right,' said Ellie surprisingly. 'Why do you ask?'

Pascoe began to laugh. It was a good sound so Ellie did not interrupt it, puzzled though she was.

'It's the thought of old Uncle Andy phoning about your health!' he explained. 'It's always business with that one.'

Quickly he described his own telephone conversation with Dalziel the previous night. Ellie was less than rapturous about the implied theory.

'You mean Etherege is a fence?'

'In a small way.'

'And he jumped me last night just to get that pendant back?'

'Well, not Etherege,' admitted Pascoe. 'He's probably got an alibi.'

'Ah, I see! A good friend of his, you mean, who just happened to think he'd do his mate a handy turn by putting a bag on my head and shutting me in a broom cupboard? All for an old pebble?'

'The pebble's the key,' said Pascoe, hastily retreating from the uncertain ground Ellie was challenging him on. Quickly he told her about Mrs Cottingley's collection of stones.

'Perfectly safe, really,' he concluded. 'But if you were the first to buy one and he then realized, as he did, that you were a copper's moll, it's the kind of thing that might niggle. So when he sees you cavorting with Detective-Superintendent Fat Dalziel, he decides to act on the spur of the moment.'

'Who? Not Etherege, you say. Who then?'

'Yes. There's the rub, I'm afraid,' said Pascoe thoughtfully. 'Who else would be sufficiently concerned? Only one answer. The guy who did the robberies. Which would mean he was in the Jockey last night.'

217

He laughed.

'Pity Dalziel didn't think of that. He could have lined all the customers up and made them pee in a kettle.'

'What?'

'Don't you remember I told you what this villain did? Well, we had the stuff tested and it turns out he's a diabetic. A slender lead, but a lead.'

'And he's also the man who murdered that estate agent? Lewis?'

'Probably.'

Ellie shuddered at the memory of the gloomy corridor in the Jockey. Something else connected with the Jockey which she ought to tell Pascoe nearly surfaced for a moment, then was gone.

'Perhaps I was lucky,' she said.

'Perhaps,' said Pascoe, putting his arm round her shoulder. 'I think it's nearly time to go.'

Dalziel felt lucky as he drove out to Birkham. If Pascoe were right and Etherege was doing a bit of fencing, Andrew Dalziel was the man to lean on him. He could be sympathetic. *People are bound to take advantage of a man in your position.* Promissory. *You tell us what you know and I'll see you all right. A nod's as good as a wink, eh?* Threatening. *There's a murder involved here, you know. Withholding information can get you ten years.*

But first he had to establish that this wasn't just something dreamed up by a man who'd been knocked on the head. He'd play the customer to start with. Have a look round. Size up the man.

He was quite looking forward to it.

It was about time he had a break. There was all that stolen property unrecovered, a murder unsolved, Sturgeon's forty thousand sunk without a trace – all these things somehow linked as well. One good break could settle the lot. Perhaps he was on his way to it now. He began to whistle a selection from *Oklahoma!* bursting into off-key song when he reached 'Oh what a beautiful morning!'

'I realize, Mr Backhouse, that it might not be desirable for you to give us a detailed account of your investigations into these tragic and terrible deaths, but insofar as anything you have discovered might relate directly to this present court's business, we would be grateful to hear of it.'

French's tone was reasonable, deferential almost, but the gaze he fixed on Backhouse over his reading spectacles had something of defiance in it.

Pascoe looked round the crowded schoolroom. The desks had all been stacked outside in the corridor, but it still bore the unmistakable signs of its normal, more innocent function. Children's paintings adorned the walls and a chart immediately behind Backhouse demonstrated that Celia was the tallest in the class, taller even than James and Antony. Poor Celia. He hoped that time would redress the balance for her.

Backhouse was explaining with his usual combination of efficiency and courtesy that he was not yet able to contribute very much officially to the proceedings.

Ellie nudged Pascoe.

'Where's Pelman?' she whispered.

He glanced round the room again. The Culpeppers were there; the Dixons, Bells, Hardistys; the sisters Langdale from the post office; Jim Piss Palfrey; Anton Davenant making notes, but no Pelman.

'He'll have work to do, I suppose. Why?'

'Nothing. Something I remembered. Hang on.'

French had finally succeeded in what had clearly been

his aim, to have the note found in the abandoned car introduced into the evidence.

'It has been established that this note is written in the hand of Colin Hopkins, husband of the deceased woman?'

'Yes,' said Backhouse.

'And that his fingerprints are on it?'

'Yes.'

'Thank you. It is not generally the practice of this court to have notes written in such circumstances read aloud, but in this case I think it may be in the public interest to depart from practice. Such a crime as this arouses feelings of horror and revulsion in everyone, but among those who live in proximity to the scene of the crime, it must also arouse trepidation and fear of repetition. It is the task of this court to allay such fears where possible.'

French coughed twice and began to read from the paper before him. Pascoe shut down his hearing and turned his thoughts elsewhere, but phrases kept on coming through . . . *here for ever, ever must I stay* . . . *a naked lover, bound and bleeding* . . . *all is calm in this eternal sleep* . . .

'Pope,' whispered Ellie.

'What?'

'Pope. The poet. He's quoting Pope.'

She was holding his hand tightly, and he felt she was trying to keep the words intoned by French in a dry, unemotive, literary context, far removed from the rain-lashed car bumping and skidding its way towards the stinking quarry pool.

'Oh, Peter,' she said. 'It's *Eloisa to Abelard!*'

She stood up and left. There was no outburst of tears, nothing dramatic at all. It was as if she had remembered an appointment elsewhere.

With an apologetic glance at French, Pascoe followed. He caught up with her in the playground.

220

'Don't you see,' she said. 'That poem would come to mind because of us. In some way he must have thought about us at the end.'

She clung to him, sobbing now. Pascoe held her close but could not enter into her mood of emotional abandonment.

'You mean, because we were coming for the week-end and one of his little jokes was to compare us with two medieval lovers, an eighteenth-century poem on the subject would come to mind after he'd murdered his wife, two close friends, and decided to commit suicide?'

'For God's sake, Peter, do you have to be so precise and analytical about everything,' she cried, pushing him away. But the tears had stopped.

'This poem, it's years since I looked at Pope, what form does it take?'

'Well, it's supposed to be a letter from the girl Eloisa after they've been separated. Peter Abelard was castrated, you knew that? She's in a nunnery or some such place, but the fire's still there. It's a very passionate poem.'

'A strange choice. Look, love, I want to push off for a while and work something out. Do you mind?'

One of Ellie's many virtues was that she knew when not to object.

'All right. I'm all right, I'll go back in now.'

'Fine. One thing. What are you going to say about Pelman?'

'Well, it's not about him really, not directly anyway. It's just that I remember something more about that holiday in Eskdale. That awful farmer who kept hanging round, the one who rented us the place? Well, he lived by himself and the locals in the pub said that his wife had run off with one of his farmhands a few years earlier. No one ever saw them again.'

Pascoe grasped the railings of the playground with both hands and stared unseeingly at the sunlit field on to which the school buildings backed.

'You're right,' he said. 'I remember. And didn't Colin, and Tim, I think, haunt him one night when they were a bit stoned? They dressed up in sheets and ran down the fellside behind his farmhouse as he was driving home.'

'That was it,' said Ellie, smiling widely. 'I remember.'

For a moment they were all alive again.

'I'll go now,' said Pascoe gently. 'See you later.'

'All right.'

She watched him stride athletically across the yard and through the gate. Something made her call after him, 'Take care!' but she didn't think he heard. Incongruously she now remembered what she should have told him about the Jockey. But it would keep. This morning had to be got through first.

'I don't know much about antiques,' said Dalziel, 'but I know what I like.'

'Really?' said Jonathan Etherege, a smile spreading over his round pleasant face. 'I can only hope you have an expensive lack of taste. Would you like to browse?'

'Aye,' said Dalziel, enjoying his fat philistine role. Role? he thought. I *am* a fat philistine!

But the thought merely added to his enjoyment.

'Been in the business long, Mr Etherege?' he asked, as he strolled around the antiques section of the shop checking the articles he saw against a mental list of stolen property. It was a matter of routine rather than hope.

'Long enough,' said Etherege. 'I started in the scrap business and worked my way down.'

'You're very frank,' said Dalziel. 'Why do you say *down?*'

'Half a joke.'

'And the other half?'

'Well, if I'm selling you a couple of hundredweight of lead-piping, you know the going price and either want it or don't. With this stuff everyone thinks in terms of value. It's not just a matter of so much a hundredweight.'

'I still don't follow why you said *down*,' grunted Dalziel, trying unsuccessfully to open the top drawer of a handsome Victorian desk. Etherege leaned over, pulled, and the drawer slid effortlessly open.

'Price is always above value, sir,' he said. 'So it must be down.'

'Too bloody clever for me,' said Dalziel. 'Still you sound like an honestly dishonest man. You like brass, eh?'

'I've been without it,' said Etherege. 'I won't be again if I can help it.'

'No. This all local work?'

They had moved into the craft section.

'A lot of it. Fancy a basket for your wife? Or a horse brass?'

'For my wife? Not very complimentary,' said Dalziel. He could see no sign of anything like the pendant Ellie had described. He began to poke among the ornaments displayed on a large wooden tray.

'Very nice,' he said. 'But I'd like something for the neck. No, not a collar either. A whatsit.'

'A pendant?' suggested Etherege. 'We have a couple here. A simple rather plain design, if you like that sort of thing.'

'No. No,' said Dalziel. 'Something a bit more decorative than that.'

'I'm sorry. We did have some rather nice ones with local stones in a ceramic setting, but, alas, they've all gone now,' answered Etherege. 'Such a pity.'

He knows, thought Dalziel suddenly. The sod knows.

He knows who I am and what I'm after. Shit! If he's that sharp, it's going to be difficult to touch him.

He looked at his watch. It might be worthwhile getting a search warrant and really turning this place over. But he doubted it.

Etherege was looking at his watch too.

'Will you excuse me a moment?' he said. 'Feel free to poke around as much as you like.'

Cheeky bastard, thought Dalziel, as he watched Etherege disappear into what looked like a small office behind the stamp display. He's probably gone off for his elevenses so I can convince myself there's nothing here.

The thought of his usual mid-morning coffee and two doughnuts set his stomach rumbling. He'd even been reasonably successful these past few days in cutting down on the drink, and the cumulative effect was not one he could foresee himself becoming resigned to.

He looked around the converted barn in frustrated distaste. His own tastes, so far as they could be called tastes, in living styles were what was generally know as old-fashioned. But that was because they had been formed by the material and moral aspirations of a working-class family in the 'twenties. This self-conscious pursuit of the aged was not something he understood. He liked the old oak table off which he ate his lonely breakfast (and precious little else since his wife had left him) because it was his and had been his parents'. Probably his grandparents' too; he had no idea how old it was. It didn't signify. But if he had to get another, it would be something new. This stuff was just second-hand. Evidence of your own family's use and misuse was one thing; other people's scars, scratches and grime was something quite different.

No, there was nothing for him here, either profession-

224

ally or personally. He turned to go, then on impulse went through the stamp section and pushed open the office door. He intented only to leave Etherege with some kind of thinly veiled threat. Dalziel was a man who did not like to feel mocked.

The significance of what he saw when he opened the door took a moment to sink in. Etherege was sitting at a table with his jacket off and his left shirt-sleeve rolled up. In his right hand he held a hypodermic syringe. He looked up angrily at the intrusion.

'Please wait outside,' he said sharply. Dalziel didn't move. 'It's all right,' said Etherege, still sharp, but mocking now as well. 'I'm not having a fix. It's merely my insulin shot.'

'You're a diabetic,' said Dalziel, stepping into the room. 'Well, well, well.'

He smiled broadly. This was the morning of the lucky break, after all. He had had things the wrong way round. Etherege wasn't merely the greedy fence. This was where the action was worked out in detail. It made much more sense.

'Is it a crime?' asked Etherege. 'Better call a policeman.'

He really did think he was sitting pretty, thought Dalziel. He believes we can't touch him. Perhaps we can't, but we'll have a bloody good try.

He leaned over the antique-dealer and picked up the insulin pack which lay on the table.

'You know, Mr Etherege,' he said, 'you shouldn't go around peeing in other people's kettles.'

Etherege became absolutely still. It was almost possible to see his mind rushing to a realization of what Dalziel meant.

'The world is full of diabetics,' he said with an effort at

225

coolness. Dalziel noted the effort, and looking grim, he placed his hand heavily on the man's left shoulder.

'Jonathan Etherege,' he intoned. 'I must ask you to accompany . . . Jesus!'

He leapt back, sending a chair, a card-index and an electric kettle crashing to the floor, and gazed at his wrist. Dangling grotesquely from it was the hypodermic which Etherege had thrust violently upwards. The sight made him nauseous and quite unfit to deal with the attack that followed. Etherege's knee caught him in the stomach and drove him back into the sharp edge of a filing cabinet. Memories of the potential – and realized – violence of the man they had so long been looking for mingled fragmentarily with black shapes of pain which were trying to join together and bring complete obscurity.

There were a few seconds' respite, enough for sight impressions to return, albeit blurred and wavy. Etherege, he realized, hadn't given up the good work by any means. He had merely been casting around for something to kill him with. The answer to his problem was a large pot dog. A King Charles spaniel. Staffordshire-ware. Seven pounds a pair. Dalziel's grandmother had had a couple till the young Andrew had taken the head off one with a cricket ball. His mind threw up the absurd thought that this might be its mate come to exact a terrible vengeance.

Later he said that he was given strength by the thought of the amusement it would give his enemies to hear he'd been done to death with a china dog. Now it was just the instinct for survival. He drove himself forward under the descending dog, wrapped his arms around the dealer and grappled him to the floor. For a moment he thought that his mere weight superiority was going to be enough to keep him there, but Etherege's outstretched hands came into contact with the electric kettle and he brought it crashing round into the side of Dalziel's head. Stunned, he could not prevent himself from being rolled over, but Etherege's first kick acted as a restorative and when the man drove his foot a second time towards Dalziel's rib-cage, the fat man caught him by the ankle and pulled him off balance. He fell backwards through the open door into the shop.

They both rose at the same time and as they looked at each other they knew that their roles had reversed. Through Dalziel's being a tide of terrible anger was running fast and free, driving out the aches and pains. Casually he pulled out from his wrist the remains of the hypodermic and dropped them to the floor.

'Now, Mr bloody Etherege,' he said, and stepped forward.

Etherege turned and ran, but his over-filled shop hindered rapid movement. The ceramic display-case went crashing down as he blundered past. A grandfather clock by Barraclough fell into Dalziel's path and chimed its last as the fat man trod carelessly on the disembowelled works.

Etherege, realizing he could not make the door, took to the heights, bounding desperately across chairs and tables, cabinets and bureaux. The late Victorians took it well, but much damage was inflicted on earlier pieces, especially when Dalziel followed.

His simple unambiguous aim now was to hurt Etherege. He did not know where this incredibly violent desire stemmed from, nor did he care to investigate. It was as if the repressed violence of three decades in the police force had finally asserted its right to exist.

Etherege knew it and the knowledge made him incred-ibly agile. As Dalziel cumbersomely surmounted a mahog-any dresser, the dealer skipped lightly across a set of genuine fake Chippendale dining-chairs and made for the door which opened as he reached it. A man and woman stood there, blocking the exit and gazing in amazement at the scene before them. Etherege perforce hesitated and next moment Dalziel was on him.

He pushed him across a table and began driving blows into his body and face. The man offered no defence, hardly seemed to be conscious.

'Look here,' said the newly arrived customer, stepping forward, but stepping more rapidly back when he saw Dalziel's expression.

Something deep inside, however, was telling him he must stop. This was wrong. He had never lost his temper like this in his life.

There was a disturbance behind him and someone seized him by the shoulder.

'Get the police!' said a man's voice and he felt himself being pulled back from Etherege.

The fury came back. He turned and saw an indignant-looking man in his late thirties. Dalziel did not care for the look or the touch of him. He balled his fist and smacked into the stranger's face with all the strength he could muster.

Chapter 5

The first thing Pascoe did on reaching Brookside Cottage this time was to search the place. Lounge, dining-room and scorch-marked kitchen; then upstairs through the bedrooms, bathroom and junk-room. When he was satisfied that he was alone, he returned to the lounge and began to run his eye along the bookshelves. What he wanted wasn't there, and he turned away in disappointment and stood thoughtfully looking around.

'The bureau!' he said aloud. It was a nice piece of furniture and when he found it was locked he felt some compunction about breaking into it. But one thing he had learned from Dalziel was that once you launched yourself on a course of action, you followed it through with force and determination to no matter how bitter an end.

The lock yielded easily to the knife borrowed from the kitchen. He nodded in satisfaction as he picked up the book and pushed back on the writing-paper ledge. Quickly he thumbed through it and nodded again. It was always nice to be right. He'd learned that from Dalziel too. Or perhaps what the fat man had said was that it was nice to be always right. He was an egotistical bastard. But Pascoe wished he were here now.

He sat down for a while and applied his mind to the problem. It wasn't a problem at all really, he finally admitted. The facts as he saw them suggested a theory. It was a theory. It was a theory he could easily test. It would also be easy to pick up the phone and ring Backhouse, but that wasn't the way. Not this time.

With a sigh he rose and went out into the garden. He stood beside the sundial for a moment and looked down. The carpet in the dining-room still had the dark, disfiguring stains on it, but out here rain and dew and sunlight and the cycle of growth had left no trace on the thrusting green shoots.

His shadow was on the dial and he stood aside to see where the point of the gnomon fell, but an edge of white cloud trailed across the sun momentarily and he did not wait until it cleared. Instead he went down to the stream and with little difficulty leapt across it into Pelman's woods. The water was slow-moving and not very deep, but beautifully clear for all that. Long water-grasses wavered in it, pointing downstream, and he followed their directions. For twenty or thirty yards it was possible to walk parallel with the stream, but then the trees began to close in on either side, and the tangle of briar and whin forced him either to move farther out into the woods or to descend the banks of the stream itself. Unhesitatingly he chose the latter.

At first he attempted to stay dry-shod by treading carefully along a narrow margin, but this soon disappeared and after the first immersion of his feet he bothered no more but trod boldly on.

Soon the end of his journey was in sight, the ridge of land which carried the track up from the road to Pelman's house. The culvert which carried the stream under the track was visible as a dark semi-circle above the water's surface which sparkled in even the few rays of sunshine penetrating the vault of trees.

Pascoe stopped about thirty yards away. A tremendous lethargy seemed to have gripped his leg-muscles, as though the stream had bathed his feet in some slow poison. The woods were full of noises which asserted themselves now that the splashing of his progress down the stream had ceased. Birds called sharply, musically, warningly, languorously; leaves rustled in the breeze, still a rich sound though the parchment edge of autumn was beginning to be heard; a bee murmured by; and somewhere in front of him he heard, or imagined he heard, the buzzing of many flies.

Then came a sound he hadn't imagined. Something moved among the trees to his left. He crouched low against the bank and remembered walking up the lane to Culpepper's, hearing the passage of his pursuer through the night.

Cautiously he raised his head above the level of the bank and glimpsed a figure moving slowly towards the stream. Too quick a glimpse for identification, but long enough to recognize the object the man carried before him, carefully, like in a Holy Day procession.

A shotgun.

Pascoe began to move. It was foolish. It was bound to cause noise. But it was beyond him to lie quietly against the bank while the gun-bearer approached. After a few steps, he realized that even the little care he was exercising was just a waste of time. The noise he was making sounded tremendous, like a herd of cows splashing through a ford. He began to run in real earnest.

'Who's there?' called a voice.

He had to get out of the water-course. The trees on the voice's side were thinner, but he didn't fancy clambering up there. Instead he tore at the sallows which grew like a fence on the other side and pulled himself up.

'Stop!' commanded the voice.

If, thought Pascoe, if once I can get a few nice trees between me and him, if once I can head him down to the road, if once I can get back to the village, that'll be it; no lone investigations for me, I swear it, God, make a bargain, please, if once. . .

Behind him the shotgun spoke, a curiously undramatic noise, something whipped along the side of his head, he turned and slid slowly back down the bank into the water.

On the opposite bank, about thirty yards upstream, the smoking gun in his hands, was Angus Pelman.

Was that one barrel of two? wondered Pascoe. Will he have to reload?

But it didn't matter. For gloriously, wonderfully, there were other voices in the woods and Backhouse appeared behind Pelman, and Ellie came leaping into the water towards him with love and terror in her face.

Curiously, he did not feel too bad till they told him that he had been hit by a small branch splintered from a tree by the shotgun blast. It was then he recalled what he was doing here.

'If you go on up to the culvert,' he told Backhouse slowly and clearly, 'and look inside, I think you'll find Colin's body.'

Then he knelt on the soft cushion of rich leaf mould and was very sick.

'You know,' said Dr Hardisty, 'dressing your wounds is becoming a habit.'

'Yes,' said Pascoe.

'I'm normally a very discreet kind of man, minding my own business,' continued the doctor. 'But do you mind me, on this occcasion asking what the hell's going on?'

They were back at the Crowthers'. Pascoe had not the least desire to talk further to the doctor, and he shot an appealing glance at Ellie who politely but firmly took the man to the door.

'You did that well,'Pascoe said.

'I know,'she said.

They spoke no more for a while. They had stayed in the woods until one of Backhouse's men armed with a

232

torch had penetrated the dark barrel of the culvert. When his shout of mingled discovery and aversion had reached them, they had gone away and let themselves be driven back to the village.

'How did you know?' asked Ellie finally.

'I began to wonder. There were lots of things, lots of "ifs". If Colin didn't commit suicide, then someone wanted us to think he did. If someone wanted that, then presumably it was to direct suspicion from the real murderer. If it was worth planting the car and the note, then Colin must be dead. If Colin was dead, then his body must be hidden somewhere. And so on. Today when you said that those quotations came from *Eloisa to Abelard* I was suddenly certain. It was one of Colin's gags. Rather, it was going to be. You didn't see the bedroom, did you?'

'No,' said Ellie.

Briefly Pascoe described it, the pillow decoration, the sign.

'He'd been going to add something else. And with his passion for aptness, he picked on Pope's poem. I found a complete Pope in the bureau. All the lines in the so-called suicide note had been marked. Just listen to the stuff! *Soft intercourse. I come, I come! He best can paint 'em who can feel 'em most.* Not the outpourings of despair, but all lovely dirty double meanings! Probably they did it together, Rose and Colin; Timmy and Carlo too. But he never got any further than jotting a few things down.'

'Why?'

'Oh, nothing dramatic. Dinner perhaps. Or they got a bit drunk. Something. Later of course, it happened.'

She was trembling, he realized. He stood up, felt dizzy for a second, then crossed to her and put his arms around her.

'But why, Peter?' she demanded. 'Why?'

'Perhaps Pelman will tell us that,' he answered.

'You might have been killed too,' she said.

'Perhaps. But I had to go up that stream. I kept on remembering that fellow, Bell, going on and on about the water, about something polluting the stream. He said things had suddenly got much worse in the past few days. And I thought of the heat and the time it takes for . . . well, it filled my mind and I had to see.'

He laughed uneasily and without humour.

'You know, in a way, I'm glad I was interrupted before I reached the culvert.'

'I'm glad Pelman was interrupted before he reached you,' said Ellie. 'Backhouse asked where you were after the inquest and seemed very keen to get after you. He must have suspected something.'

'What happened at the inquest, by the way?' inquired Pascoe.

'What?' said Ellie. 'Of course, you won't have heard. They brought a verdict of murder against Colin.'

Some time later Pascoe was standing looking down at the water-ravaged face of Colin Hopkins. Curiously he felt very little, as if the day's events had been successfully cathartic.

'Yes,' he replied to Backhouse's question. 'Yes. I can identify him. Colin Hopkins.'

'Fine,' said Backhouse, and the concealing sheet was drawn over the face once more.

'This makes French look a little foolish,' said Pascoe as they left the mortuary. He felt the need to nurture his normality with a little idle chatter. Something was over. His interest now would be professional. And distant. He was ready to go home.

'Yes,' said Backhouse. He was rather withdrawn, even for him. Pascoe felt there was something he wanted to say, but was equally certain that it was not going to be said.

Perhaps he wants to thank me for my help, he thought. But he knew it wasn't that. And he wondered again why the man wasn't himself interrogating Pelman.

'You'll keep me in touch, sir?' he asked.

'Of course. Though you will remember you are just a witness, Inspector? Congratulations on your promotion, by the way.'

'Thank you.'

'We'll go back to the station now and you can sign your statement. You're heading back to Yorkshire straightaway?'

'Yes. Miss Soper too. We're driving in convoy. Unless you want me to stay for anything else?'

'No. I don't think so.'

They drove back slowly through the busy streets, a strong contrast with the quiet thoroughfares of Thornton Lacey.

Ellie was waiting in Backhouse's office at the station. A constable appeared with his typewritten statement, handed it to him and murmured something in Backhouse's ear. The superintendent left the room as Pascoe quickly scanned through the statement and signed it.

'Ready, love?' he said.

'Ready,' said Ellie. He took her hand.

At the door they met Backhouse looking perturbed.

'Goodbye, sir,' said Pascoe. 'We're on our way.'

'Inspector,' said Backhouse, 'I'm afraid I've got some rather strange and disturbing news for you. I've just been checking on a rumour which one of my sergeants had picked up. Do you know a man called Burne-Jones?'

'I know of him,' said Pascoe.

'Well, Mr Dalziel has been arrested for assaulting him and breaking his jaw!'

235

'Poor old Dalziel,' said Ellie as they headed to the car-park. 'Do you think he's flipped at last? Oh, Peter.'

'Yes?'

'Something I remembered. It got submerged in all this and it's probably irrelevant anyway. You said something about a diabetic? Well, Etherege, when he came and talked to us in the Jockey that day, he was holding a bottle of tonic water specially prepared for diabetics. Could it be important?'

Pascoe stopped and turned back to the police station.

'It might,' he said. 'I'd better get them to pass the word. Better to be safe than sorry!'

Chapter 6

The first person Pascoe met on his return was Inspector Headingley who laughed heartily at his anxious inquiry.

'No, he's not in the cells. He's upstairs. He'll be pleased to see you. We got your message about Etherege. Very grateful Mr Dalziel was!'

He found the fat man in his office watching a couple of detective-constables unpack the contents of several cardboard boxes which had a ripe fishy smell.

'Welcome back,' said Dalziel. 'A bit late, aren't you?'

'Things happened,' said Pascoe.

'And here. If you'd had your flash of insight a bit earlier, you might have saved a great deal of pain.'

For one moment Pascoe thought the Dalziel was referring sympathetically to Burne-Jones. Then he held up a bandaged right hand.

'I broke my bloody thumb,' he said. 'And I found out about Etherege the hard way.'

'He's our man then?'

'Certainly. He stuck a bloody great hypodermic needle into me to prove it. That turned out to be a mistake. Evidently a dose of insulin can make a non-diabetic irritable to the point of irrationality, particularly if he's got an empty gut. Me, I'm on a short fuse at best. And I've been starving myself for days. So when Burne-Jones grabbed me from behind, I hammered him.'

'He's hurt?'

'Nothing much. A cracked jaw. It was quite comic.' The fat man laughed heartily at the memory, pressing himself against a desk edge to get a free scratch on his

237

shaking buttocks. 'There was an old couple there. They called the police and an ambulance. A right officious little snot turned up. He didn't know me and I was still far from normal! So the silly bugger arrested me! It was soon sorted out when the quack had a look at me and heard what had happened. There may still be an inquiry, but I'll survive.'

'I'm sure,' said Pascoe looking with interest at the assortment of articles the DCs were taking out of the fishy boxes. Some of it he recognized, though seeing it for the first time.

'You found some of the loot then?' he said. 'At Etherege's?'

'Not on your life! He's not daft, that one. No, we had a stroke of luck. Burne-Jones was in on it too. Not actively, he claims, but we'll see about that. Anyway, my right hook softened him up a lot, and when he heard his partner had got himself under a murder charge while he was on holiday, it was only his broken jaw that slowed him down to a gabble! And guess what? You remember my little idea about the kennels?'

Suddenly everything jumped together in Pascoe's mind. He sniffed the fishy odour and nodded.

'Jim Jones, the cat-meat man!' he said. 'Who is he? His brother?'

'Cousin,' said Dalziel grumpily. 'It's getting to be a nasty habit, this being wise after the event. You're right, though. Burne-Jones is really just plain Jones. Jim Jones travels round a dozen or more kennels, delivering food. Plenty of chance to glance at the list of inmates. I believe a lot of the silly sods put placards with name and address of owner on the bloody animals' cages! He'd pass it on. His cousin and Etherege would pick out what they thought was worthwhile and do it. Easy.'

'What about disposal?' asked Pascoe.

238

'Etherege and Burne-Jones probably did quite a bit themselves through the trade. But we reckon the really hot stuff was moved through a third man. Burne-Jones clammed up here. I think he was regretting talking so much and his jaw was beginning to hurt. But he said enough. Jones-the-cat-meat claims to know nothing about him except that he exists. He sounds to me like a middle-man who knows interested and not too curious purchasers for a certain kind of item. At a signal from Etherege he comes along and pokes around in the latest haul.'

'Any chance of getting on to him?' asked Pascoe, looking sadly at the little array of items which seemed to match stuff stolen from Sturgeon's house. There was little of real worth there. And no sign of the most valuable article, the old man's stamp-album.

'A good one, I reckon,' said Dalziel gleefully. He picked up a small diary from a desk top.

'As you'd expect, there was precious little at Etherege's shop, but this we did find. His diary. Nothing incriminating, but look at this.'

He jabbed his forefinger at the page for February 8th, All that was written there was a time. 11 A.M. He flicked over the pages. March 1st 6 P.M. March 23rd 1 P.M. April 20th 9.30 A.M.

'And so it goes on,' he said.

'So?' asked Pascoe.

'So all these dates fall around the periods during which we know the break-ins happened. On the couple of the occasions when we know the exact date, these dates in the diary come three days later. Now I reckon these are appointments with his distributor, someone who would take the more valuable and identifiable stuff away. It's clever, really. You see, generally the stuff would be moved before the house-owners came back from holiday and even discovered they'd been robbed. No risk!'

'I see,' said Pascoe thoughtfully. 'Now Lewis's house was done last Monday, which would mean there should have been a meeting last Wednesday or Thursday.'

'Well done!' said Dalziel condescendingly. 'One was made for Wednesday, it's been crossed out. See. Now it seems it was remade for this morning, but see, it's been crossed out again.'

'They were having difficulties. Perhaps it was just as well, sir. Even with insulin, you might have found it hard to take on three of them.'

'Very funny,' said Dalziel. 'Tomorrow morning I'm going to be alone though. And there'll only be one.'

'Sorry?' said Pascoe. Then it dawned on him. 'You mean that . . ?'

'That's right, Inspector. 10 A.M. Tomorrow. Care to come along?'

'Excuse me, sir,' said one of the detective-constables.

'Yes, Ferguson?'

The youngster pointed at by far the largest group of articles.

'This lot seems to have come from the Lewis house, sir. It's almost all there. They can't have had time to dispose of it.'

Dalziel gave Pascoe his mock awe-stricken look.

'The future's safe, Inspector!' he said.

The young man was unperturbed. He picked up an ornately inlaid cedarwood box of Oriental origin.

'There's some papers in here, sir. They look interesting.'

They were. Matthew Lewis had felt the need to keep a detailed financial record of his Scottish transactions. It was all here. The amount paid for the Callander land by the mysterious Archie Selkirk, the sum (more than twenty times larger) paid by Sturgeon for the same land, details of solicitor's fees, hotel and other expenses for 'A'

240

('Atkinson', said Dalziel) and, most interestingly of all, expenses to be set against gross profit by 'C'.

'Well now. This could be useful to the fraud boys,' said Dalziel, rubbing his hands. 'Certainly it should stand up nicely in court.'

'Court?' said Pascoe, puzzled.

'Yes. When Sturgeon sues Lewis's estate, as I presume he's going to. There wasn't much before, you know.'

'It might establish something else as well,' said Pascoe, pointing at the 'C'.

Dalziel shrugged.

'I doubt it. There's precious little in a name, and there's bugger all in an initial. No. If Cowley was in on this deal, it's going to take more than this to trip him up. There's been a lot of quiet checking going on and there's nowhere obvious that he's got forty thousand stacked away. Anyway, what the hell would his job have been? I can't imagine Lewis cutting him in for love.'

Pascoe was reluctant to give up. He studied the papers again.

'There's something else here,' he said. 'Or something not here. Look, sir. At "C"'s expenses. Right? Now what's missing?'

'Selkirk's expenses,' interrupted Ferguson brightly. 'Which could mean "C" and Selkirk are the same person.'

'And I used to think *you* were bright, young and horrid,' said Dalziel to Pascoe. 'All right. But you realize this cuts out Cowley altogether?'

'Why, sir?' asked Ferguson. Pascoe did not need to ask. In fact he answered.

'Because not only does Cowley deny he's ever been anywhere near Lochart, on the week-end Sturgeon actually met Selkirk he's got a nice alibi.'

'Nor does he fit Sturgeon's description,' said Dalziel.

'Still, we never showed him a picture of Cowley, did

we? Wasn't there one in the *Evening News* bit on Lewis's murder? Ferguson, cut along and see if you can dig a copy up. Has Sturgeon been moved up from Doncaster yet?'

'Yes, they reckoned he was up to being transferred to the General today,' said Dalziel.

'Good. Then we'll go and see him.'

'Will we?' asked Dalziel. 'I suppose we will. Do you know, I think that injection of insulin did me good. I used to have these delusions that I was a detective superintendent in authority over all kinds of people. Strange, wasn't it?'

He left the room, shaking his great bull-head.

'What are you grinning at?' said Pascoe to Ferguson. 'Go and find that newspaper and be quick about it!'

Sturgeon, having decided to recover, was recovering apace. He was sitting up in bed, surrounded by flowers and fruit, and there were the beginnings of a healthy colour in his cheeks. He greeted them warmly, like old friends.

'Everyone's been very good. To Mavis too. That's what's best,' he said when they'd settled down, Dalziel in the bedside armchair and Pascoe on the edge of the bed.

'We've brought you something too,' said Pascoe. He began to exhibit the contents of the box.

'Aye, that's mine. That too. And that. Aye, it's all ours. What about the stamps?'

'I'm sorry,' said Pascoe gently. 'No stamps.'

'No? Well, I reckon they'd get rid of 'em quick because they were valuable, eh? Not to worry. Does this mean you've got him as done it, then?'

'We think so, Mr Sturgeon. Now I'd like you to look carefully at this picture.'

242

Pascoe produced an envelope and from it took a piece of newspaper which he passed over.

'No,' said Sturgeon. 'Vaguely familiar. You know. Like I might have passed him in the street or something.'

'Try this,' said Pascoe. He took out a ball-point and sketched in the spectacles and shaggy moustache Sturgeon had mentioned in his description of Archie Selkirk.

Sturgeon looked at it puzzled.

'It's his hobby,' said Dalziel kindly.

'Does that look anything like the man Selkirk?' asked Pascoe desperately. Dalziel groaned at the leading question.

'Aye. A bit,' said Sturgeon cautiously. 'But if you did the same to yourself, lad, you'd look like him too, I reckon!'

In the hospital lift, Dalziel looked at Pascoe assessively.

'You've been hit on the head twice,' he stated, referring for the first time to the twin stripes of plaster adorning Pascoe's head.

He began to tell the superintendent what had happened, but Dalziel stopped him.

'I rang Mr Backhouse after your interesting message about Etherege's drinking habits came through. He seemed disappointed I wasn't in the Tower of London. But he told me all about your day.'

Pascoe was touched by the fat man's solicitude for a moment.

'If I'd been Backhouse, I'd have torn you to shreds,' he went on. 'You think this chap Pelman's your man?'

'He could be,' said Pascoe, not wanting to sound too certain of himself.

'Aye. Backhouse seemed none too happy either,' said Dalziel to his surprise. 'Anyway, you've had a hard day. Don't start cutting corners by trying to force everything to fit your own notions. Forget Cowley. Have an early night.'

'I think I might do,' agreed Pascoe.

'You do. You need your rest, sergeant. Sorry, *Inspector*. Now you've been promoted I suppose I should call you by your first name. The accolade, eh?'

They had come in their own cars. In the car-park Dalziel clapped him on the shoulder.

'Get yourself off home now,' he said. 'Straight to kip. Good night, Paul.'

He strode away powerfully.

'My name's Peter,' called Pascoe after him, but he didn't think he heard.

His plans for an early night did not last long. The phone was ringing when he entered his flat. It was Ellie, who was reacting very differently to the trying events of the day.

'Peter, if your head feels up to it, I'd like to go somewhere nice and bright and noisy, and have a big meal with a bit of music.'

'That sounds like the Dick Turpin,' he said, referring to the biggest and brightest of the night-spots which had erupted locally in the past five or six years as sophistication crept north.

'That'll do,' said Ellie. 'I feel like getting a little bit high.'

The Dick Turpin was booming even this early in the week and they were lucky to get a table. A five-piece band beat its own original trail through the current hit-parade and the small dance-floor was awash with shuddering flesh.

'Let's dance,' said Ellie as they waited for their prawn-cocktails to arrive.

'This is a side of your character you've cleverly kept

concealed,' said Pascoe as he followed her reluctantly to the edge of the arena.

Fortunately after a couple of minutes the musicians either relented or became exhausted and the tempo decelerated to a dreamily slow shuffle. Ellie hung close so that Pascoe was almost carrying her round.

'What happens now, love?' she asked suddenly.

'What do you mean?'

'It's not really over yet, is it? You know, driving home from Thornton Lacey, I half imagined it was. But now I see it's nowhere near. I mean, there's everything still; investigation, trial, appeal; it just goes on. It's only in stories that everything stops when you get your murderer.'

And it's only in stories you can be certain you've got him, thought Pascoe. But he didn't speak.

'I'll never get them out of my mind,' Ellie went on. 'At one moment on that Friday night they were there, all four of them. Happy, a bit tight, certain they had each other. Then bang! it was all gone.'

'Shall we sit down, love?' asked Pascoe.

'No. I like this. I'm OK, I promise. Peter,' she said drawing back a little from him, 'it's made me realize how much I need the illusion of permanence. Let's get married. Or shack up together. I don't mind which, only I suppose being married wins more friends and influences more people in your business. What do you say?'

The band had a quick recovery rate. Without warning they burst into a new chaos of sound and Pascoe would have found it difficult to make an audible reply. But in fact he made no effort to do so.

His attention was fully concentrated on the far corner of the dance-floor. There, his face flushed with effort, eyes gleaming, mouth set in a twisted smile, body snapping back and forth like a rutting ape, was James Cowley.

But it was his partner who really caught the eye, with

her long red hair, large sensual mouth and deep-cut dress which concealed hardly a square inch of her breasts as they shook mightily in the exertions of the dance.

Pascoe's first thought was that she fitted perfectly the albeit sketchy description of the woman who sometimes accompanied Lewis to Lochart.

His second thought was that this was not the only reason for her familiarity.

And his third thought which set the jackpot showering into his amazed mind was that beneath the fiery hair, the bright make-up and the clinging dress was the dowdy, retiring personage of the firm's senior secretary, and the better half of Cowley's Scottish alibi, Marjory Clayton.

Pascoe played it very cunning, much to Dalziel's later approval and Ellie's present distress. He escorted her quickly back to their table, picked up their bits and pieces and dragged her away, not without protest, from their approaching prawns.

'There's someone I don't want to meet,' he explained.

'Why? Who? I thought criminals were supposed to hide from the law, not the other way. And what about my dinner?'

'We'll go somewhere else. And the answer's *yes*.'

'I don't want to go anywhere else. What answer?'

'To your question. Now where shall we go?'

'Oh. In that case, I'm not hungry.'

They had fish and chips in the car a couple of hours later.

Marjory Clayton, back to her Ugly Duckling plumage, was picked up the following morning as she left for work. She was more than happy to go down to the station to help with their inquiries into poor Mr Lewis's death, but shouldn't she let Mr Cowley know she was going to be late? Some of the warmth left her smile when she was

246

assured Mr Cowley was going to be too busy to notice her absence.

And the smile itself disappeared when Dalziel, wearing his most unsmiling expression, greeted her by slamming down a notepad on the table before her and bellowing, 'Right! Quick as you like! I want details of the account where you've got Sturgeon's forty thousand. Every second you waste now could mean a month on your sentence.'

It took two attempts for her to write it legibly.

Pascoe had a tougher job with Cowley who refused to be prised way from his office and very rapidly became very irate. Finally he picked up his telephone and started dialling. Solicitor? wondered Pascoe. But he was wrong.

'I have had more than enough of this badgering and I intend to have a word with your superior,' snapped Cowley.

'Dalziel,' said Pascoe.

'What?'

'Mr Dalziel,' he repeated, and sat poker-faced as Cowley got through with remarkable speed and launched into a not very elegant series of complaints. Finally he finished and with an air of triumph passed the phone over to Pascoe.

'He wants a word with you.'

'Pascoe? Listen, the girl's talking so fast, it's taxing Ferguson's shorthand. The gist is she was in love with Lewis, didn't know he was doing anything dishonest ha! ha!, was happy to do him a favour by banking the money in a little account she had opened in Leeds. She denies any knowledge of Cowley's Selkirk act, but she's lying. She does agree that it might have been a week earlier that they did the accounts last May. Says she could have got mixed up with the Spring Bank holiday and Whit! We've chatted to the Collinwood girl who agrees. She's so thick she'll agree with anything! Bring Cowley in, will

247

you? Give him a fright if you like. Then shut him up till I get back.'

'Sir?'

'I've got an appointment with Etherege's leg-man, remember? Sorry you won't be able to make it. I'll be back by eleven. Cheers.'

Pascoe put the phone down quietly.

'Right,' said Cowley. 'I'm sorry to have had to do that, but you really must learn. . .'

Pascoe ignored him and stood up.

'James Cowley, you are not obliged to say anything at this time, but I must warn you that anything you do say will be taken down and may be used in evidence. I would be grateful if you would accompany me to the station, now, where I believe you may be able to help in our inquiries.'

'This is outrageous,' said Cowley. But he didn't sound as if he believed it.

Dalziel did not get back until eleven-thirty, not in the best of moods.

'No luck?' asked Pascoe.

'No. Not a bloody soul went near the shop all morning. They must have heard.'

'Unless it wasn't the shop, sir. We just have a note of a time, not a place.'

'Aye. I thought of that too. But the best I could do was keep Jones-the-cat-meat's store-house watched as well. Nothing. And I had a couple of lads get details of everyone who stopped in Birkham between ten and eleven. All three of them, all looking for a cup of coffee. One of them was a Methodist Minister!'

He held out a sheet of paper as if determined to prove the existence of such an extraordinary creature.

Pascoe glanced casually at it, then with more interest.

'What's up?' asked Dalziel.

'Who spoke to these people?'

'Ferguson or Dove. Why?'

'They'll be in the canteen now, I suppose. Excuse me, sir.'

'Yes,' said Ferguson. 'Or rather, he spoke to me.'

'What do you mean?'

'Well, I was keeping an eye open for anyone showing an interest in the shop when this car pulled up. Chap wound down the window and looked out. I went across to him and he asked me if there was anywhere nearby where he could get a cup of coffee.'

'And?'

'I told him I was a police-officer and pretended to be interested in his car. He knew the registration number, his licence and insurance were OK. I apologized and sent him on his way.'

'How far was he from the shop when he stopped?'

'Oh, about thirty, forty yards. On the other side of the road.'

He went back to Dalziel's room which was now empty, and picked up the phone. It took a little time to get connected.

'Ellie?' he said.

'Peter. You've dragged me from a lecture. What's up?'

'They won't miss you. Listen, love, has Anton Davenant been in touch with you today?'

'No. Why should he?'

'No reason. Just check, will you? See if he left a note or a message or anything.'

'Hang on.'

Dalziel came back, rubbing his hands gleefully. 'I've just had a look in at Cowley. Just an accusing glare. He's a bag of nerves. We'll crack him like a nut.'

'Yes, sir,' said Pascoe. 'Hello, love.'

'Hello,' said Ellie. 'No, nothing. What's this all about?'

'I'll tell you later.'

'You won't have time later. You'll be too busy buying me a big, vulgar ring.'

'Goodbye.'

'Did she say something about a ring?' asked Dalziel as Pascoe replaced the receiver.

Pascoe didn't answer, but stared thoughtfully at the telephone as though memorizing the number.

'Jesus Christ!' said Dalziel. 'Have I been sent to Coventry?'

'I'm sorry, sir. It's just that one of these men who were spotted in Birkham was Anton Davenant who's distantly connected with the Thornton Lacey business.'

Quickly he explained who Davenant was.

'So?' said Dalziel.

'Well, last Wednesday when the first post-Lewis appointment was noted by Etherege, Davenant was up in this part of the country. Ellie ran into him and he said it was her he was on his way to see. But it was all a bit vague.'

'Interesting,' said Dalziel. 'Now, there was a cancelled appointment for yesterday as well.'

'And yesterday,' said Pascoe, 'Davenant attended the inquest at Thornton Lacey.'

'Nice,' said Dalziel approvingly. 'Just one more coincidence, and I'll buy the whole thing. He gets around a lot, this guy?'

'Yes. It's part of his business. Hang on,' said Pascoe. 'I might just be able to give you that last coincidence.'

He picked up the telephone again and after a moment's thought dialled the local reference library.

'Clever boy,' said Dalziel when he had finished. 'Now I'll buy.'

250

Now I'll sell, thought Pascoe. The librarian did not have space enough to keep all the Sunday colour supplements, but because of its peculiar local interest, yes, he had kept that one.

The *Observer* article on Birkham in general and Etherege's antique shop in particular, published the previous autumn in glorious Technicolor, had been written by Anton Davenant.

Chapter 7

It was a busy day and Pascoe had little opportunity to consider his future with Ellie, though from time to time his surface thoughts would be disturbed by undercurrents of commingled pleasure and unease. A rational ordering of his feelings only produced the disturbing realization that he had it in him to be a very solitary man. But whether this was a reason to marry or stay single he could not decide. Solitariness was not far removed from loneliness and this he feared. He believed he could recognize similar characteristics in Ellie, but how good a basis for marriage this common area would be he could not speculate. Equally far beyond contemplation, however, was a life without Ellie. Which is as good a definition of love as I'm likely to get in a police station, he told himself. Motives for marriage are at least as various and unexpected as motives for murder. That sounded like the kind of cold comfort Dalziel would doubtless offer!

He brought his mind back to bear upon his work. It was mainly a question of listening at the moment as everyone seemed to be in the mood for talking.

Etherege was awake and recovering.

As soon as this news reached them, Dalziel sent Pascoe to the hospital to interview him. 'I doubt if he'd talk to me,' he said.

The antique-dealer admitted cheerfully to the twelve break-ins which were laid at this door. The only regret he expressed was in breaking his pattern. He had had a job lined up in the usual way for the beginning of the week, but the people had changed their plans and stayed at home. Matthew Lewis, it turned out, had been a customer of his and had had the misfortune to mention that there would be no one at home that week to take delivery of a table Etherege was renovating for him.

'Normally I wouldn't dream of doing a customer,' said Etherege virtuously, 'but when the other thing fell through, it seemed a pity to scrap everything. The devil finds work for idle hands, you know.'

'I see. Was that why you killed him?' asked Pascoe. 'Because he recognized you?'

'Nonsense!' declared the antique-dealer. 'I was wearing a nylon stocking. I merely tapped him on the head in self-defence when he attacked me. The purest accident, I assure you.

Pascoe didn't believe a word of it but it was not his business to decide on the nature of the charge to be brought.

'What did Davenant say when he heard you'd killed somebody?' asked Pascoe casually.

'You don't think I went about telling everybody,' protested Etherege. 'Oh dear. Was that a trap, or did you really know about Anton?'

'We knew,' asserted Pascoe. 'How did you warn him off?'

'We had a little system. I would put a rather hideous Victorian conversation piece in the side-window if all was well for a conversation. Rather clever.'

'What happened last Wednesday?'

'Oh, I couldn't face the fellow, not with the Lewis business so fresh in my mind and my partner not here to comfort me. I was deeply distressed by it all, you know. He rang later. He made an appointment for yesterday, but he cancelled that and that awful fat man came instead. Hey, it wasn't Davenant who put you on to us, was it?'

253

'We're not at liberty to divulge the source of information,' said Pascoe gravely. Etherege nodded as if his suspicions had been confirmed and when Pascoe left ten minutes later, he had a detailed list of every item Davenant had ever received from Etherege.

Back at the station, Dalziel was having less success than he had anticipated with Cowley and Clayton. Like Etherege they were trying to strike a balance between confessing what was undeniable and denying what was most culpable.

Cowley started with a complete denial of any knowledge of his partner's activities, but when faced with the girl's allegations, he shifted his ground rapidly and claimed instead that his complicity had merely been one of silence. Dalziel went along with this until he had squeezed every last admission possible out of the man on these terms. Then he accused him of being Archie Selkirk and laughed raucously at his denial.

'We've got men checking Lewis's cottage for fingerprints,' he said. 'Yours will be there. You couldn't keep your gloves on all the time!'

Cowley thought for a moment.

'Yes, of course,' he said. 'I've been to the cottage, so my prints might well be there.'

'You said you'd never been near the place.'

'Did I? I'm sorry, I'd forgotten.'

'I suppose while you were there, you might inadvertently have handled the legal papers concerning the land transfer from Selkirk to Mr Sturgeon?'

'Very likely. Lewis showed me some stuff, but I passed it back straightaway. I didn't want to be involved.'

'Wise man,' said Dalziel. 'Tell me, did Mrs Lewis know about the fraud?'

'She probably knew there was something going on. A business deal. Nothing more.'

'Just like you?'

'Right.'

'And the girl. Why should she be making these accusations against you?'

'To cover herself, of course. You're not altogether thick, are you? Anyway, does she say that I disguised myself as this man, what do you call him, Selkirk?'

She didn't, of course. Despite her obvious fear, or because of it, she was still able to see that to admit that she possessed certain pieces of knowledge was to incriminate herself still more. But she did give them a few new lines on the man, Atkinson, and Dalziel had set matters in train for their investigation in London.

Also, as soon as Pascoe rang in from the hospital, a hunt for Anton Davenant was instigated. At Pascoe's suggestion, they contacted Thornton Lacey, and by the time he returned to the station, it had been established that he had booked out of the Eagle and Child the previous afternoon, destination unknown.

But there was some other more disturbing news for Pascoe.

'They've let Pelman loose!' he told Ellie that evening.

'My God! Why?'

'No evidence'

'No evidence! But he tried to blow your head off with a shotgun!'

'He claims he'd no idea it was me. He heard a noise, saw a trespasser, probably a poacher, scrambling out of the stream bed, shouted at him to stop, and then blasted off over his head to give him a scare. It appears that he is most distressed that I got hit by a splinter!'

'Backhouse must be mad. I never thought I'd prefer fat Dalziel's kind of copper-ing, but Christ! I'm sure he wouldn't have let Pelman walk out of it like this.'

'There's a bit more to it,' protested Pascoe. 'He's got a

255

reasonable alibi, it seems. The Amenities Committee meeting finished at eight-thirty that night. Now we know that Rose left the Queen Anne at eight-fifty, and all the evidence, circumstantial and medical, indicated the murder took place about then. Now, according to Marianne Culpepper, she stayed behind in the village hall after the meeting to sort out some clerical work with Pelman and he didn't go off until nearly nine. That would make it impossible for him to have done it.'

Ellie snorted vigorously, a most effective sound. Pascoe suddenly had a picture of her snorting disbelievingly across their dinner table at something the chief constable had said. She will be the missing Dalziel part of me, he thought, and was somehow cheered by the thought.

'Surely Backhouse isn't going to take much notice of anything Maid Marianne says to defend Pelman, is he? If she'd said he'd spent the next few hours rolling around the vestry with her, then it might have made sense!'

'Perhaps in her own modest way that was what she was saying,' suggested Pascoe. 'Anyway it seems to have satisfied Backhouse.'

'And that means it's even further from being over than I thought, Peter. What the hell? It's over for me, I swear it. I'm going to pile great heaps of joy between me and that Saturday morning. Great, insurmountable mountains of joy. For both of us. Right?'

'Yes,' said Pascoe.

They were drinking in the Jockey at Birkham once more. Pascoe recalled that Etherege had refused to admit any knowledge of the attack on Ellie. Pascoe was certain he was lying, just as he was equally certain it had been Jones-the-cat-meat who had committed the assault. Probably it had been the sight of Ellie in Dalziel's company which had convinced the man that it was dangerous to leave even the faint clue of the pendant in her possession. The handbag had been a mere cover. But Jones was admitting nothing, probably wisely. Assault on a woman could get him a couple of extra years.

'Having doubts?' asked Ellie, breaking in on his thoughts.

'About what?'

'About accepting my proposal. Not that it matters. I had a tape-recorder strapped to my thigh.'

'I didn't notice,' he smiled. 'No. No doubts. In fact I think I'm getting more certain by the minute. I was just a bit distracted, that was all. I don't know why, I just thought of Mrs Lewis. Mountains of joy made me think of her. I don't know where she's going to get them from. Husband gets murdered. There's no money left in the kitty. Two young kids. Now she's going to have to find out that her late dearly beloved was having a bit, or rather, a lot, on the side with his secretary. From what she says, the next step would have been the big move-out, leaving Mrs Lewis and family high and dry.'

'It sounds as if she may be better off with him dead.'

'Never say that,' said Pascoe seriously. 'The next step then is the gun, or the knife, or the poison.'

'Constabulary philosophy! There's a thing. What you're trying to say is that relatively we're lucky?'

'Relatively,' said Pascoe, 'I hope we will be. Thornton Lacey is a non-place from now on. Let's start shovelling up those mountains!'

But Thornton Lacey had not yet finished with Pascoe. As he prepared to leave his flat the next morning, the phone rang. It was Dalziel.

'I've just had Backhouse on the line. It seems that Constable Crowther's inquiries about Davenant were not altogether unproductive. He got an anonymous phone call last night to say that Davenant was back in Thornton Lacey staying guess where?'

257

'The Culpeppers'?'

'You used to be fun to play with! Naturally he let Backhouse know. And Backhouse for some peculiar reason seems to think it would be a good idea for you to get down there and pick him up. He's expecting you by twelve noon so get your skates on. Ferguson'll go along to hold Davenant's hand on the way back. I'll have him and a warrant waiting for you at the desk.'

'Thanks,' said Pascoe.

He went back into the bedroom where Ellie, who had a morning free from teaching, was lying half-awake.

'I'd have made your breakfast,' she admonished, 'if you'd given me a push. Are you off?'

'Yes,' he said. He hesitated a moment, then bent down and kissed her. 'See you tonight.'

At his front door he turned back and re-entered the flat.

'That was Dalziel on the phone,' he said. 'I'm going to Thornton Lacey to pick up Davenant. He's at the Culpepper's. Goodbye, love.'

He left feeling happier. The future might hold plenty of things not to talk about and plenty of times when there would be no time to talk. But not now. Not yet.

Chapter 8

The journey to Thornton Lacey was swift and uneventful in objective terms. Detective-Constable Ferguson pleased to be out of the office routine for a while, chattered away with the brightness of one who feels no career height to be unscalable, and the radio filled in the few gaps left by his near-monologue.

Pascoe drove. (He was a bad passenger. Fortunately Ellie was a good one.) Ferguson's voice did not bother him. He hardly heard it. It was a glorious morning and a light mist rose to the sun from the roadside fields. The car seemed to be moving more and more slowly through a world where sound was deadened as though by winter snow. He drove by instinct; in fact the car seemed to drive itself, drifting round bends, floating over the crests of hills, as though in some relationship quite other than mere movement with the countryside around it.

His mind, not usually given to the wilder flights of imagination, was strangely supine, ready to accept that this journey should somehow go on for ever in a region of non-time. Or that time should have been tricked and that once more they were on the road that Saturday morning twelve days earlier with nothing to fear at the end of their journey.

'Thornton Lacey,' said Ferguson approvingly. 'You've made good time, Sergeant. Sorry, *sir*.'

'Yes,' said Pascoe.

He drove directly to the police station. Crowther was behind the desk.

'Morning,' he said.

'Morning,' said Pascoe. 'I believe you've got someone for us.'

'Mr Backhouse is having a cup of coffee in the sitting-room sir. Shall I have Mrs Crowther bring one through for you?'

'That would be kind,' said Pascoe without enthusiasm. He had hoped he might be lucky enough just to pick up Davenant and get away.

'Hello, Peter. It is Peter, isn't it?' Backhouse rose, smiling, like a gentleman farmer welcoming a luncheon guest.

Suddenly it's Christian names all round, thought Pascoe. Perhaps the word's out that I'm earmarked for Commissioner.

'Yes, sir,' he answered. 'This is Detective-Constable Ferguson. Do you have Davenant here for us?'

'No. No, in fact we don't,' said Backhouse. 'Sit down, will you? Ferguson, perhaps you'd like to see how a small country station like this functions, would you? Constable Crowther would be delighted to show you round, I've no doubt.'

Ferguson stood uncertainly for a moment. The thing was, when Dalziel gave you a choice, it was a real choice. When he wanted you to go, he just told you to shove-off.

Pascoe looked significantly at the door and Ferguson left as Mrs Crowther brought the coffee in.

Alone at last, but with none of the romantic overtones of the phrase, the two men sipped their coffee in silence for a while.

'Davenant's gone, sir?' prompted Pascoe.

'No, no. He's still at Culpepper's. I have a man watching, never fear. But there were one or two things I thought it worth discussing with you before picking him up.'

'In which of my capacities, sir?'

'I'm sorry?'

'As a police officer or. . .'

'I see! Or as a not very co-operative witness, which has been your usual role in Thornton Lacey! I'm not sure. I'm not at all sure!'

Backhouse settled more comfortably in his chair, placed his coffee cup on the floor, and touched his fingertips together in a parsonical gesture.

'First,' he said, 'let me tell you about Pelman. Naturally, even when it looked as if Colin Hopkins was very much a front runner, I was having a close look at other possible candidates. Pelman was, at best, only an outsider and I was pretty surprised when I found him pointing a smoking shotgun at you.'

'More surprised than you were to find Colin's body with a bellyful of shot?' asked Pascoe.

'Yes,' admitted Backhouse. 'Yes, I think so. That was always on, though I never thought he'd be so close. Anyway, the more I talked to Pelman, the less likely he seemed. I'd almost made up my mind before you left on Tuesday.'

'I thought there was something else,' said Pascoe.

'How perceptive. Anyway, when Mrs Culpepper confirmed the time he left the village hall that night, there was no more reason to hold him. He's very contrite about shooting at you. He's sensible enough to know the limits of a landowner's rights. Oh, by the way, one thing I did discover. It *was* Pelman who cut through the wire round the clay pit.'

'What?' exclaimed Pascoe.

'Yes. He's been using the pool as a dumping ground for all the chicken-dirt from his battery. Hence the vile smell. He's very contrite about that too.'

'I suppose it did strike you,' said Pascoe diffidently,

'that Mrs Culpepper's evidence might not be altogether unbiased here.'

'I should be very careful about suggesting such a thing,' cautioned Backhouse with a smile. 'Mr Pelman's contrition might not be enough to countenance the smearing of a lady's honour. In any case, you really must permit me to be the best judge of evidence here.'

'I'm sorry, sir,' said Pascoe.

'I'm just as ready to concede you the same superiority in respect of what happens in Yorkshire,' said Backhouse. 'Which is why I was intrigued to learn of your interest in Mr Davenant. Mr Dalziel gave me all the details. He's a great admirer of yours, as doubtless you know.'

'He does occasionally let me go home before midnight,' said Pascoe modestly.

'So it seems that Davenant has managed to appear on the fringes of two murder cases. A striking coincidence, don't you think?'

'Why?' asked Pascoe. 'It happened to me. And to Miss Soper.'

Backhouse raised his eyebrows and smiled.

'You want to act the devil's advocate? All right. In your case, it's not so unlikely. Your profession puts you in constant proximity with crime. When you found yourself involved at a personal level, it was not strange that elsewhere you were engaged in a professional investigation. Indeed, it would have been strange had you not been. But Davenant. . .'

'Davenant too had a professional connection, sir. It seems likely he's a criminal. So the same applies.'

'Reasonable. There's still the coincidence that it should be the same crimes as you he's involved with. And, like you, professionally in Yorkshire, and here in Thornton Lacey – personally, emotionally, would you say?'

'Certainly. He was deeply involved with Timmy, it seems.'

'And the source of your information?'

Pascoe was puzzled.

'Well, I think . . . Davenant himself, of course, and Ellie, Miss Soper. He told her a great deal . . .'

He tailed away. Backhouse said aloud what he was leaving unspoken.

'On an occasion when he required a reason for being in your area, I believe. What did Miss Soper gather was the purpose of his visit?'

'It was all very vague,' said Pascoe. 'But why should he . . . he seemed genuinely concerned!'

'Perhaps so. I've been looking very closely at Mr Davenant. I took note of him when he first appeared, of course. And since the events of Tuesday I've been having a closer look at everybody. One or two interesting things emerge. Mr Davenant is, you would say, a homosexual?'

'Why, yes,' answered Pascoe.

'It sticks out a mile, you feel? Perhaps too far. Discreet inquiries made by some of my London colleagues seem to indicate that in fact his sexual interests are enthusiastically hetero. This might of course just mean that he is – what is the word? – not *ambidextrous*, you know what I mean. Certainly informed opinion seems to be that a grand passion for either of your friends was unlikely.'

Pascoe's mind was racing, but he felt that Backhouse still had some cards left unplayed, so he held his peace though the superintendent's quizzical gaze invited him to speak.

'Very well,' said Backhouse finally. 'So it wasn't love that brought him rushing to Thornton Lacey from Oxford. He *was* in Oxford, I checked that, of course. And he booked out of his hotel on the Saturday morning. What is more interesting, however, is that no one recollects seeing him on the Friday night. The hotel garage attendant is fairly sure that Davenant's car, a Citroën GS, still rather a distinctive car in this insular realm, was not in its place at eleven P.M. when he went off duty. Early enough, you say? I agree. However, in our efforts to check sightings of the Mini-Cooper around the village on Friday night, was asked a lot of questions about cars. A couple of people mentioned a strange Citroën. One of my brighter constables made a note. And I read every report anybody makes.'

Pascoe stood up and made for the door.

'Whither away?' asked Backhouse.

'I came to collect Davenant, sir. I think it's time I did just that,' said Pascoe. 'He's got questions to answer.'

'What is there about this place with turns you into such a *sudden man*?' demanded Backhouse helplessly. 'All these qualities Mr Dalziel finds in you, why do you leave them behind in the north?'

'I'm sorry, sir. What you've said seems to me to urge immediate interrogation of Davenant.'

'*Sit down and listen!*' bellowed Backhouse.

Stony-faced, Pascoe obeyed.

'That's what's missing, is it? Andy Dalziel's fog-horn voice! I'll remember. Look, I haven't brought you all this way just to let you try to shake something or other out of Davenant. There are problems here, and many possible solutions. You're peculiarly well-equipped to help. Look at the facts. Davenant's in the area at the time of the murder. Davenant's alleged sexual connection with your friends seems likely to be a lie. Davenant is suspected of being a kind of travelling fence, a middleman between the thief and the purchaser of stolen *objets d'art*. As a policeman, what's your hypothesis?'

Now at last Pascoe saw it. He had been uncharacteristically obtuse. He remembered saying with pity of Mrs

Lewis that death brought some strange surprises and here was Backhouse starting a few in his face.

'You think that Colin and Rose might have been involved in the Etherege-Davenant racket?' he said steadily.

'Or the other two. Or any one of the four. Or all of them. What do you think?'

'Was anything found?'

'No. But you wouldn't expect it to be, would you? Not if Davenant had anything to do with the killings.'

'Is there any piece of hard evidence I don't know about?'

'No,' said Backhouse, after thinking judiciously for a moment. 'No. But the Continent is the most obvious market for the more easily identifiable stuff. And Timothy Mansfield worked in Brussels for some time, travelling frequently from Britain to Belgium, as well as touring extensively in Europe. Davenant did meet him there, as he told Miss Soper. But it wasn't their first meeting.'

'You can't have unearthed all this since you spoke to Dalziel,' said Pascoe accusingly.

'No,' said Backhouse. 'I try to keep many steps ahead of blind chance. But sometimes it comes along and bumps you in the back, as when out of the blue, you tied Davenant in with your investigation. Till then it had been just so much background information. Your friend, Mansfield, had to resign his job in Brussels, did you know that? There was some currency fiddle being worked. He kept out of serious trouble, but only just.'

'Knowing Timmy, it would be in a good cause,' protested Pascoe weakly.

'What the hell have you or I got to do with causes!' exploded Backhouse. 'For a policeman, understanding motives is just a means to an end. That end's catching crooks. I dare say whoever it was that shot your friends

265

will come up with a good motive. It might even impress a judge, or a jury, or a psychiatrist, or just his grey-haired old mother who know he's basically a good lad. Now, you want Davenant. I might want him too. I had a little plan, but I'm not sure how far I can rely on you. I was going to suggest that you go up to the Culpeppers' and get him, giving the impression that police interest in him is restricted entirely to his connection with your antique-dealer, Etherege. Be a bit diffident, uncertain, if you like, as though you've got less on him than you have.'

'Which is only Etherege's word,' said Pascoe.

'Is it? I'm sure Mr Dalziel won't be standing still. Anyway, come the old-pals act, take a trip down memory lane with him, reminisce a bit about your late mutual friends. In other words, see if you can catch him napping in Thornton Lacey while he's too busy keeping fully alert in Yorkshire. That's what I was going to suggest. Can I trust you, Inspector? That's what I've got to know.'

'I think so, sir,' said Pascoe. Appearances deceived. Compared with this man, Dalziel was Mother Hubbard.

'Then I would suggest you go and bring him in. Give the impression you're just dropping back here to sign a form or something before taking him north. It might work.'

Pascoe rose and made for the door.

'Just one thing, sir,' he said. 'The Culpeppers. Why is Davenant there? What's the connection?'

Backhouse groaned loudly.

'Stay in Yorkshire, my boy,' he advised gently. 'You'll never make the grade down here. It's obvious, surely? Aesthetic Mr Culpepper, your connoisseur of fine porcelain, is probably one of friend Davenant's regular customers!'

Chapter 9

'Stop here,' said Pascoe. Ferguson obeyed him as literally as possible and despite their low speed managed to skid noisily on the gravel drive.

I was right to drive all the way down, thought Pascoe with a shudder as he climbed out.

'I don't anticipate any trouble,' he said through the open door. 'But keep you eyes skinned. Poke around the garage and see if you can spot the Citroën.'

He slammed the door and a hand gripped his shoulder. Dalziel's philosophy included the dictum *if anyone grabs you from behind, don't think, give 'em the heel and the elbow*.

Pascoe turned slowly and smiled at Culpepper's mother. He was glad he had ignored Dalziel's advice, not just out of chivalry but also because he doubted whether his judo could cope with the vicious-looking secateurs she carried.

'That could ruin a machine!' snapped the old woman, pointing at the scattering of gravel the car-wheels had sprayed on to the lawn. 'Have you no consideration?'

'Sorry,' said Pascoe. 'Ferguson, see that all these bits of stone are returned to the drive, will you?'

'What are you after anyway? You're that policeman, aren't you?'

'Yes. I'm *that* policeman. I'd just like a word with your son,' said Pascoe, walking across the lawn towards the front door. The old woman accompanied him, matching him stride for stride.

'I knew there'd be trouble,' she said suddenly.

267

'Sorry?'

'When I was young, police coming to the house always meant trouble.'

'We only trouble those who trouble us,' said Pascoe with a smile.

They had come to a halt outside the front door. He had not spotted any movement through the windows.

'I liked your friends,' she said as she pushed open the door. 'Some things beat explanation. Step inside.'

'Thank you,' said Pascoe. He glanced back down the garden. Ferguson was on his knees in search of gravel, a light breeze spilling his longer-than-regulation hair over his face.

'You can say goodbye to the good weather,' said the old woman ominously, and as though in confirmation a rout of beech leaves came scuttering round the side of the house and preceded them into the hallway.

The Culpeppers were seated in the lounge and Hartley rose and held out his hand in greeting when he saw his visitor. He looked perfectly at ease, not without cause Pascoe was sure. If there had been anything of doubtful provenance in Culpepper's collection, it was probably long gone now.

'You're fully recovered, I hope, Pascoe? I was talking to Pelman last night. He was in a terrible state, terrible. Poor fellow, to come so close to injuring you was bad enough, but then to realize he was under suspicion for the murders!'

'Yes, I'm recovered, thank you.'

No one seemed very keen to ask what he wanted, Pascoe noted. He hoped Davenant wasn't slipping quietly out of the kitchen door. Or if he was, that Ferguson had abandoned his gravel hunt and was fully alert.

'It's difficult to know what to say,' Culpepper went on. 'No one who knew him ever really believed it was possible that Colin did the killings, but we didn't want him proved innocent in this way.'

'Some believed it,' objected Pascoe. 'The coroner's jury and the coroner for a start. But it's none of my business, officially anyway. Mr Culpepper, I believe Anton Davenant is staying with you at the moment.'

The doorbell rang. Only old Mrs Culpepper showed no desire to answer it. Her son and daughter-in-law both seemed keen to get out of the room, but Marianne won by a short head.

'So it's Davenant you're after? Well, well. Would you care for a drink or is it too early?'

As though in answer to his query, the door opened and Major Palfrey came in clutching two brown-paper-wrapped bottles.

'Morning, Hartley, morning, Mrs Culpepper.' He noticed Pascoe and gave him a neutral nod.

'Sorry to butt in, but as I was just saying to Marianne, you've caught us on the hop, old boy. Pity I hadn't been around when you rang. That potman of mine's a bit dim! The thing is, we're very low on spirits at the moment. Can manage a couple of bottles, but boxes are out of the question. Sorry.'

It was a more than usually gruesomely hearty performance, Pascoe felt. But why? Because I'm here? Do I always bring out the worst in people?

'Don't fret about it, JP,' said Culpepper equably. 'Sam Dixon will probably be able to cope. Give him a ring, will you, Marianne? They do quite a large off-licence trade at the Anne, I believe.'

'I suppose they do,' said Palfrey as if he suspected a slur. 'You must give us warning if you're going to start spreading business locally. So you're with us once more, Sergeant Pascoe? What brings you back?'

269

'I really wanted a word with Mr Davenant. Is he here, Mr Culpepper?'

Culpepper exchanged glances with his wife, but before either could speak, his mother burst out. 'Well, if he is, they've kept very quiet about him. I've not seen hide nor hair of him.'

'Thank you, Mrs Culpepper. Well, sir. Is he here?'

'Of course he is, darlings. Though he almost wasn't.'

Standing at the door, one hand on his hip, the other behind his head, was Anton Davenant. Behind him in the hall, Pascoe caught a glimpse of Ferguson.

'I had no idea you were here, my dear fellow. And I was just setting off for a little circumambulation in search of Nature, red in tooth and claw, when I ran into your boy.'

Boy came out beautifully round and succulent. Pascoe held back a smile. It must have been a good test for Ferguson's temper under stress.

'I'd like a word with you if I may, Mr Davenant,' said Pascoe.

'By all means. Here?'

'Would you care to use my study?' intervened Culpepper before Pascoe could suggest retiring to the station. It seemed a good idea to start here at least. Things were on the boil, though he was far from sure what the dish was going to be.

'Thanks,' he said. 'That's kind.'

Culpepper led the way across the hall to a room next to his porcelain room.

'I'll ring Sam Dixon now,' said Marianne suddenly. 'About that drink.'

'Do, darling,' said Culpepper. 'In here, gentlemen.'

Pascoe paused as he passed Ferguson.

'Nicely fielded,' he murmured. 'Get on to Backhouse and tell him I'm opening up the batting here.'

The study was more like a businessman's office than the gentleman's retreat Pascoe had for some reason expected. Modern desk with typewriter, a book-shelf filled mainly with reference and technical volumes, a filing cabinet; nothing here which showed any desire to emulate the landed gentry.

'At last we are alone,' said Davenant.

'So we are, Mr Davenant, what were you doing in Birkham village yesterday morning?'

'Passing through, dear boy.'

'It's a little off the beaten track.'

'That depends on where you are beating your track *from* and *to*.'

'And where was that?'

'Which?'

'Which?'

'*From* or *to*?'

'Begin at the beginning, please,' said Pascoe, quite enjoying himself. Dalziel would have been clenching his fists and making sinister grunting sounds by now. The only thing which darkened his mood was the cloudy connection between this man and Brookside Cottage.

'Well, let me see. From first? From Barnsley then.'

'*Barnsley!*'

'Why so amazed? Contrary to rumour Barnsley is not a volcanic cavity full of flames, fumes and the stench of sulphur. A trifle naïve, yes; something of a frontier town, yes. But not without its attractions, one of which is a superb restaurant, the delights of which I check annually for the *Gourmet's Guide*. So I left Thornton Lacey on Tuesday, after the inquest, missing all the excitement and the tragedy too, of course, and headed for Barnsley.'

'So. From Barnsley to – ?'

Davenant threw up his hands in exasperation. 'It's self-evident surely! To *here*! I arrived here yesterday evening, so I must have been heading for here, mustn't I?'

'I don't know if you consult maps, Mr Davenant, but Birkham would take you many miles out of your way.'

'Of course. I see your difficulty. I wanted to take a look at the Old Mill about five miles to the north. Do you know it? Fascinating. Do you know I spent a week in Birkham last year doing a feature article and I never found time to get to see the Old Mill! So when I was in Barnsley . . .!'

He was doing a very good job, Pascoe had to admit. Fitting everything nicely into a reasonable pattern. So nicely that Pascoe had to keep on reminding himself of all the other little bits and pieces. All? Mainly Etherege's agreement that Davenant had been the middleman!

He stared down at Culpepper's desk for inspiration. It was empty but for a tray which held one of the Sunday paper business supplements. Egotistically, it was opened at an account of Nordrill's annual general meeting held the previous Wednesday afternoon.

At which time, the thought popped into his mind like a well-browned piece of toast, Culpepper was wandering around Sotheby's, wishing he could afford to bid.

Which thought prompted one obvious question and a second not quite so obvious.

But now was not the time to ask them.

'Is this about poor old Jonathan Etherege?' asked Davenant.

Pascoe looked up, pleasantly surprised. His musings on Culpepper had had an unforeseen spin-off, the breaching of a minute gap in Davenant's unperturbability.

'Who?' he said.

'Etherege. I read about him in the papers and it just struck me that this is why you people are suddenly finding anything to do with Birkham so fascinating. Mind you, there must be a mistake! Jonathan as a burglar is too much. As a *killer*, it's not on!'

272

'Many people find it in them to be killers,' Pascoe said flatly.

The doorbell rang and at the same time there was a tap on the study door. Pascoe opened it. Marianne Culpepper stood there with a coffee tray, but she was looking down the hallway to the front door.

'Angus. How nice to see you. Come in, please,' said Culpepper.

Pascoe peered out, rudely pushing his head almost up against Marianne's. Pelman was just stepping into the hall. He stopped short as he spotted Pascoe, then came forward quickly.

'Pascoe. I heard you were here. I'm sorry I didn't have a chance to see you again on Tuesday. Let me say how sorry I am. It was a terrible thing. Terrible. I was more distressed than I can say.'

He was referring to the discovery of Colin, Pascoe realized, not the shooting. The priorities were right, he had to admit.

But Pelman hadn't finished.

'And I'm sorry too about taking a pot-shot at you. Or rather over you. The superintendent was on me so quick that I didn't even know you'd been hit by a splinter till later. Is it OK?'

'Smiling was painful for a while,' said Pascoe.

Pelman laughed.

'Good man. I thought you were a blasted poacher. Anyway, to make some amends, I put a brace of pheasants in the car when I heard you were about. If you've been shot for a poacher, you might as well go home like one. Hartley, give us a hand, will you?'

The two men went out of the front door once again and Pascoe retreated into the study. There was something about Pelman he could admire. The man had said nothing at all about his own ordeal as a suspect for several hours.

He turned back to Davenant who was pouring out the coffee.

'Black?' asked Davenant.

'Thanks,' said Pascoe. He was getting nowhere. Backhouse wanted him to play it cool, but if Backhouse insisted on keeping his own hand so well concealed, then he could get with his own bloody game!

'Etherege says it was your idea for him to organize the burglaries,' he said conversationally.

Davenant hardly flinched.

'Which burglaries? You don't mean. . .? Good Lord, how clever! he must be trying for a plea of insanity!'

'I thought you said it was impossible for him to be guilty?'

'So I did. But that's not the same as it being impossible for your lot to *prove* him guilty!'

'My word,' said Pascoe. 'I thought you loved us bobbies?'

'A simple country boy's got to be careful who he loves, Inspector.'

'Like you loved Timmy?' There, that did it. He was well off the rails laid down by Backhouse now.

'Perhaps,' said Davenant. 'But he's dead, isn't he? Pity you couldn't have got there on Friday night. It might have helped.'

'Why?' asked Pascoe, keeping a tighter rein on his temper than was yet necessary. 'You managed it and that didn't help at all.'

Davenant put his coffee cup down and his gaze flickerred momentarily around the room, finally coming to rest steadfastly on Pascoe.

Escape? or a weapon? wondered Pascoe. This hygienic, functional study offered little chance of either.

'No,' said Davenant sadly. 'It didn't, did it?'

For a moment Pascoe was unable to grasp the significance of the words.

'You were there?' he said finally. 'You admit it?'

'Yes,' said Davenant. 'I was there.'

Outside in the hallway there was a crash and the sound of upraised voices. Pascoe was glad of the diversion and opened the study door to peer out yet again.

Just inside the front door stood Sam Dixon holding a cardboard container in his arms. Another lay on the floor at his feet and a damp stain was spreading quickly from it. There was a strong smell of whisky. Old Mrs Culpepper stood alongside Dixon, glaring at him angrily, while her son and daughter-in-law came out of the lounge to investigate the noise. Pelman and Palfrey were close behind.

'What's happened?' asked Culpepper.

'Sorry,' said Dixon. 'Bit of an accident. My fault.'

The old woman muttered something inaudible and stamped off into the garden.

'Your birds are on the back seat of your car,' said Pelman to Pascoe. 'Don't forget 'em! I really must be on my way now, Marianne, Hartley. Work to be done!'

He set off up the hall but his passage was impeded by yet another arrival. This time it was Backhouse with Crowther close behind.

'May I come in?' asked the superintendent, sniffing. 'This smells interesting. You're not trying to corrupt Inspector Pascoe, I hope?'

He came down the hallway, nodding at Pelman as he passed. Even now the way out was now clear, Pelman's impetus seemed to have been completely spent and he made no attempt to leave.

'Sorry to intrude, Mr Culpepper, but I wanted a word with Inspector Pascoe.'

'By all means,' said Culpepper.

Pascoe backed into the study where Davenant still stood. He had lit a cigarette and looked perfectly at ease.

'Well?' said Backhouse.

'He admits he was there.'

'Where?'

'At Brookside Cottage on the night of the murders.'

Backhouse rolled his eyes heavenwards in mock-appeal.

'How right I was to come so quickly,' he murmured. 'You seem incapable of following instructions, Inspector. I suppose I should think myself lucky he hasn't been beaten unconscious! Wait outside now, will you? Crowther, step in here, will you?'

'Sir,' said Pascoe and went out, passing Crowther in the doorway. He was beginning to feel once again the simmering fury which seemed to be his normal emotional state in Thornton Lacey.

The hall was empty now; everyone had retired to the lounge, doubtless to discuss the constabulary goings-on. Pascoe, in no mood for small talk, made for the front door. On the steps he took a couple of deep breaths of fresh, cool air. It was perceptibly colder now. The old woman had been right. This was the bouquet of winter.

The drive in front of the house was like a car-park. Pelman's Land-Rover was still there, Palfrey's car, Dixon's van, and of course Backhouse's official limousine.

'Excuse me, sir,' said Ferguson behind him.

'Yes?'

'I don't know if it's important, but when the big fellow came out to get those birds from the Land-Rover, he gave something else to Mr Culpepper.'

'What?'

'A packet of some kind. About so big. White paper wrapping.'

'Did they know you were watching?'

'No. It wasn't surreptitious or anything like that. Just quick, if you know what I mean. Not much said. That's what made me take notice.'

'What did Culpepper do with this packet?'

'Stuck it in his pocket. But after that, I don't know what. It was quite bulky and he's got rid of it somewhere, I noticed just now.'

'Well done, Hawkeye,' said Pascoe.

He turned and re-entered the house. Everything was quiet. A man of Culpepper's money and taste didn't build doors which let ordinary conversation trickle through. He wondered again about Culpepper and Davenant. How guilty was the collector? Just suspicious of the source of the sale items? or with definite knowledge they had been stolen? The law made little distinction between the two states, but the individual conscience was a much more refined beast, able to pick and crop at definition and qualification.

These thoughts ran through his mind as he made his way silently and swiftly upstairs. Davenant was using the room which Ellie had occupied. There was surprisingly little evidence of his presence – pyjamas, toilet articles, all with his initials monogrammed on them; but nothing really personal.

He left the room and stood a moment on the landing. Still silence below.

Now he moved on to what his memory of the geography of the house told him was Culpepper's room. While it was clearly a man's room there was sufficient evidence of occasional female occupation to indicate Marianne's departure from the marriage bed was by no means a permanent move.

What am I doing here? wondered Pascoe as he gazed at the Chinese watercolours which decorated the walls.

Backhouse would not be pleased if Culpepper found me and started making a fuss.

Stuff Backhouse.

He began searching. It didn't take long.

No attempt had been made to hide it. It lay beside the pastel-green telephone on the bedside table.

The Sellotape binding was still intact. Whatever the packet contained, Culpepper hadn't felt the need, or perhaps had the time, to check.

Unpicking the Sellotape as neatly as possible, Pascoe pulled the white wrapping paper open.

It didn't look very much at first glance, but a quick check gave him the exact figure.

It was surprising how little space was taken up by a thousand pounds in fivers.

Chapter 10

It took Pascoe a moment's thought and a five-minute telephone call to decide what to do. The time had come for drama.

He pushed open the lounge door, stepped in, and threw the money on the coffee-table. They all looked at him in amazement. A slow-motion camera and a trained psychiatrist might have made much of the kinds of amazement displayed, but Pascoe had to make do with snap judgements. Honest bewilderment from Palfrey and Dixon, but something else from the other three. A reasonable division.

'There's a thousand pounds there,' he said. 'What's it for?'

Culpepper was white with indignation.

'What right have you to search my house? This is an outrage!'

'Yes. Why did you bring it here, Mr Pelman?'

Pelman and Marianne exchanged glances, not easily readable.

'I think that's my business, don't you?' said Pelman.

'Perhaps. Blackmail is a crime, of course. And that's my business.'

Pelman looked flabbergasted, then began laughing. It sounded genuine.

'I'm glad you can be amused, Angus,' said Culpepper. 'I'm sorry, but I can't be. Excuse me.'

He strode from the room.

'What the hell's going on?' asked Dixon, his open face

creased in puzzlement, while Palfrey reached for the coffee-pot, eyeing the money greedily.

Culpepper returned. With him was Backhouse, with Crowther and Davenant bringing up the rear.

'Superintendent,' said Culpepper, 'I should like you to explain by what authority a police officer, uninvited and without warrant, can search a private house.'

'The end sometimes justifies the means,' said Backhouse. 'What did you find, Inspector Pascoe?'

Wordlessly Pascoe showed him the money.

'Interesting, but not incriminating. I presume you've got a theory.'

He's not going to blow his top, thought Pascoe. Not yet. He's going to let me do his dirty work for him.

'This is not the point,' said Culpepper angrily.

'Yes, sir. I've got a theory. Mr Pelman brought this money with him. Let's call it a loan for the moment.'

'He thinks I'm being blackmailed,' interjected Pelman. 'What I'm supposed to have done this time, God knows! Oh, and Hartley, too, as I presume he's doing the blackmailing.'

'This gets worse!' said Culpepper.

'I trust not,' said Backhouse seriously. 'Inspector!'

'Let's call it a loan,' repeated Pascoe. 'The more important question at the moment is why did Mr Culpepper want it so quickly and in cash? My suggestion is simple. You wanted it for Mr Davenant.'

'But why should I wish to give Davenant a thousand pounds?' asked Culpepper.

'Why? Because he has been supplying you with pieces for your collection which you may have known or suspected to be stolen. Now he's in a hurry to get on his way. He realizes we're on to him. He heads straight down here, and is just hanging around for the money to arrive when unfortunately I turn up.'

Culpepper smiled. His anger seemed to have left him now, which was a pity. He looked cool and alert.

'You tell a good story, Inspector. But it's a fairy story, of course. You're very welcome to inspect my collection for stolen articles.'

'I don't doubt they've been removed since Mr Davenant's arrival,' replied Pascoe. Pelman, he noted, was looking more worried now than at any time hereto, which was interesting. It was time Backhouse made a move. He had been very insistent that the Brookside Cottage case was his. Pascoe had delivered into his hands Davenant, who admitted he was there on the night of the murders, and now also Pelman, who had just delivered a thousand pounds in used notes to the house of the woman whose story supported his alibi. Let the superintendent pick the bones out of that.

But Backhouse showed no sign of being ready to make a move. Palfrey glanced at his watch and stood up.

'I think this is outrageous, Hartley,' he said, shooting a malicious glance at Pascoe. 'If you want any witnesses to this gross misuse of police authority, just let me know. But I've got to push off now and see to my pub.'

'Thanks, JP,' said Culpepper. 'Your story falls down elsewhere, Pascoe. For example, if I wanted money in that much of a hurry, why should I go through the complicated business on contacting Angus? Why not just get it myself?'

He smiled round as if he had produced a rabbit out of a hat.

You poor bastard, thought Pascoe.

He felt reluctant to go on. A man had a right to his areas of privacy. Why should Culpepper's small secret be revealed here?

Because, he told himself looking round at the ring of

expectant faces, because it had or might have or could have something to do with a crime.

And perhaps also because of something in those faces – wariness, expectancy, warning, or in the case of Marianne Culpepper, supercilious disinterest. That especially.

'Because, Mr Culpepper,' he said, 'you no longer work for the Nordrill Mining Company. In fact I believe you no longer work for anyone. You are unemployed, have been unemployed for six months and are practically destitute.'

If he had expected this to be an explosive revelation, he was disappointed.

True, Culpepper stood very still, his expression freezing as though a film had stopped on a single frame. But the others were manifestly unsurprised.

'I don't see what Hartley's financial affairs have to do with you,' said Pelman scornfully.

'So what?' said Dixon with a surprising amount of aggression.

Even Palfrey risked a contemptuous sniff, and Marianne merely turned away.

Only Davenant looked surprised.

'You all knew?' he said. 'Well, well. Isn't that an interesting thing? They all knew, Hartley, old son.'

'So much for your bombshell,' murmured Backhouse, taking Pascoe into the window bay. 'Even I knew. It was in Crowther's first batch of background notes. How did you find out?'

'I rang up Nordrill, put on a bit of an act,' admitted Pascoe, feeling suddenly rather shamefaced as well as very foolish. 'There were some discrepancies, the date of the AGM and Sotheby's sale clashed, for instance; other things. I thought I was being pretty clever.'

'It's cleverer than getting into fights, anyway. But I fear you've bowled over our genial host.'

Culpepper certainly looked unwell now. The little colour in his cheeks had ebbed away and he seemed able to pay little attention to the attempts at polite chat which the others were directing at him. Only Marianne was not joining in the general rally-round-Hartley movement. Presumably she had known – or had he imagined he had kept his insolvency a secret from her also? Impossible. Pelman knew and Pelman would surely have told her.

It was Pelman who returned to the attack now.

'We've had a lot of accusations and hints of accusations, Superintendent,' he said to Backhouse. 'I think it's time we saw some cards on the table.'

'A splendid idea. Perhaps you'd begin, sir, by telling us why, when you knew Mr Culpepper was in financial straits, you were so willing to lend him a thousand pounds?'

Pelman momentarily looked uncomfortable, but recovered quickly.

'Why, you've just said it! Because I knew he was in a bit of trouble financially, that's why. What better reason for giving a neighbour a loan? You don't lend money where it's not needed, do you?'

'I didn't realize you were such good friends, sir,' said Backhouse with a smile. There was a thoughtful pause.

Surely, thought Pascoe, he knows Pelman's got something going with Marianne. It's conscience money, if anything. The important thing is, what was Culpepper going to do with it? Davenant was still standing at the periphery of the group, apparently casual and very much at his ease. It would be a good idea to get him out of the room and isolate him from the present discussion. But before he could suggest this, Backhouse started talking again.

'The question still does remain,' he said, addressing himself to Culpepper who all this time had retained his

283

statue-like pose by the doorway, 'what, in fact, were you going to do with the money?'

'I think I ought to clear up something first,' interjected Davenant. 'Everyone's entitled to have all the facts, don't you think so, Superintendent? I've already told you that I was at Brookside Cottage that night. Oh yes. Gasp gasp all round. But I left shortly after seven when all was still well and made my way to dear old Hartley's pad where we sat sipping his super whisky and talking of matters cultural until – when was it, Hartley, my love? – about half past ten?'

Damn! thought Pascoe. This is what he had been afraid of. He couldn't understand Backhouse's policy. Separation of suspects and witnesses was usually as essential to a case as separation of yolks and whites was to a soufflé. Now here was Davenant publicly inviting Culpepper to give him an alibi. Or reminding him of what they had agreed.

But Culpepper's response could have brought little comfort to Davenant. He stared coldly, almost unseeingly, at him, turned and left the room. Marianne, with a quick perfect-hostesses's apologetic smile at the gathering, followed him.

'Well now, Mr Davenant,' said Backhouse. 'I'm sure Mr Culpepper will be able to confirm your story when he's feeling better. Or is there anyone else who can help us? Did Mrs Culpepper come home while you were there?'

'No. No. Not exactly,' said Davenant. 'At least, I didn't see her. For all I know, of course, she came in earlier, heard Hartley and me talking, decided not to interrupt and went up to her room. Now that's a possibility of course. Oh yes, that's a very distinct possibility.'

The cocky bastard! thought Pascoe. He's inventing alibis publicly as he goes along and putting them on display for all to see. Marianne's not here to hear it, of course. But her boyfriend is. And Davenant knows!

Slowly a picture was forming itself in Pascoe's mind. It was not yet complete, but its main outlines were clear. And as he examined it and found its composition more and more balanced, the ball of rage in his breast began to swell and swell till it was ready to burst in black hatred.

Against Davenant.

Against Davenant who had turned up at Brookside Cottage on that fatal Friday night. Against Davenant who had sat and talked and drunk with Rose and Colin and Timmy and Carlo. Against Davenant who for reasons still not clear had taken up a shotgun and blasted Timmy and Carlo out of this world. Who had met Rose in the garden and left her lying by the sundial, bleeding to death. Who had pursued and murdered Colin and stuffed his body into a dark oozy culvert for the flies to discover.

Think logically, he commanded himself. Think! All right. Davenant knew Culpepper lived locally, had visited him before on his 'fencing' trips. Perhaps he did go to see him that night. Perhaps it was just a useful invention to have in the background in case it was ever needed. And it had been needed. Pressure was on him from all sides. From Yorkshire where Etherege's little empire was crumbling. And down here where his car had been spotted in the area that Friday night.

So back he comes to Culpepper. He needs two things. An alibi and money. By threatening to reveal their business relationship – fence and receiver – he aims at getting both out of Culpepper. But Culpepper has no money. Borrow it, suggests Davenant. Who from? Why not try Pelman? says Davenant with a significant glance at Marianne. Yes, he would have dug up that bit of information pretty easily. And Pelman's willing to play

285

ball. Conscience? Fear of scandal? To protect Marianne? Who knows? A detail to be filled in later.

But Davenant's plan was in jeopardy. The public revelation of Culpepper's unemployment had thrown the man off balance. Perhaps that had been an element in the blackmail threat also? Certainly it had seemed to matter a great deal to Culpepper, relegating to second place his concern for the immediate future. Now was clearly the time to be talking to him while he was still off balance and before he recovered sufficiently to support Davenant's story.

But Backhouse did not seem ready to make a move in that direction. He was talking to Pelman, Palfrey and Dixon, none of whom now seemed disposed to leave despite the casual reasons for their presence. The door opened and Marianne Culpepper came in. She looked worried.

'He's resting with his porcelain,' she said to the unspoken question which met her. 'He was a bit upset. He's been trying desperately hard for months now to find a new post, but only jobs in selling, or factory accounts offices, that level of thing, were ever available.'

'You could have helped, got a job yourself,' said Pascoe sharply, stung by the tone of *that level of thing*.

Marianne looked at him wearily, dismissively.

'Mr Pascoe,' she said, 'why don't you piss off?'

The expression uttered in those smooth-vowelled tones, was surprising, almost shocking. And worse, Pascoe felt himself somehow justly reproved.

'Perhaps you'd take Mr Davenant back into the study and see if you can get an ordered account of his movements from him,' said Backhouse.

At last he's woken to the danger, thought Pascoe. And off I'm sent to do the dirty work again.

'Yes, sir,' he said.

In the hall by the front door stood Ferguson, drinking a cup of coffee.

'The old lady made it for me,' he said defensively.

'You bring out the mother in us all,' said Pascoe. 'Is he still in there?'

He jerked his head at the porcelain room. Ferguson nodded.

'Good. In here please, Mr Davenant.'

'Do you ever get a feeling of *déja vu*?' asked Davenant as he entered the study once more. 'As the bishop said in the strip-club.'

'Let's cut the comics,' said Pascoe, closing the door. 'And you can drop the queer act too.'

'Don't you love me any more?' asked Davenant advancing coyly, hips wiggling, arms stretched out appealingly.

Pascoe poked him in the stomach, not hard, but hard enough to double him up and send him crashing into a chair.

'Jesus Christ!' gasped Davenant, holding his arms across his waist. 'So it really happens! The rubber truncheon bit. I never believed it.'

'I'm glad we had you fooled. Are you sitting comfortably? Then let's begin.'

'What the hell do you want?' asked Davenant, eyeing the door speculatively. Pascoe was interested to note that his accent and style of speech had changed completely. The long drawn vowels and rising rhythms were gone. What remained was flat, almost monotonous, with a touch of the north in it.

'How long have you been a fence?' asked Pascoe, ready for denial and wondering what he would do when it came.

'About ten years. Six on a regular basis. I started shortly after I accepted my first bribe for mentioning

287

someone's stinking restaurant in a piece I was doing. You must have noticed how one thing leads to another crime.'

'You're being very frank,' said Pascoe, slightly taken aback.

'Look, sonny, you're a frightening man. I reckon you've flipped just a bit because of this business. But not so much that you'd beat me up in front of witnesses. I don't like being beaten up *anywhere*, so I'll talk to you. But like your beatings, not in front of witnesses.'

'How old are you?' asked Pascoe.

'Forty-three.'

'You look younger.'

'Thank you kindly,' said Davenant, relapsing momentarily into his old manner. 'It's marvellous what fiction and false hair will do for you. Truth is dead.'

But now as Pascoe looked at him he no longer saw the fashionable ageless swinger, cynical and sophisticated, but a middle-aged man dressed up for a costume-party he no longer wants to attend, with lines of worry running from the eyes and the mouth to complement the deeper furrows of age on the brow.

A frightened man. Pascoe knew from observation how easy it was for a frightened man to kill. Just as he knew from experience how easy it was for an angry policeman to strike. He clenched his fists in his jacket pockets and tried to keep his voice calm as he asked, 'Why did you kill them?'

'For God's sake!' said Davenant. 'What a stupid question!'

'You mean the answer's obvious!'

'No! Yes. Yes, it's obvious. I didn't. I've told you the truth. I was there. I went on business; you don't like that, do you? I left at seven. I went to Culpepper's. When I left there. I went straight back to Oxford.'

'You're a liar,' said Pascoe, taking a step forward.

Davenant leapt up in fear, his chair shot backwards and overturned. The door opened and Ferguson's head appeared.

'You all right, sir?'

'Yes. Listen, Davenant, you think you've got an alibi, don't you? Well, we'll see about that. Nobody's said a thing yet that supports your story. I don't think they are going to. Ferguson, stay here and watch him. Don't be taken in by the whipped poodle expression. The beast is dangerous.'

He turned and left the study, the fury in him burning high now. Culpepper was the key. Without his supporting story, Davenant was done. The group in the lounge seemed to be still in session, which was good. He was better with Backhouse out of the way.

In the porcelain room Culpepper stood between the two huge pseudo-Chinese vases with his back to the door. Lights were on in all the display niches and the pieces of his collection tranquilly radiated their cold beauty.

'Why not sell them?' asked Pascoe. 'That would tide you over for a bit.'

'What? Oh, Mr Pascoe. Yes, I suppose it would, I suppose it would.'

The words expressed agreement but the tone was the kind used when agreeing with an importunate child.

'What were you going to do with the money Pelman brought?'

'That? But you know that already. It was for Davenant.'

This was better than he could have hoped for. He thought of stepping out and fetching Backhouse, but was afraid of breaking the atmosphere.

'He was blackmailing you.'

'In a way.'

289

'Because some of your collection had come through him?'

'In a way.'

'What else did he want from you?'

'I'm sorry?'

'Did he ask you to do anything else? Was he really here that Friday night?'

'Oh yes, he was here.'

'And what time did he leave?'

'I forget.'

'Come on, Mr Culpepper! He says he was here till after ten. What do you say? Is that true?'

'Oh no. He definitely left before half past eight.'

Pascoe let out a long sigh of relief. His hunch had been right. Culpepper was in no mood at the moment to play alibis. He might be sorry later, but later would be too late.

'Thank you, Mr Culpeper,' he said, turning away. Behind him was old Mrs Culpepper.

'You going?' she said.

'Yes. We won't bother you much longer.'

'Oh aye.' She shook her head, whether in negation or to clear it was not certain.

'Hold on a moment,' she said, stepping into the room.

Pascoe watched, impatient to get back to Davenant to present Backhouse with his killer, to go home. Slowly the old woman moved forward and stood behind her son.

'Yes, Mother,' he said.

'The clever policeman's going, Hartley. Don't you want to talk to him?'

She said nothing more but stood in silence looking at her son's unyielding back. Then she did something amazing. She turned and threw all her old weight at one of the Chinese vases. Pascoe leapt forward to catch it as it toppled off its plinth but he was too late.

It hit the ground and exploded into green and blue and white shards. Something lay among them like a gift in a child's chocolate Easter egg.

A shotgun.

Pascoe moved fast, but the old woman was in the way and the shotgun was in Culpepper's hands before he could get by her.

'I'm sorry, son,' said the old woman. 'I waited long enough, too long perhaps. You should have told him yourself.'

Pascoe's mind was spinning. There was no room for fear there, or at least only for the fear that he might never hear the truth.

'Why?' he cried. 'But why?'

'Your friend was going to tell everybody,' said Culpepper, his face twisted in a plea for understanding. 'He had no right. You understand that? And I didn't realize that everybody knew already. But I never meant . . . but I never meant . . .

In the lounge they heard the almost simultaneous double blasts of the shotgun. For a second no one moved. Then they poured into the hallway and gazed with varying degrees of incomprehension at the scene before them.

Pascoe, old Mrs Culpepper and her son were standing in the porcelain room looking at the damage the double blast from the gun which still smoked in Hartley's hands had wreaked on his collection.

Some of the pieces were still untouched. Now Culpepper stepped forward and smashed these with the gunbarrel. Satisfied at last, he dropped the weapon and came out into the hall where he stood and gazed unemotionally at his wife who was sobbing rhythmically in Sam Dixon's arms.

Dixon? wondered Pascoe, surprised at nothing now.

The study door opened and Davenant and Ferguson stepped out.

Davenant looked into the porcelain room and shook his head at the shambles. Then he turned to Pascoe.

'Pity,' he said. 'I hoped he'd blown your bloody head off.'

Chapter 11

Statement of Antony Neville Dick made at Thornton Lacey Police Station, Oxfordshire, in the presence of Detective Superintendent D. S. Backhouse.

I am a free-lance feature writer, working under the name of Anton Davenant. The nature of my work has brought me in close contact with many people connected with art and antiquities and I have from time to time acted as an agent for dealers. At no time have I had reason to suspect that any dealer I worked for did not have full title to the goods I handled.

'Can he get away with this?' asked Pascoe, almost in admiration.

'We can only hope you do a better job of work in Yorkshire than you've managed down here,' said Backhouse.

On Friday September 17th at about seven P.M. I called at Brookside Cottage, Thornton Lacey. My purpose was partly social as I knew the owners, Mr and Mrs Colin Hopkins, and partly business. Mr Timothy Mansfield, a house-guest, had brought with him a figurine which I had agreed to pick up from him and show to a local collector, Mr Hartley Culpepper.

'Is there anything other than Davenant's assertion to tie Timmy in with this business?' asked Pascoe.

'Circumstantial stuff only.'

'But you believe it?'

'It seems probable, that's all.'

'And the others?'

'Customers, perhaps. A couple of things went missing from the cottage at the time of the fire. I suspect Davenant picked them up just to get any evidence out of harm's way.'

'He started the fire?'

'Left a gas tap on, I believe. Eventually the pilot light ignited it. But it's all beyond proof.'

I had dealt with Mr Culpepper before. Indeed he owed me almost four thousand pounds from a previous business deal, so I was naturally concerned when his name was mentioned in connection with the book Mr Hopkins was working on. Its theme was poverty in the affluent society and it was concerned not so much with breadline poverty as with credit living, conspicuous waste, executive unemployment, that kind of thing. Mr Hopkins had gained access to information from one of the big executive employment agencies and had noticed the name of his new neighbour there. He was intrigued to find that Culpepper was still maintaining the pretence that he was employed by the Nordrill Company and he had hopes of ultimately getting the man's co-operation in using his experience as material for the book, though no approach had yet been made.

Shortly after seven-thirty I left Brookside Cottage and called at the Culpepper's house. He expressed an interest in the figurine but said he had not sufficient cash on hand to pay for it and asked me to add it to the price of his previous debt. In view of the information I had just received, I refused and told him why. He denied it at first, then became very angry and demanded to know how I had found out. I told him about Hopkins's book and suggested it might be worth his while financially to co-operate with Hopkins, and even offered to act as his agent should he decide to dispose of his porcelain collection. At this he became so incensed that I left and returned to Oxford.

'And that is all we are going to get out of Master Davenant, I fear,' said Backhouse.

'And Culpepper?'

'A long and rambling statement swinging between self-justification and recrimination. I don't think you'd care to read it.'

'No.'

'It's pretty clear what happened. He went down to Brookside to protest to Hopkins. Mrs Hopkins had just gone off to the pub. He and Hopkins had a row in the dining-room. Your friend was quite drunk, of course, and perhaps did not realize just what this business meant to Culpepper.'

'What did it mean?' asked Pascoe.

'It meant the shattering of a self-image as well as a public one,' said Backhouse slowly. 'He came from a poor background, you know. Achieving the position he had done was his life's work. More. His life perhaps. Suddenly Hopkins must have seemed the focus of everything that threatened him. He picked up the nearest suitable object, which happened to be the shotgun your friend had borrowed from Pelman, and struck him on the head with it. Half unconscious, Hopkins staggered through the french window into the garden. The other two now came through the lounge to investigate. He brought the gun up and pressed both triggers. At that range you don't have to be any kind of gunman.'

'And Colin?'

'Hears the gun and sets off down the garden into the stream bed, follows the flow of water. He's on the point of collapse, remember. Culpepper's only made more furious by what he's done. Hopkins *made* him do it – that's the way he's thinking. There's a box of cartridges on the sideboard. He reloads it, sets out after Hopkins. Unfortunately, Mrs Hopkins arrives home at this point and comes round the back of the house to re-enter through the french window. Nothing is going to stop Culpepper now. He shoots her down without a thought and goes after Hopkins. He catches up with him by the culvert.'

'Oh God.'

'And that's that. As some kind of rationality returns, he sets about tidying things up. He goes back to the cottage and unearths your friend's notes for his book. These he must destroy. Then he comes across the jottings from the poem and sees how these might just sound like a suicide note. So he sets it all up. He's lucky. No interruption and later it rains so heavily that all traces of Hopkin's passage up to the stream are obliterated. Back home. His wife is out – with Sam Dixon, of course – and he's safe. Except that his mother sees him, and then or later discovers the gun. Poor old woman. She suspected something, but with Hopkins still missing and apparently the killer, she persuaded herself all was well. Later however . . . Not a good way to end your life.'

'No,' said Pascoe. 'Davenant must have suspected?'

'He claims he believed like everyone else that it was Hopkins. I believe he went back to the cottage to remove the dangerous pieces and also got hold of the notes for the book. He was worried in case anyone coming across the reference to Culpepper might stir things up and he wasn't very keen on Culpepper in his present frame of mind having any pressure put on him. Pure self-interest, of course. He tried to set fire to the cottage in case the manuscript was still there somewhere, and he searched your bedroom just in case you'd got hold of it as Hopkins's friend. But once again, this is pure speculation. Nothing to show in court.'

'It makes sense. More than anything I ever speculated about the case. I had it all worked out. Every premise a false one! I sometimes wonder it I'm fit for this business.'

'Not for this particular bit of it, perhaps,' said Backhouse gently. 'But that's not surprising. I'm sure you do sterling work back home.'

'Home,' said Pascoe. 'That's a nice word. It's only a

scruffy old bachelor flat, but it'll do for the time being. That's what I'd like to do now. Go home.'

'There's no place like home,' said Dalziel, like a man making a completely original discovery.

'True,' said Pascoe.

'That's where they got that fellow Atkinson, in an old folks' home in Romford. Told them he was seventy-two! He's an old con artist from way back. He felt seventy-two when I'd done with him! But we've got enough to put Cowley away for a long time now.'

'I'm glad,' said Pascoe, relaxing in his chair and looking round the room with pride.

It was remarkable what a pleasant civilized place his flat had become. The candles on the table had seened a little too much in the light of the afternoon, but now they were perfect. A woman's touch worked wonders. Oh yes indeed.

He and Dalziel were sitting opposite each other, finishing off the sharp white wine which had accompanied their baked trout.

'It taught me one thing,' said Pascoe suddenly.

'What?'

'Information. If you're cut off from local channels, you're lost! Everyone knew about Culpepper except me. Everyone knew that it was Sam Dixon who was having a bit on the side with Marianne except me.'

'Backhouse always did play his cards too close,' said Dalziel. 'I hope your promotion doesn't get you transferred anywhere near him. You made a lousy impression!' He laughed. 'But he's not such a hot judge. He reckons nowt to me either!'

'Amazing,' commented Pascoe. 'Anyway it was Dixon who rang Crowther and told him Davenant was at the Culpeppers'. Marianne mentioned he'd come back and

297

Sam was jealous! Not of her husband, mind you, No competition there. Old Mrs Culpepper knew what was going on, of course. She knew everything. That's why she was so angry when Dixon turned up at the house. She made him break half a box of scotch!'

'Tragic,' said Dalziel. 'But if he knew Culpepper was broke, why was he willing to supply the stuff anyway?'

'Culpepper's usual tradesmen were beginning to dig their heels in. The bills are huge, it seems. That's why he turned to the local pubs for booze. Palfrey wasn't going to play. He brought a couple of bottles to keep on the right side, so to speak, and shot a line about his low stocks. Dixon now, well, Dixon was in love. It made him willing to act quite irrationally. I told you it was him that banged me on the head at Brookside.'

'Yes,' said Dalziel. 'A bloody ghoulish place, that, for a lovers's tryst.'

'Too true. Pelman had run into Marianne in the village and mentioned he'd met me where I was going. She dived for the nearest phone to warn Dixon. Rang twice, a pre-arranged signal so he'd know who it was. Naturally, he didn't want me to answer and recognize her voice. So bang!'

'A violent lot in Thornton Lacey.'

'Yes. Not just me! Then off Dixon goes, worried sick about me. Picks up his car and drives back to find me 'accidentally'. But good old Sergeant Palfrey's done the job for him. So his guilty secret is safe. Was safe. The proud Marianne's come out in the open now. Poor old Molly Dixon! They seemed perfectly matched.'

'Aye. Well, it happens,' said Dalziel dourly.

'What happens?' asked Ellie cheerfully, coming in from the kitchen with a vegetable tureen.

'Policemen do the decent thing and get themselves

298

engaged,' announced Dalziel with heavy jocularity. 'What's next? It smells good.'

'Surprise,' said Ellie, grinning at Pascoe as she went out again. She had not been over-enthusiastic at the prospect of playing hostess to Andrew Dalziel, but somehow it had seemed a necessary thing to do. Why, she could not imagine! In the event she was enjoying her role tremendously and deriving much pleasure from the fat man's vacillations between hearty, old-fashioned guestmanship and his more customary blunt vulgarity.

'So Dixon was a dark horse,' resumed Dalziel when he felt Ellie was safely out of earshot. 'But his part was only incidental really, wasn't it?'

'Oh yes. Though he frightened the pants off me when he followed me up the drive at Culpepper's that night on his way to his rendezvous with Marianne!'

'This fellow Pelman sounds more interesting.'

'He was,' said Pascoe. 'Backhouse told me afterwards that, alibis apart, he couldn't really suspect anyone being motivated to such a crime who could cheerfully dump loads of chicken-crap into the pool where his wife and her lover had killed themselves! Odd reasoning!'

'Not at all,' said Dalziel. 'It's being able to reason like that that makes you a superintendent! I don't understand why he was willing to loan Culpepper a thousand quid. They weren't great mates, and he knew the old man was pretty well bust.'

'Oh, it wasn't sentiment, rest assured of that!' laughed Pascoe. 'Culpepper went to see him the previous night to ask for the loan. And he took as security half a dozen pieces from his collection – all the bits, naturally, that Davenant had flogged him and which he wanted to keep out of sight for a while!'

'Cunning old Culpepper,' said Dalziel.

'Yes,' said Pascoe with sudden passion. 'I hope he's not so cunning that they don't put him away for ever!'

'Easy,' said Dalziel, glancing warily at the kitchen.

'Sorry, sir,' said Pascoe. 'It's just that it's relatively so easy to be objective and impersonal in out business. You strain after it all the time. X kills Y. Find him. Charge him. Forget him. X has many names, we spend all our lives looking for X. He's not unique. But sometimes Y has one particular name. Y is unique. Something has gone which to you personally is irreplacable. And then you, begin to think it's like this every time. For someone.'

'Forget names,' urged Dalziel. 'Stick to X and Y. Life's a series of wrecks. Make sure you're always washed up with the survivors.'

'Gosh,' said Ellie at the kitchen door. 'Does promotion get you a course in philosophy too? Sorry to interrupt the Socratic moment, but here we are!'

Triumphantly she brought to the table a large serving dish on which lay side by side two roast pheasants.

'Jesus!' said Dalziel in admiring anticipation. 'Well, that's buggered my diet!'

They all laughed. Pascoe, watching Ellie's genuine uninhibited amusement, felt the springs of his own laughter dry up. He busied himself with the carving knife and sharpening steel. It would be easy to become permanently suspicious of happiness, to taste no joy without glancing sharply over the shoulder to check who was watching. Perhaps this was the formula for survival that Dalziel would offer, though he could not think so, looking at the fat man this very moment.

But then, to look at Ellie now, proudly explaining the subtle modes by which the birds had been brought to their present fragrant succulence, who would know that a few hours previously he had found her standing in tears,

300

looking down at the unplucked pheasants whose plumage's iridescent green and purple gleamed on the kitchen table like the silk of a woman's evening gown?

To be a look-out, to keep alert, was not a bad role. Particularly if you did not make a great show of it.

He put down the sharpening steel and approached the pheasants with the knife. Poker-faced, he jerked his head at Dalziel and said to Ellie, 'Which one is his?'

They all began laughing again. This time Pascoe laughed to the finish.

Deadheads
Reginald Hill

Life is a bed of roses for Patrick Aldermann when Great Aunt Florence collapses into her Madame Louis Laperrières and he inherits Rosemont House with its splendid gardens.

But when his boss, 'Dandy' Dick Elgood, suggests to Pascoe that Aldermann is a murderer – then retracts the accusation – the inspector is left with a thorny problem.

By then Police Cadet Singh, Mid-Yorkshire's first Asian copper, has dug up some very interesting information about Patrick's elegant wife, Daphne.

Superintendent Dalziel, meanwhile, is attempting to relive the days of Empire with Singh as his tea-wallah.

'Their [Dalziel and Pascoe's] double act . . . is one of the delights of English crime fiction'   *The Times*

ISBN 0 00 649991 0

The Wood Beyond

Reginald Hill

A ravaged, cratered wood, a man in uniform long dead – this is not a World War One battlefield, but Wanwood House, a pharmaceutical research centre.

Away to the south, Peter Pascoe is attending his grandmother's funeral, and scattering her ashes leads him too into war-ravaged woods in search of his great-grandfather who fought and died in the Passchendaele campaign.

Seeing the wood for the trees is a problem for Andy Dalziel and Edgar Wield, the latter in his investigation into the bones found at Wanwood House, and the former in his involvement with an animal rights activist, despite her possible complicity in a murderous assault and her appalling taste in whisky.

The Wood Beyond presents a cast of fascinating characters and a mind-bending puzzle, leading us to the wild side of the pastoral, through fields where nothing may safely graze, into woods where no bird dares sing . . .

'Hill's wit is the constant, ironic foil to his vision, and to call this a mere crime novel is to say Everest is a nice little hill'   *Mail on Sunday*

ISBN 0 00 647994 4